SELF CARE

SELF CARE

A NOVEL

RUSSELL SMITH

BIBLIOASIS
WINDSOR, ONTARIO

FIRST EDITION
10 9 8 7 6 5 4 3 2 1

Library and Archives Canada Cataloguing in Publication
Title: Self care / Russell Smith.
Names: Smith, Russell, 1963– author.
Identifiers: Canadiana (print) 20250140837 | Canadiana (ebook) 20250142112 | ISBN 9781771966245 (softcover) | ISBN 9781771966252 (EPUB)
Subjects: LCGFT: Novels.
Classification: LCC PS8587.M58397 S45 2025 | DDC C813/.54—dc23

Edited by Daniel Wells
Copyedited by Martin Ainsley
Typeset by Vanessa Stauffer
Cover designed by Kate Sinclair
Cover photo by Roman Odintsov

Biblioasis acknowledges the support of the Canada Council for the Arts and funding support from the Ontario Arts Council and the Government of Ontario, including through the Ontario Book Publishing Tax Credit and Ontario Creates.

PRINTED AND BOUND IN CANADA

for Jessica Latimer

1.

FLORIAN ALWAYS CLOSED HIS HAND around her throat and squeezed when he was about to come, and that seemed to hasten it for him, but still Gloria didn't really like it, or at least didn't like not being asked, and recently she had started pulling his hand off and saying no, which was never an issue; he would say sorry quickly and continue. Now she felt his hand squeezing her neck and she said *no* rather insistently. He removed it but was already too excited to notice, and he came in his usual quiet way and went heavy on her. He rolled off, careful as always to hold on to the condom. He wouldn't let Gloria take it off, as he had once caught a girl dipping her finger into the used tube to smear inside herself when he wasn't looking. Most of the guys Gloria knew were careful about this too.

Florian pulled it off and tied it neatly and dropped it off his side of the mattress, then turned back to hold her. He was polite in this way.

He said, "I wish I could make you come."

She closed her eyes. "It's fine. I'm fine. It's still nice."

"Nice."

Gloria exhaled. "It's my medications. I already told you. It's not you."

He stroked her hair. "It must be so frustrating."

"No. No, it's still nice."

"Nice."

"It's wonderful," she said, keeping her voice even. "Fantastic."

"What can I do? What do you think I can do? Do better, or do new, or whatever."

She hesitated. "There really isn't anything. I mean you try so hard, I mean you do a lot. But that can be frustrating. For me. It makes me feel like there's pressure on me? In a way?"

"I understand. That's bad. Pressure is bad."

"So there's nothing, really. It's the medication. It's been like that for like months now. Six months, eight months anyway. And the medication is good for me. So it's a trade-off. I don't want you to worry about it."

He was silent. He picked up his phone and she thought the conversation was over. But then he put it down again. "It makes me feel frustrated."

"It makes you feel frustrated? Are you trying to make me feel bad about not being able to come?"

"No, no. It just makes me think that it's not you. It's me that can't make you come."

"No one can make me come," she said.

He made a short sound that may have been a sigh or a cough. Then he did pick up his phone. He angled it slightly away from her as he scrolled. He had the frown of concentration when he did this.

It was late afternoon. The window was open a little, as the heat in Florian's building was always excessive, even well into the spring, so there was a sliver of wet cold in the dryness. The radiators were too hot to touch. If you dried socks on them, as Florian often did, they would go hard and crusty in an hour. There had been a conversation going on the whole time, just outside, on the street under Florian's second-floor window, which Gloria had caught bits of, and now it was getting loud.

"Where you going? Where you going?" the woman was shouting. "You leave me the fuck alone. You leave me the fuck alone."

The man yelled something from a distance, possibly from across the street.

"That's right, that's right," she yelled. "Where the fuck you think you're going? You're not going anywhere."

His voice came back closer, probably right under the window, too, but it was still muffled.

"Leave me alone," said the woman. "Leave me the fuck alone."

Gloria propped herself and peeked down at King Street. The woman, she had seen before—walking a jerky walk up and down, in sparkly sneakers and leopard-skin leggings and crop tops under short hoodies. She was very thin and ropy. She had a wrinkled face, but it was impossible to tell how old she was. Sometimes she rode a kid's scooter. She had a little gold purse on a gold rope that was always over her shoulder. The guy was someone new, a heavy white guy in long satiny basketball shorts and a huge camo parka and a toque. He came close to the woman to be shouted at and shook his head and moved away across the street, moving implacably through the cars as they honked at him, and then yelled from across the street and came back.

It was still a long way from summer. Summer was rough at Florian's place because he kept the window open and there was a lot of this. Plus the streetcars and the sirens.

The woman who yelled had always been excessively polite to Gloria when she had spoken to her on the street, asking her how she had such pretty hair, and if Florian was her boyfriend, and could she spare a cigarette or a toonie, or get her a Coke, and thanking her and godblessing her a lot when she said *no*.

Florian said it was good to have these people outside, as they were a kind of neighbourhood watch, and they would tell you if anything new or weird was happening, but also that some of the people in his building said the woman stole packages off porches. You had to buzz to get into Florian's building, though, so he had no packages left for him ever, not that Gloria could imagine him ever ordering anything for delivery anyway. Florian resisted commodity fetishization.

"Hey," she said. "You okay?"

"Hmm?" He did not look away from his phone. "What?"

"I want to ask you something."

"Okay." He was typing a text now.

"Hey, you know how we talked about the choking thing?"

He did not answer. She looked over and he was typing intensely on what looked like an Instagram thread.

"Hey."

"Sorry. What?"

"I mentioned the choking thing. Last time."

"Oh. Did I do it again?"

"Yeah."

"I'm sorry. I forgot. I'm sorry."

"Yeah."

Florian put down his phone. "Hey. I'm sorry. Are you upset?"

"No. No. I just want to know why... like, do you not remember?"

"No. I don't remember. I just really thought you liked it. It made you come once."

"Huh. I don't remember that." Although she did. It had been probably the first or second time they had been together. Before she was on the Cipralex.

"I bet you do remember. And you liked being tied up. And spanked. And all that."

She thought about this a minute. "I liked very much that you wanted to do it to me. I liked that it turned you on so much."

"Huh. And you don't now?'

"I guess I kind of have to plan it. I kind of have to think about whether I want to or not." And there was also, she knew, the anxiety about liking it, the sense that she shouldn't like it, just like porn of gangbangs, which could also make her orgasm, at least in the past it could, and the slight shame that the orgasm brought, which she wasn't going to talk to Florian about. "Why don't you let me do it to you? How do you know it wouldn't make you come?"

Florian snorted.

"You remember we tried that once when you let me play schoolmistress or whatever it was. You came pretty hard then."

"You didn't choke me."

"I tied you up," she said, "and I teased you and wouldn't let you touch me. I slapped your cock. I did all kinds of things to you, and you liked it. You seemed to like it."

"Of course I liked it. Anyone likes being ... I don't know."

"Dominated?"

"No," he said, "not dominated. Like, tended to. You don't have to do anything, you can just sit back and be, you know. You're the centre of attention. It's like you're being pampered. It's not far off getting a massage."

"Huh. I guess. But the choking thing—"

"Thing is," he said, "I don't even like massages. It doesn't come naturally to me. Relaxing. Being the passive one. Makes me nervous."

"Nervous! Like I'm going to do something bad to you?"

He snickered. "No. Not that. It's more like it's not really me. Not really how I see myself. I'm an in-control kind of guy."

"You mean," she said, "that you're stuck in old-fashioned gender roles and you're afraid of being unmanly."

He sighed. "I think that manliness is a pernicious concept, you know that."

"I know you say that."

They lay together and he picked up his phone again. Gloria definitely could now, and should, get up and get dressed.

She said, "You're passive when you get a blow job. And you don't mind blow jobs. At all."

"I kind of do though. Makes me nervous."

"When you say nervous," she said, "and when I say nervous, we mean different things. I am nervous that, yes, something bad might actually happen to me, like I might get hurt or, that's the choking thing, like it's actually dangerous. And you never know with guys. You're nervous you might look weak."

"I get nervous that you're not having fun," he said. "If I'm flat on my back and you're the one doing all the work. It feels selfish. I mean what's in it for you if you're the top or whatever? See, I don't even feel comfortable saying *top*. It's so ... it's like a pamphlet from a gay information centre. The only people who talk about topping and bottoming all the time are, like, fat bloggers with pronouns."

"You know that when you say *fat*," she said, "every woman you are talking to is wondering if you think she's fat."

"Oh, for. And every man who ever hears a woman ask him if she thinks she's fat is instantly bored. That is so boring."

"I am sorry I am boring."

"Okay, sorry, I mean body-positive bloggers. Body-positive bloggers with pronouns."

She laughed at this because she knew she shouldn't. She said, "The one time we did it when you were passive I did like it. I liked having the control and I liked how excited you got."

Florian was scrolling through people's photos: burritos, sweaters, cats, dance floors, muffins, sunsets, a cat in a frog outfit. Perhaps he did not remember how excited he got.

Gloria did, very clearly: she remembered him begging to come and whimpering. She had never seen him so excited. She said, "I don't need to be the centre of attention all the time. And also ... I only like sort of scary games if they're not scary at all. I don't want to be actually wondering if you—or

I mean not you necessarily, anyone—if they're going to slap me too hard or choke me. So I guess I could be more relaxed if I was the top or the domme or whatever the pronoun people would say."

He glanced at her sharply. "But you're not, though. That's not really you. You have a big submissive side, believe me."

"And maybe I don't like it." She was looking at his screen. "Is that Anicka Soberman's cat? The poor fucking thing."

"Who, Anicka or the cat?"

"She should just have a baby already."

"I didn't know you knew her."

"I don't want to know if you fucked her or not."

"Hey," he said, "you're not really worried I'm going to slap you or anything? You think I'm like that?"

Gloria was remembering the times she had let him pin her down. They were at the beginning. She said, "The thing is, you only let someone do something like that to you if you really like them and you want them to like you."

"And you don't like me?" he said.

"I'm freezing."

"So, are you pissed off now?"

"Do I seem pissed off?"

"Well. It's a bit. It's like you're ... like now we're done and you're telling me what I did wrong. And I already feel like whatever I'm doing doesn't work. It doesn't make me feel great."

"No," she said. "That's not what I."

"*You're not going anywhere*," yelled the woman outside.

"I just wanted to talk about it," she said. "About that one thing, not about how you ... like about sex in general."

Now her phone buzzed and lit up. She turned it over so she wouldn't see who it was.

"Okay, I'm sorry, all right? I'm sorry."

He picked up his phone again and so she picked up hers too. Like him, she angled it away. The text was from Scott.

Great mix, with a link to one of his sort of industrial drum and bass djs. *How are you?*

Gloria had not heard from Scott since they had had sex about two weeks or possibly six weeks before. She had not been thinking about Scott much and had been at once relieved and surprised that he had not texted her. There was some pleasure or, at least, piqued curiosity in receiving this.

"Most girls do like it," said Florian.

"Sorry?"

"Women. Most women like it I guess."

"So why are you telling me that?"

"Didn't you just ask me to talk about it?"

"Yeah, okay." Gloria lay there with her phone face down against her chest. She wanted to get up and text Scott and put her clothes on.

"*That won't work with me,*" the guy outside was yelling. "*That's not going to work with me.*"

"Do you ask them?" said Gloria.

Florian snorted. "Sometimes they ask me. It seems to work for them."

Gloria pictured all the girls lying in this very bed, on this mattress, asking Florian to choke them, and she felt tired. She picked up her phone and texted Scott.

Not bad. Superbusy with work.

Then she went to her socials and scrolled. There were a couple of posts expressing condolences for someone, a name she didn't immediately recognize. Avi Leibovitz.

"I knew a girl who couldn't come without it," said Florian.

Avi was a sensitive and erudite man who will be much missed.

Avi left us too soon.

Professor Leibovitz was a huge influence on my thinking and a valued member of the department.

There was a picture and then Gloria recognized him: Professor Leibovitz, her prof in first year, her prof in Introduction to Social Critique of Narrative, a course he had designed and taught for some years that everyone had told her she should take. She had liked him, she thought, although she couldn't remember much about the course. He had been rather quiet and gentle and very unattractive.

Comments on his death were all prefaced with content warnings, and then they went into carefully worded discussions of how the community's mental health was the community's responsibility, and that if you ever have a sense that someone is struggling you should reach out and check in on them.

She looked up a girl called Kayleigh McGavin who she thought might have been in Avi Leibovitz's class with her, and messaged her.

Did Prof Leibovitz off himself?

On the wall of an anti-suicide activist named Shanita Johnson someone had written, *There was a note, we all know there was a note, and you won't hear about it in the media.*

Kayleigh responded right away: *It's so awful isn't it? When is it going to stop!!*

Gloria wrote, *When is what going to stop?*

K: *Second suicide this year of someone we know?*

G: *Who elsei*

K: *Hilary Hong!!*

G: *Oh right I din;t really know her. When was that*

K: *Before Christmas and nobody knows why. Her gallery was doing great.*

G: *Did Leibovitz leave a note*

"Hey," said Florian, "I'm going to bartend for Jamal tonight at Bunny's."

"Okay."

"You should come by and hang out."

"Maybe."

Kayleigh wrote, *Part of it was like an anti-racist essay. Like he knew he was taking up too much space. He said it was time to step aside and make room. But it was kind of self-pitying too.*

G: *Jesus.*

K: *There's a memorial service next weekend we should go and we can hang out*

G: *where*

K: *on campus*

G: *maybe but it's far from where I live*

"Helena is DJing," said Florian.

"Oh god," said Gloria. "Is it that like ironic hip hop?"

"It's eclectic," said Florian. "I don't know if it's ironic or not. It suits the vibe."

"My prof died," said Gloria, "A prof I had. He killed himself."

"That sucks." Florian typed a bit on his phone. "Are you sad?"

"Kind of. He was a nice guy. I'm a little surprised. He had everything going for him."

His two courses had been cancelled, wrote Kayleigh.

"Most of the people in his class went on to do comms or content. So, if I go to his memorial I could maybe, I mean this is not the only reason I would go, but I could make some contacts and get some work. I'm a terrible person."

Florian was typing.

"I know some of them went into film. And TV. I don't know if anyone still does film though. Are there still like TV shows?"

"There are a lot of reality shows," said Florian. "Cooking competitions. I think."

Gloria thought for a minute about whether she could work for a cooking show and then got up and looked for her underwear.

"So, are you coming tonight?"

"I don't think so." Gloria stood in the window as she dressed and looked out. Across the side street was another low-rise building, and in the window opposite was a sign that said SUGAR FREE FOR 579 DAYS. She was pretty sure it had said *579* for the last three days though. She knew this because she had passed by to see if Florian's light was on.

She didn't have any plans for the evening.

"That's too weird about your prof," said Florian. "A prof of mine killed himself just last week."

"Who? One of *your* profs, now? Who?"

"No, a guy from a while back, not really a prof, actually, just someone I took a course with in undergrad, a creative writing course. A writer. You probably wouldn't have heard of him because no one ever heard of him. But he was an okay guy. I liked the course."

"When did this happen?"

"Last week or the week before? Devon Rumpel. Did you hear about this?"

"Nope."

"He was old though. And he was getting all twisty about being kind of forgotten, you know, a has-been. I guess he left some kind of angry note."

"That is weird. That is kind of creepy."

"He was a has-been, though, it's true. His books were all about white people remembering the war and their families and who died in the war. He used to get a lot of grants and published a lot and then it all stopped. Anyway. There are a lot of pills going around, I guess."

"What do you mean by that?" she said.

"I mean everyone's on meds, right? We all have enough of whatever we're on to just call it a day on whatever day we want. Like, if you took all your antidepressants plus all the clonazepam in one prescription, you could do that any time you want."

"This is kind of a creepy talk."

In another window on the street, in a house right next to the sugar-free building, there was a poster that read WE'RE ALL IN THIS TOGETHER.

And taped on the telephone pole right outside was a photocopied sheet that said BECCA GIVE ME BACK MY PHONE.

If she went home now it would take over an hour; there were two trains and a long bus ride to get to her place. Gloria could not afford to live even here where Florian lived; even this corner, now, was not really accessible to people like her who freelanced. Florian had a roommate, and they split the rent. But then so did Gloria.

Isabel had said she had some family thing tonight, so Gloria had no one to hang out with, and it was Sunday, and tomorrow would be just the computer and stupid work all day again, so it would actually be a bad idea to go all the way home and just stay in all night. So she knew she would end up going to Bunny's and watch Florian bartend.

FLORIAN ALWAYS LOOKED VERY COMPETENT behind the bar. He wore deep V-neck T-shirts and a black scarf knotted at his neck. He didn't work out, but his arms were still strong. His beard was neat and trimmed and he wore heavy, square, black plastic glasses. He greeted every boy who came in by name, and shook their hands or hugged them, and if it was a person of colour or even vaguely Arabic or something, he would do the rock-and-roll thumb handshake instead. He did not hug the girls who leaned over to kiss him, but he let himself be kissed and asked them all very thoughtfully about how they were and if they were still working at whatever restaurant or caterer or still doing fundraising for the dance company or theatre. Several of his friends sat to talk to Gloria but they didn't stay long. Helena's music was too awful, really, for anyone to sit near the speakers for long: she was playing Michael Jackson and Stevie Wonder and hip hop from the 80s and then sort-of-folkie stuff by her friends. Helena was wearing a tank top and no bra, so nobody cared.

Gloria tried to entertain herself with her phone; she texted Scott and she texted Isabel: *I'm at Bunny's come rescue me.*

Isabel had posted on Instagram and it was another unbelievably sexy shot, in a diaphanous nightgown, with her hands up over her head, piling her hair up in a bun, and some of the hair falling down over her face. Her eyeliner was a little smudged and you could see her nipples through the nightgown. She had written simply, *Dumb vain shot.*

This was a little odd because it was Isabel's everyday account, not her sexy one which was only for nudes and near nudes and which didn't show Isabel's face or name and was called Boredcitygirl.

Gloria checked Boredcitygirl and there was a new bikini shot, on Isabel's bed, and a slightly blurry one of her ass in a thong as she bent over a bathroom sink somewhere. It did not look like Isabel's apartment. Gloria wondered who had taken that. She could have just set the phone on a chair. But then it wouldn't be blurry.

Every now and then one of Isabel's pictures would be censored and taken down, and she had even had brief bans, after which she would post rants about censorship and the sexualization of the natural.

Gloria had asked Isabel why she put these up for free on Instagram when she could be making a ton of money from them on OnlyFans and Isabel couldn't give a clear answer except to say that people really expected to see a face if they were going to pay for an OnlyFans subscription, and she couldn't show her face because of her work. Gloria didn't really buy this.

She wondered again who had taken the bathroom shot. She did not know Isabel to be seeing anyone new, and Isabel told her everything. She had probably put the phone on a chair.

Florian was in front of her with a glass and vodka in it. He pushed it towards her and leaned forward, "That's the last one I can give you free," he said in her ear, "sorry. Vuong is here, he's in the back room." He sprayed soda water in it from his hose.

"That's okay," she said. "I'm not staying long." But she was happy to have the vodka.

Scott texted, *I can be there at 11.*

She thought about this, about how long she could make her vodka soda last, then replied, *I won't make it that long*. Also, she realized, she did not want to have sex with Scott, that night at least, so it would not be wise to ask him to show up at eleven.

Tomorrow?

She replied, *Might work.*

He replied with three flames, which was a little forward, she thought, so she did not continue the exchange.

Then came a strange text from Surinder, her boss, or at least the person she submitted her copy to, the person she had to invoice every week; he could hardly be called a boss if she had no job. He only texted late if there was some breaking health news or celebrity breakdown he wanted her to mention on Daily Self Care, which she wrote, not daily in fact but weekly, so for something to be urgent so late on a Sunday, somebody must have died.

Hey, wrote Surinder, *what's this about artists killing themselves?*

Gloria sighed. *Which artists are you referring to?*

UofT prof yesterday? Did you know him?

Yes.

I'm sorry for your loss.

Gloria waited.

Which makes three in like six months.

Prof wasn't really an artist, she typed. *But i guess close. I think it's a coincidence.*

What was name of art lady?

Hilary Hong. Feminist gallery called Erishkigal. Months ago though.

Then the writer. Pretty odd coincidence! Three people same community less that one year is statistically epidemic.

It is not an epidemic, wrote Gloria. She knew what was coming but didn't want to encourage him.

Could you mention in Daily Self Care this week? Important conv about suicide in arts. Talk to experts on prevention. And reaction from city maybe, ok?

Yes, typed Gloria.

A tall guy who did not appear to know Florian sat heavily beside her. "How you doing."

Gloria gave him the most barely perceptible nod she could get away with. The guy's hair needed a wash.

Hey r u still at Bunny's? Isabel texted.

Yes

Because of bartender?

yes

Get out of there!!!!

Ok

You know, Isabel texted, *I have great business idea for you.*

What

You start this website called Foster Girlfriends

Okay

You be a girlfriend to sad boy and take care of him until he finds his forever home

Gloria laughed and put away her phone. She waved goodbye to Florian. He waved but did not come over. She slid off the stool and pulled on her coat and looked the dirty-hair guy in the eye and said, "Have a good night." He looked startled.

Outside it was mild and wet. She passed a construction site and on the billboards someone had painted FUCK CONDOS GO VEGAN. Her phone buzzed again.

Her mom had sent her a long text asking if she wanted to come to Fort Erie to be with her for the May long weekend. She reminded Gloria that she could come and visit at any time and just spend a weekend, even if it wasn't a long weekend, and that she could bring her boyfriend, of course.

Sure if I don't have work, Gloria texted. Then she typed *I don't have a boyfriend* and walked quickly towards the subway.

2.

GLORIA'S ROOM HAD A SMALL window that looked onto a wall across a driveway, and in that wall was another window, into another house, so she kept a lace curtain closed and didn't get much light. Her desk was under her window and so she looked out through the lace curtain at the alley to see if the sky was grey, and it usually was. This may have been because of the lace curtain.

She usually tried to get dressed and eat something and brush her teeth before she sat down to produce her content, because it was easy to go a little crazy if you just moved from your bed to the desk in the morning, in your pyjamas, just stepping over that metre and a half from bed to desk soon became pointless, and then you started to work in bed with your computer on your lap. This was a good way to put on weight very fast.

But this morning there was a lot to do because of Surinder's great idea about a suicide epidemic, so she wasn't dressed when she called a city councillor's office to get a comment. She had slipped into the kitchen and grabbed an energy drink very quickly because Autumn was already in there boiling her eggs, which was the only thing Autumn said she could eat in the mornings, being on paleo or keto or whatever it was. Gloria's door was tightly closed against the smell of the boiled eggs, and she wore her college sweatshirt over her pyjamas, and socks.

She left a message with the city councillor who would most likely know something about the arts, a gay guy from downtown, and then with her usual suicide-prevention experts, doctors at the mental hospital, and a particularly cooperative private psychotherapist who liked to promote her blog.

She read about Hilary Hong, who had run the Erishkigal Gallery and who had just gone down to the basement one night and taken all her anti-anxiety and bipolar II meds.

Gloria wrote,

> Hilary had been a mentor to many young artists and was known for the vibrant fundraisers she arranged, some of which had caused notoriety for explicitly excluding white cis males and even a small group of white feminists who had signed the Open Letter to the Kahlo Rape Crisis Centre.

Then she deleted the last bit about the notoriety as it was too complicated to explain, and it sounded a bit judgy.

> The Erishkigal Gallery was facing eviction due to an unprecedented rent increase—a result of the new government's elimination of the rent controls and

> the zoning laws—and the refusal of an expected annual operating grant (also a result of the new government's cuts).

She would try to get that past Surinder though he might find it too political.

About Devon Rumpel she wrote,

> Devon Rumpel had been longlisted for all the country's major literary prizes, and his 1998 novel, *The Lighthouse Keeper*, was shortlisted for the Governor General's Award and the City of Hamilton Book Award. His long-time publisher, Churchill House, had effectively ceased to exist some six months before, as it had been absorbed by Jianguo Transmountain, the media multinational that also owns SpinCycle, Radmom, Celebnudes and The Hype Report.

She felt it odd to report this—because Daily Self Care appeared in The Hype Report; that was who she worked for—but she knew that many would come to her articles through links on their phones and didn't know what website they were really reading, so it needed to be pointed out. Surinder would probably delete this connection anyway.

Her friends reminded her about the big anti-immigration demonstration outside the provincial legislature that afternoon and that there would be neo-Nazi groups there and everyone had to mobilize and counter-demonstrate.

The Hype Report would not be focussing on this. Surinder liked to keep things positive and not get bogged down in politics.

Her friends also told her that Devon Rumpel had apparently used all the Percocets he had for his hip, the Risperdal he had for anxiety, and a great deal of Xanax. There was a strict policy against reporting suicide methods, so this had to be excluded. But already she had seen quite a bit of discussion over how effective the various SSRIs and SARIs could be in causing death if you combined whole bottles of them with benzos or some kind of depressant. The general consensus seemed to be that they were pretty useless for causing death even in large quantities. SNRIs like Effexor were way better but no one was prescribing them anymore.

As she wrote, she watched the trickle of gossip grow on one side of her screen. The blog posts suggesting some kind of suicide surge had already appeared. People she knew were already making social media posts about the importance of self-care, and the importance of reaching out for help, the need to explore past trauma, and the need to increase one's meds if necessary. Shanita Johnston wrote out a lot of stats about how people working in the arts or arts-related industries were at higher risk of suicide. She asked, "Why don't we talk about arts suicides the same way we talk about opioid deaths?"

The city councillor's assistant called her back and said she could come in and interview him this afternoon.

"Oh no," said Gloria, "I don't need to see him in person. A phone interview is fine. Or even just emails. I only have a couple of questions."

"Oh, so it's not a video interview?"

"No no."

"Don't you need a photo?"

"Yes, I do. I was hoping you could send me one."

"Councillor Bencic prefers to do media interviews in person."

Oh for fucking Christ, Gloria resisted saying. She looked at her puffy face in the mirror on the closet door and made a sad clown face and said, "Sure, if that's more convenient."

ON THE BUS TO THE subway she kept scrolling through growing commentary about "arts suicides." There was a lot of shock going around about some nasty mocking X accounts. Someone had written quite a funny "trauma" poem that sounded like every poetry reading she had ever gone to.

I language
the wounds written
in the body
since they refused my grant

Someone else had posted a cartoon of scientists watching a group of "artists" in a lab. The artists were all transgendered in some obvious way and fantastically unattractive, skinny men with beards and dresses or fat women with large breasts and beards and purple hair and piercings. A computer had just been put in their cage, and they gathered around it puzzled, as if unsure how to turn it on. The scientists outside the cage were shaking their heads and making notes.

The thing about this cartoon that made it so dumb, Gloria thought, was not so much that it was crudely offensive but that it was only men who would find it funny.

Someone had posted a poem.

I think of my people:
My father
My mother
My grandparents
None of us ever learned to code
Our trauma is intergenerational

Gloria knew she would be called on to denounce this, so she spent a few minutes doing so. She added some angry-face emojis to the array that were already there and added a comment that this was hateful. It really was quite awful, she did admit that.

The bus rolled into the subway station and she joined the slow queue shuffling down the stairs into the tunnels.

COUNCILLOR BENCIC DID NOT MAKE her wait. He brought her into an office with glass walls and smiled a lot. He seemed to be about her age and had a brown suit and red socks and some architectural glasses.

"I'm very sorry for your loss," he said.

"Oh, I didn't—I wasn't really close to anyone who..."

"I'm sorry for the arts community. I know these tragedies have a real ripple effect, and I hope, I really really hope everyone is taking advantage of support services, reaching out if they need support."

Gloria asked him if he could provide a list of these support services, and he said his assistant would put one together for her. He was creating a crowd-sourced fund, too, for the survivor families of "fallen arts workers," and was wondering what Gloria might think of the idea of some kind of symbol of solidarity everyone could wear, like a black ribbon? She didn't answer this right away so he went on that recognition of the stresses that arts workers face is so vital because the arts are so vital to a healthy culture.

"Why?" said Gloria.

"Sorry?"

"Why?"

"Why what?"

"Why are the arts vital to a healthy culture?"

"Oh!" He smiled tightly and sat back. "Oh, because..." He held his palms outwards. "The arts are...the arts are everything. I mean." He sighed and started again. "It's a difficult question, to explain, but we all just feel it, don't we? I mean we all experience the arts on a daily basis."

"Sorry," said Gloria. "It isn't really a part of the story anyway. I was just curious."

"You don't think the arts are important?"

"Of course I do. But it just looks, from here, right now, like anything but a healthy culture."

"Oh I see. Right." He nodded and looked serious and puzzled.

"I guess you're aware that there's been some really, um, tasteless backlash to the news of these deaths? Like on social media?"

He frowned and shook his head.

She got out her phone and showed him some of the nasty stuff, and he was genuinely shocked and seemed to have seen none of it. She wondered why *she* had; her friends must have been looking hard to find it in the first place.

Councillor Bencic denounced it all as offensive and having no place in an inclusive society and said that this atmosphere of hate and hostility was precisely why people working in the arts were so vulnerable.

Gloria was about to ask him if he thought other people, then, were responsible for these weird suicides, and who those other people might be, specifically, but he had looked at his watch and glanced at his computer screen so she decided to wrap it up. She told him she had enough, because she knew she would just quote him as saying the arts are important to a healthy culture and that hate had no place in an inclusive society, and she thanked him and stood up.

ON THE SUBWAY THERE WAS a seat and so Gloria was able to open her laptop and start on the piece. But then the train slowed and stalled between two stations and there was an announcement: the next station was closed because of the demonstration at the legislature.

"Crowd control," said the man beside her, grimly. "The station gets overcrowded. Crowd control." He nodded. "Want to control us all, I guess."

Gloria got up and went to the doors to wait.

She saw her face in the harsh light, and past it the tunnel walls that always seemed furry with grime. She tried to breathe and do the exercise where you try to note all your surroundings. There was a yellow pipe running along the wall. The number 357 was stencilled in white paint. She tried to be conscious of these things. The yellow pipe was thin and so was possibly a gas line? Someone had told her that gas lines were always yellow.

She wondered for a moment, trapped in that tunnel, whether she were actually an "arts worker" and whether that made her at risk of suicide.

When the train finally lumbered past the closed station and into the next one, the platforms were already packed with people fleeing the demonstrations, and some of them were decked out in red and black and they had badges with the black emblems and the white fists. Many were carrying flags. They were all men, a mix of ages, some biker types with long ponytails and cowboy boots, some college boys in polo shirts and bad skin. The boys had their heads shaved on the sides and the hair slicked back on top. It looked both fascist and punk and she didn't mind it, if she had to think about it.

They lined the platform so tightly that when the doors opened no one on Gloria's train wanted to get out: the knot of people on the train just stood on the threshold staring at this pack of white faces and black jackets and nobody moved.

Behind the front row, someone was still holding up a placard. It read WOKERATI KEEP KILLING YOURSELVES. Gloria was standing and had to pee.

The boy at the front of the pack of fascists himself looked frightened, and his fists were clenched at his sides. He was almost handsome, this boy, or he would have been had his lips not been so thin, and his short hair was combed and parted. It wasn't shaved on the sides. He turned his head and shouted, "Back up, back up, boys. Let the people off the train." And he spread his arms and made a sort of corridor, and the guys behind him backed up, and the people in front of Gloria stepped off.

As she approached this boy, now standing respectfully to one side, Gloria caught his eye, she didn't know why, possibly because she was so pissed off at him for this nonsense, possibly because she knew he was timid, really, and she knew he might show some deference to her, which she wanted, really, even if he was a fascist, for why not, no one else was going to show her deference. She said without smiling, "Thank you for letting us out," and it didn't come out quite as sarcastically as she had hoped.

The boy pursed his lips and frowned and looked pious and said, "We respect rules, ma'am." And as she heard this she saw the badge on his bomber jacket, among his many badges, the sad face logo. She knew this logo from the news although she had never seen anyone actually wearing it, and she knew "respect rules" meant his rules only, and a great desire to hurt him coursed through her.

She turned to face him and shook her hair out over her shoulders. She put a hand on his chest, right over the sad-face button, and she said, "You're kind of cute."

A tiny spasm passed over his face, a spasm that could only have been pain. His eyes were wide and his mouth was open.

The people pushing past them had not seen anything, had not heard her. The fascist boys passed onto the car and he stood there and she stood there.

One of them called after him "Darren! Get on!" and he frowned, and he jumped in just before the doors closed. She watched his face slide away, a face of confusion, possibly anger, the face of a child about to cry. She smiled and waved.

IN THE PHARMACY NEAR HER home she had to wait in line to get her prescriptions refilled. She saw Shannon Hayek, from the now-closed Erishkigal Gallery, and pretended not to, because all Shannon would talk about was the loss of her friend and boss. She would talk about grief and self-care. Shannon had put on a great deal of weight and was walking with a cane, and Gloria did not want to hear what medications had caused this weight gain and whether or not they were working.

By the time she got home Gloria was hungry and she hated Autumn for being in the kitchen baking her chicken breasts. The keto diet meant that every evening she had to cook meat and prepare a kale salad with pumpkin seeds that was good the first few times but unimaginable as a staple, and Gloria was a vegetarian, at least now she was, or was trying to be, since finding veganism impossible, and was also attempting to reduce both gluten and dairy, which Autumn was not being helpful about. So Gloria was on a high-carb low-fat diet and Autumn was on a high-fat low-carb diet and liked to offer Gloria some of her chicken breasts or tilapia fillets, which Gloria would occasionally eat, hungry as she was for protein, and then be resentful about, as Autumn knew that she was trying to avoid it and was easily tempted. And so the smell of the oil and the meat, particularly in the small kitchen with its slot for a window that looked onto a wall, had become triggering for Gloria and a symbol of much that she resented—not about Autumn per se but about her own impatience with Autumn, which was utterly unjustified—Autumn was fundamentally sweet, really—and yet unavoidable. (Autumn was not even doing well on the keto, so what was the point anyway? Not that this was any of Gloria's business, and she should not think about it.)

Gloria ate some crackers and cheese, aware of both the gluten and the lactose she was consuming, and a little bit fuckit about it, and wary of the fuckit as well. She went to her room and opened her laptop and filed the interview with The Hype Report. She ticked off Task Completed in Basecamp, and when the list of To-Dos immediately popped up she felt a wave of panic like bile and swallowed it down and closed the app as if it were on fire. Her room was cold.

Her dad had emailed her, from Thunder Bay, where he now lived because he had found work there in some kind of office. The message was a link to a job posting for a "communications specialist" in Kirkland Lake, Ontario. And three happy faces.

Autumn had tweeted something about decolonization that ended with *Chi-miigwech*, which was something she was saying a lot, now that she had decided it was true that her grandmother was Metis. Autumn was Metis now. She didn't even say *grandmother* anymore, she said *kookum*.

Gloria remembered the boy on the subway platform. She googled "sad face logo" and various incel sites and threads came up. Toronto Beta Males. Toronto Blackpills. She looked up the news photos of today's demonstrations and saw only one shot of the pale boy Darren, from the side, in a marching crowd. He did not appear to be shouting or waving a flag. He looked worried.

She read through some of the discussion threads—she had seen stuff like this before, about whoring Staceys and smug Chads, and about how women smelled disgusting between the legs and the different ways in which they could be murdered; she had even written a Q & A about it for The Hype Report, and she was not shocked. She did not see any username that could obviously be him.

The smell of the sesame oil for Autumn's kale salad was too strong in her room. For a second she wondered whether she was going to cry—a possibility she looked at as if from afar, with neutrality—but it passed. She took her Pristiq, her Latuda, and her Imovane. She was supposed to go up a half tab with her Latuda today, but she didn't.

She knew she was supposed to do her breathing exercises for anger, but she was too angry. This was all fuckits, and she had written about this too, and how to fight it. She lay down and waited for sleep.

3.

THE NEXT DAY SHE WORKED in her room. She had to finish the arts suicide piece but also find a subject for the next Daily Self Care.

She was a little surprised that Scott had not been texting her. Whenever she opened the door to him a little like that, he usually got quite excited. Perhaps even Scott was sick of her now. Or afraid of her. Or maybe even Scott had found some fantastic woman who was a real estate agent and was writing at that very moment a long Facebook post about having finally found happiness.

That Florian had not texted was not at all a surprise; he rarely initiated communication and she had stopped feeling troubled by that. In all honesty, genuinely, she had. Even the thought of having sex with him now brought up the awkward conversation about the choking and about her not coming and it wasn't worth that. And the fact that he would only notice in about a week that she hadn't contacted him was another thing that was becoming less and less attractive.

Not that she wanted to control anyone, not that a relationship should be a series of rules, not that she wanted to imprison anyone, no. She would not want to be controlled herself.

(And there was the image of the sad-face boy on the train again—a boy who wanted her terribly and hated her terribly—or were all men like that?—and whom she could almost certainly control, in his desperation, but who would want that?)

She supposed that realizing that she was not going to text Florian anymore meant she was free, and that was exactly what she had felt she wanted—it was certainly what she had told Scott, although for reasons that had more to do with his curiously soft body than with her own desires for exploration—and now this fact that there was no boy in her inbox, no boy she was trying to break up with, that she had actually done it, this fact was not upsetting or invigorating, just a silence, an empty room, the train stalled in the tunnel; the anxiety that interstice created was not a fear of being alone, it was more a problem with attention span; it was the anxiety that comes of not having a signal for your phone and a long time to wait. You would then have to pay a lot of attention to the grey tunnel wall and the yellow pipe and the sign with a meaningless number. It would be a kind of meditation, and she had always failed at meditation.

And this, this emotional silence, was a situation she had not experienced for a year or two, not since the end of school. She would have to learn to read again or something.

Or work, do nothing but work and make a little more, which she should have been doing anyway.

She thought she might pitch another single-by-choice piece, but she had already interviewed all the experts. She had even interviewed Autumn.

She updated the blog feed with some advice to protect your mental health by setting boundaries and learning to say no.

She ended up pitching something for next week on exercise as possibly triggering for people who had suffered trauma, particularly the trauma of harassment at gyms, and she got a psych prof from the university to give her a couple of quotes. She had already used this prof for a piece on fat acceptance, so now she couldn't use her again for a few months.

She herself had not been to the gym for three days. The main problem was that it was the university gym, downtown because she had an alumni membership and that entailed a bus and two trains, which she knew meant she wasn't going to work out if she got busy, and so she would end up writing a lot more stories about fat acceptance and gym trauma, which would get embarrassing eventually.

Gloria herself was not fat, not by a long stretch, and that was not a word she would use anyway, and she knew that her roundness did not make her any less attractive to men and was only a thing women worried about and she was perfectly happy with her curvy body, even her bum which was not something she would likely post a lot of pictures of, and curvy was not a useful word because it simply meant *fat* to some of the women she knew and obviously to every woman posting pictures of herself online, she knew this and she told herself this again, as she did every day. She was sick of thinking about this and writing pieces on fat acceptance was not helpful.

She shaved and put on makeup and shiny leggings and her running shoes and drank a lot of water, and went outside, which was like being born except painful.

Her phone trembled and it was Isabel, who texted, *I'm doing French on Duolinguo and did you know that garbage bag is ordure sac?*

She stopped and wrote, *Do I know it? I am an ordure sac.*

Okay so one drink never hurt anyone.

Gloria wrote, *What, now? I'm on way to gym.*

You don't need gym. You need mojito at Ether.

I'm in gym clothes.

So you look more hot. Winner/gagnant. Luckily Ether close to gym.

I'm Fatty Gay.

We're all fatty gay. So cocktail perks up. Meet half hour?

"IT'S A PICTURE OF, LIKE, four cats, photos of cats, against different backgrounds, like one's on a beach and one's in a gym, and it says 'guys over forty on dating sites' and I was like, that is exactly it, exactly so exactly it. They look identical, like totally nervous and stiff and petrified, or just so fat they can hardly move." Isabel had her hair up in a high ponytail and a black leather choker on and little puffy sleeves, and she looked as delicate and dangerous as any woman Gloria had ever seen, which was never really a source of envy for Gloria, more a kind of longing—not so much to be Isabel as to be able so effortlessly to combine the innocent and the forbidden on her person in any way as beautifully as this—and also a kind of fear, for she feared, when she saw a certain insensitivity in Isabel, that she could be insensitive this way herself and wasn't sure whether to cultivate it or not. It would probably not be useful to be insensitive unless one was as hot as Isabel.

"Why do you have it set at that age group in the first place?"

"Oh, like I'm going to go on a date with a guy my age. We're going to meet in a pub with a pool table and like hockey on TV screens. He's going to suggest we meet after dinner because he can't afford to pay for dinner. And he's going to tell me about his favourite profs. Because he has read Jung and like Joseph Campbell and he wants to know if I have read *The Hero's Path* or whatever. And then he's going to send a dick pic, and I'll be like, whatever, that's sweet. Then we have sex and then he doesn't call me."

"So are the older guys better?"

"Some of them. They're more confident. They have more money and we go to nicer places. They work out a lot, it's not like they're not attractive. The problem is the wives and families."

"You mean like ex-wives or current wives?"

"It's hard to tell. They lie a lot about that. I dated this one guy for about eight weeks, and he stayed over at my house every time, and I could never come to his house, and he invented this elaborate story about his daughter living there part-time, until I figured out he just lived with his wife, and then he stopped calling anyway. As soon as I found out he just ghosted me."

"That's horrific."

Isabel shrugged. She sipped her cocktail, which was grey and cloudy. Gloria's was red and bitter. "The sex was getting a little weird," Isabel said. "He was very dominant but not in an entirely healthy way."

"Like you were afraid of him?"

"No, not afraid, exactly, it was just a little mean and maybe wasn't so playful. I'm up for anything, but . . ." She held her hand out flat and tilted it side to side. "*Neener-neener.*"

This was a thing that Isabel did: she illustrated her speech with sounds, her own personal library of sounds that were meant to represent clear emotions, such as wonderment or fear or embarrassment; but one could never be exactly sure if one had understood them correctly. Gloria suspected she used them when she really didn't know what she wanted to say. Isabel would say she just wanted to, you know, just *zhhhhh*, with her hands flattening the air on either side of her, and this was meant to signify a desire to take it easy or chill, but sometimes she would describe a dinner party as being way too *neee-ow* or *whoooozh*, because she was just feeling so *vrrrrrk*, you know, and Gloria would just nod.

"They are all weird about their kids. Like you're absolutely not allowed to meet the kids. Which is honestly just fine, because I'm not all that great with kids, but it can make you feel a little like, you know. *Mooooosh.*" She pushed the air downwards with her palms. She tossed her ponytail, and it flashed like scales.

Gloria looked around to see if there were any men looking at Isabel right then, as there usually were. Ether was quiet, it being a cold Tuesday, with classes finished; there were three older women next to them, lawyers or television producers, laughing very loudly and drinking white wine, and in the window, a student couple on a date. Gloria and Isabel sat against the wall opposite the bar. Isabel always sat with her back to the wall because she said she had to see who was going to come in to shoot her before they got her, and Gloria didn't mind this for she didn't feel much like being on display, in her running leggings and sweatshirt; she felt formless against Isabel's sharp lines; but she did know that Adam, the Black bartender, was working, and she liked to look at his arms as he worked, and how he spoke so quietly to the new Asian girl working with him, and how she smiled at everything he said and listened so closely and eagerly it was as if she was just a sail to catch his energy; this made Gloria happy not because she was interested in Adam the bartender herself but because she liked to see people feeling actual attraction to each other and being nice about it.

So, no one was looking at either Isabel or Gloria.

"Are the Instagram photos for them?" Gloria asked.

"For who?"

"For the older guys with money or for someone you might actually like?"

"What are you talking about? They're for none of them."

"Are they for other women to see? I mean I do see them and I think they're beautiful but I'm just wondering if you're thinking of anyone in particular looking at them."

"No! They're for me. They just make me feel good. It's what I do when I'm bored. I'm not, you know, fishing for whatever. Are you going to get all judgy about that, too, now?"

Gloria was thinking of the last shot on the Boredcitygirl account, Isabel bending over a sink in someone's bathroom. "Do you take all those shots yourself?"

"Are we going to eat anything?" said Isabel. "I don't want to eat anything."

"Me neither."

"How are your boys?"

"I don't have one single boy," said Gloria.

"Did you get sick of Scott?"

"I guess. I feel very embarrassed talking about Scott."

Isabel laughed. "Why? Everyone's slept with Scott."

"That's why."

"It's a thing everyone has to try. Like, I don't know, bubble tea."

"I hate bubble tea."

"Right? But you tried it."

"You never felt weird at all, knowing?"

"Oh, god no." Isabel laughed. "I told him he should try for you. Didn't I tell you exactly when I told him that? I told you to get ready, he'll be coming on to you. It was all me. I thought you'd have fun and I knew it wouldn't be serious, and it was fun, right?"

"It was fun, sure, but then a little sad. Because it's Scott—he's nice and tries hard and then he just kind of wanders off, or you do."

"I told you he was kind of small," said Isabel.

"Oh, that, that didn't worry me, that was fine, he was quite fine in bed. It was just trying to talk, and him playing the folk music, and talking about skiing, it just felt like a high-school boy."

"And you're still in love with, what was it, Thomas? Was that his name? No. Gay name. Or foreign."

"Florian."

"Right! I knew it was a totally gay name, but he wasn't. Are you still . . . ?"

Gloria laughed, because it was funny, about the gay name, the kind of thing she wished she could actually say herself, and why she loved Isabel, and she shook her head.

"Oh! Sweetie. That's too bad. What happened?"

"I'm really proud of myself, actually, for getting out of it. It was unhealthy. He just wasn't that into me. At least I don't know. I need more emotional support than that."

"He was the smart one, right, like a PhD or something?"

"Well, not yet. A student. A PhD student."

"And big dick."

Gloria rolled her eyes. "Yes, okay, big dick, but he was too proud of it, and I really didn't care. Anyway, not good for me. He would just text me when he felt like it, you know. But you know, it wasn't just that either. He's really smart but also not smart in kind of irritating ways. He shakes hands differently with white guys and other guys. Guys of colour."

"*Reek?* What?"

"It's like he feels they're more emotional or authentic or something and behaves differently with them. It's so transparent and embarrassing and I can't stand being around it."

Isabel put her hand to her mouth. "Oh, my fucking god, that is so pukey. That is *pukey*. What a douchenugget. What a dickbox. What an ordure sac."

Gloria laughed and felt a rush of pleasure and love for Isabel that was not unlike the desire to be loved by boys, and it dizzied her for a second.

"Well, that's good," said Isabel. "That's strong. I'm glad you did that. So, who are you seeing then?"

"No one."

"And you're okay with that?"

"I guess. Sure. No. No, I'm not."

"Of course you're not. You deserve someone."

"Who do I deserve." Gloria said this flatly and drank a gulp of her red sweet drink. She wished she had had the courage to order a cider, or a gin and tonic, which she preferred to these bitter, sticky things that cost fifteen dollars, but she was always swayed by how pretty and sophisticated they looked. She turned around to scan the bar: now there were two business guys in short overcoats and no ties at the bar, real estate guys, the kind of guys who had done community college and didn't ever have any arguments about trans rights or astrology and who were making a hundred thousand dollars a year at twenty-four, and they were both staring at Isabel in a kind of trance. There was a blue light behind the bar—Ether always looked kind of underwater—and it gave them a grey pallor, as if they were dead. They stared out from the land of the dead at Isabel in the light. Isabel rolled her eyes briefly. Gloria said, "Who deserves anything?"

Isabel stopped smiling. "Are you serious right now? Everyone deserves..."

"What. What does everyone deserve."

"Love. Everyone deserves love. You do, especially. You're gorgeous and you're successful and you're so, so smart, and—"

"Successful? How am I successful? I am almost a complete failure. I have a university degree and I can barely afford rent in a shithole in a miserable area I don't even like, and a roommate who is depressed out of her mind, and I get work that everyone is so excited about for me that I have to be stressed about all the time and it pays me enough for like my subway fare."

"And this," said Isabel, raising her glass.

"And this," said Gloria. "Once a month. Cheers." Then, "We should drink some water. Drink a whole glass of water, right now."

"Oh drink water, right. I should drink water and do yoga and get in touch with my feelings."

"You may actually want to do that."

"Oh, believe me, I am in touch enough." Suddenly Isabel looked morose. "I have plenty of feelings. I wish I weren't in touch with them. My feelings are an ordure sac."

"No no, none of this," Gloria said. "You are not allowed to get depressed. That is not the point of Isabel."

"What is the point of Isabel?"

"To be so strong and beautiful and fabulous."

"Winner, *gagnant*." Isabel looked Gloria straight in the eye and then away again. "I'm tired of being me."

"No, no, seriously. I mean it, you are not allowed."

"What I am serious about, though," said Isabel, "is I am always so impressed by what you do, it's so cool, and you motivate yourself, and—"

"I don't want to motivate myself! You have a job! Like a real job with a paycheque!" Gloria found that she was speaking loudly.

Isabel reached over the table and put her tiny, pale hand over hers. "I am an office manager. I am a secretary. You don't want my job."

Gloria frowned. "Are you still . . ."

"Still what?"

"Well, like how down are you getting? Do you need to be . . . Are you seeing your therapist?"

"I don't need a therapist anymore."

"Okay," said Gloria, "but are you kind of . . . When you get down, everyone gets scared, because."

"Because what."

"You know."

"Because of something that happened seven or one thousand years ago."

Gloria shrugged. It seemed like a bad idea to always talk about What Had Happened to Isabel, and yet What Had Happened to Isabel never seemed so far away, even though it had been many years before, in high school, before Gloria even met Isabel. Gloria always wanted to ask her more about it and learn more details and Isabel never, she thought, talked about it enough. Isabel seemed to think it was just funny now, even though the guy should really be in jail.

Isabel said, "Go on, ask it. Am I still like pining for my lost innocence because of Mr LaRusso?"

"Well, no. I know you are not. It's just that when you get down everyone gets scared, it's normal."

"I am not going crazy again. But you just want to talk about Mr LaRusso."

"Okay, good," said Gloria. But she did want to talk about Mr LaRusso again, she did. "But I wonder how it affects how you feel for ... does it still come up sometimes, when you're dating, because you really haven't been dating anyone, and I always wonder if that has anything to do with it."

Isabel went very still for a second and stared at Gloria with an expression Gloria did not recognize. Gloria waited and Isabel looked away again.

"I date," said Isabel, looking at the guys at the bar.

"You let guys take you out on dates, which is not the same thing."

Isabel was still staring away.

"Is there something you're not telling me?"

"There's always something," said Isabel faintly, "we are not telling anyone. *Whee-wheer.*"

Gloria smiled. She did not know whether this was something to seriously pursue, or whether Isabel was just being philosophical again.

"You just want to hear about Mr LaRusso again."

Gloria nodded. "I just know the vaguest things. I don't know the details."

Isabel finished her cloudy cocktail, holding it high over her mouth to let the last drop out. She made a face. "That was like kind of melted candy cane and kerosene."

Gloria waited.

Isabel sighed. "You know all this. I don't know why it's so endlessly fascinating. Last year of high school. So, like seventeen? He was the English teacher. And he wasn't very old. He must have been just out of teacher's college so like mid-twenties? And he was just hot. Everyone thought he was hot. I wasn't the only one. Everyone would get nervous when he came by and there were a lot of jokes about his class and, you know." She took a long breath. "Want another one or should we try something else?"

Gloria waved to the bartender. "Did you come on to him or did he come on to you?"

"It was definitely me. I'd go into his classroom after class, and we were on this committee together, the model parliament committee, and so we'd have to stay late and then he'd give me a drive home. He gave me a book, like self-help or something. *Unlocking Your Potential* or something. And another book on the history of Studio 54. I know. And then once he didn't take me straight home, he went to the parking lot of the baseball diamond. We just sat in the car, nothing happened. He said nothing could happen till I graduated. And it didn't, it really didn't. Nobody believed me when I told them that, but it was true."

Adam the bartender with shiny arms was there. "Another one, ladies?"

"Something different, though."

"I want a cider."

"Me too."

Adam went away.

"So, the summer I graduated we started hanging out."

"You mean you had sex?"

Isabel laughed. "Yes, we had sex, we had a lot of sex. All the time. I wasn't a virgin, but I hadn't ever had a lot of sex like that, and I was in love with him. He had an apartment really far from the school, like not even in Scarborough, in North York, and I used to take buses for hours to see him, and it had to be secret. I was working this summer job in a store and I lied a lot. Then I moved in with him and I told my parents and they let it happen, they weren't happy about it but there was nothing they could do, I wasn't in school any more. They asked me a lot if it had started while I was in school and I kept saying no, which was almost true. And then he told me I had to move out because I was too young and immature and it wasn't right. So, I packed up my stuff and my dad came and picked me up and took me home. Then I spent a lot of days in my room, and then I swallowed a bunch of pills, and then I was in the hospital for six weeks, and that was it."

"Did they report him? What happened to him?"

"Nothing happened to him. I think he left the school but he's probably still teaching. I have resisted trying to find him."

Gloria was silent. She had herself looked up Mr LaRusso and knew he was married and a real estate agent in a place called Marathon and that he was not as handsome as she had expected him to be, but of course older and a little paunchy. She was not sure she believed Isabel had not also looked him up, in fact it was more than likely that Isabel looked him up quite frequently, but she was going to let her get away with that.

"I know you think this is why I don't date, blah blah. I don't know. I don't think it's really that."

"What is it then?"

Their ciders arrived.

Isabel said, "Do you get on with your mom?"

"My mom? Sure. I guess. She's kind of sad. She still lives in Fort Erie, she works in an office. My dad moved away so I guess I'm closer to her. She worries about me. She's nice, really." Gloria found herself suddenly sad. "I like my mom."

"That's nice. You're lucky."

"I'm very lucky."

Isabel said, "My mom is very distant. Distant from me. She's close to my brother. But we don't get along. She never..."

Gloria said, "Is it since the thing? With Mr LaRusso?"

"I guess, yes. She really didn't handle that very well. She just thought I was an idiot, I guess she still does."

Gloria drank her cider as fast as she could. She wanted to tell Isabel how wonderfully admirable she was but she couldn't say it in a clever way. "You deserve love," she said. "Sorry, that's like inspirational sloganny I know, it's cheesy but it's true."

Isabel laughed and her laugh had a hard ring. She said, "Nobody deserves anything."

"You are not allowed to get depressed, okay?"

"*Zheee!*" Isabel's fingertips all pointed upwards at once. "I'm good."

4.

THE NEXT NIGHT GLORIA TRIED again to go to the gym.

There were no demonstrations, for once, and the final subway platform, where she had seen the fascists, was not crowded.

The athletic centre was a concrete block with a big brightly lit atrium that smelled of chlorine and socks. It was a comforting space. She was almost across it and at the turnstiles, where you would swipe your pass, when she saw the slim figure in black, a man or maybe a teenager, and she stopped short. It was the gentleman fascist boy, the one with the sad-face button, but he wasn't wearing it now. He was sitting on a bench beside the help desk with his hands in the pockets of his black bomber jacket and he was jerking his head back and forth, scanning the crowd.

Gloria held back to watch him, but he had seen her, and she saw his face turn from that anxiety she had first seen to a kind of anguish or pleasure or anguished pleasure. She glanced around: she was closer to the turnstiles now than to the exit, and if she turned towards it now it would be an obvious flight. It would convey fear or disgust, and that was probably exactly what he wanted.

She walked up to him and stopped and stared him in the face.

"Hi," he said. He stood up. He was taller than her. "We met. I saw you on the train. Yesterday. The day before yesterday."

"Did you."

He nodded, but he was swallowing and jerking his head, sweeping his gaze up and down the atrium, as if he was expecting attacks from all sides. "Nice to see you again," he said, and his voice went high.

"Were you waiting for me?"

"Well," he said, and he shrugged and giggled and pulled his hand out of his pocket to scratch his nose. "Not in that way. I was hoping to see you. I thought I could introduce myself."

"And how did you know you'd find me here? Did you follow me?"

He shook his head. He pointed at her pink gym bag, which said UNIVERSITY OF TORONTO ATHLETIC CENTRE on it. "You were carrying it. And you looked like you'd go to the gym. And it was around this time."

"That's creepy and stalky."

"I'm sorry. I just wanted to introduce myself."

"How long did you rehearse that?"

"A long time. All last night and all day today."

"That's very polite. I thought you hated women though."

"No, I don't."

"Oh, bullshit. I saw your badge. I know what it means. Where is your badge today anyway? Are you scared to wear it without your buddies?"

His face still had a half smile. He was shaking his head. His hair was neatly combed, and his black jeans were not unfashionable. There were faint red bumps on his skin. He was wearing some kind of cologne. Even though he was taller than her, she probably weighed more.

She said, "Are you stalking me?" But as she said it, she knew she didn't feel the faintest fear of him. She was not even nervous. She was not turning away and walking with the students through the turnstile. She did not want to go to the gym.

"No. I just wanted to introduce myself."

"Why do you wear the badge if you don't hate women?"

"That's not what it means. That's not what it's about. We respect women."

"You respect them more than the total bastards who date them do."

"What?"

A group of girls came in laughing. He did not turn to look at them. He stared right at her. She knew if she turned now and strode away he would know he was rejected and he would not follow her. But it was worth an experiment.

She began to walk. At the turnstile she turned around. He had sat down again and was looking at the floor.

She went through the turnstile, swiping her pass, and around the corner towards the locker rooms. She stopped and waited a minute in the corridor. Then she went back and peeked out: he was gone.

She passed out again and walked through the turnstile. She crossed the atrium and pushed through the glass front doors. He was standing on the sidewalk with his hands in his pockets.

She smiled at him, and he flinched.

She said, "Were you leaving?"

He said, "I don't know. I guess. I wanted to show you I wasn't following you."

"You came here to find me though."

"Yup. I didn't know how else to meet you. Are you a student?"

"I'm not going to tell you a single thing about myself."

"Fair enough." He nodded vigorously. "Would you have time for a coffee with me?"

She shifted the gym bag on her shoulder. "I have to work out."

"You don't feel like it, though."

"No, I really don't."

"I always get my stuff together and get ready to go to the gym but half the time I don't go. I work out at home, though."

She had an idea. He might be good for an article. She shouldn't let this opportunity pass. "You can walk around the block with me and then I'll go work out. And I will ask you questions."

"Fair enough."

She walked fast down the street and he had to catch up. They walked into the dark campus where there weren't many people. They were heading for the big park where the government buildings were.

"How old are you?" she said.

"Twenty-four. You?"

"I told you I wouldn't answer questions."

"That's not really fair."

"No it isn't. What's your name?" Though she knew this. It was Darren.

"It's *Darren* with a *y*."

"Yarin?"

"*Daryn*," he said, "with a *y*."

"Ah. Daryn with a *y*. Okay. Where do you live?"

"Like Finch and Islington, kind of thing."

"I have no idea where that is."

"Etobicoke, I guess. North Etobicoke."

"Jesus. Of course. How long does it take you to get downtown?"

He looked puzzled. "Not too long. There's a bus goes right to the subway."

"You live with your parents."

"For now, yeah. Well, my mom. While I'm in school."

"School! You go to school." They were more than a block from the athletic centre now. But it was a warm evening and she liked walking around campus in her shiny legs and her running shoes. This was an excuse to do so. She said, "What do you study?"

"Murdering kittens, you know."

She turned to watch him. He had said this calmly, without a smile. "That was pretty good. You said that like a guy who's made a joke before."

"I have made jokes, yes. Guys who spend their days on the internet tend to get pretty good at making jokes."

"Oh, I know the kind of jokes they make."

They were passing a building with a cafeteria.

She said, "I'm going in here to get a juice."

He stopped. "Do you want me to wait outside?"

She shrugged. "No, I don't care."

She went in, and he followed. She turned and said, "What if you're seen with a girl? Don't your buddies have to kill you?"

"No," he said without emotion. "But I'm not allowed to tell them about it. You're not allowed to brag."

"How gentlemanly. And if you start dating someone, like if you actually got a girlfriend? Don't you have to kill yourself?"

"I would just have to leave the group, you know, whatever forum."

"And you wouldn't want to do that because you'd lose all your friends, your buddies who give you a reason to live."

"It's true," he said. "They do."

"Wow. Okay. That's bad. So you couldn't be seen with me, basically, or you would lose your friends."

"And you couldn't be seen with me."

"You are right about that. But I notice you're not brave enough to wear your sad-face pin in here."

He was silent.

In the vast lobby there were notice boards covered with student-made posters. They said REACH OUT TO FRIENDS and DID YOU REMEMBER YOUR BUDDY CHECK? CHECK IN WHEN YOU HAVEN'T HEARD FROM SOMEONE FOR A FEW DAYS! and NEUROTYPICALS CAN BE ALLIES and THERE IS NO SHAME IN ADMITTING YOU NEED HELP and they had numbers for various distress lines and self-care seminars. She saw him staring at them.

"All these posters," he said.

"I know. It's enough to make you kill yourself." She lined up and got a kombucha. She didn't ask him if he wanted anything. They sat at a plastic table.

He said, "That was you making a joke with me. So you can't hate me that much."

"You see, this is the thing," she said. "That's narcissism. You tell yourself we hate you. We don't. I can't hate someone I don't know and don't think about. You tell yourself you are hated because it makes you very sad and noble and romantic. And it gives you all kinds of excuses to do violent things and think hateful thoughts. But nobody thinks about you enough to hate you. It's egotism. It's just massive egotism."

He watched her drink her kombucha. "That sounds a lot like hatred to me."

"No, that's argument. Argument is not hatred." She looked around at all the students, all telling each other that there was hatred everywhere. "I am so sick of insisting on that. That argument is not hatred or violence or unsafe or whatever. I used to have to do it here, all the time. I'm so glad I don't have to anymore."

"What is that stuff?" he said. "What does it taste like?"

"Pee," she said. "Very much like pee. But it's good for you."

He nodded. "That's what I thought. It looks a lot like pee."

They looked around at all the students fighting hatred in their yoga pants. They were drinking large sweet drinks. This struck her as funny. "I wonder if there is a link between fighting hatred and drinking large sweet drinks."

He frowned. "I don't get it."

"No, you wouldn't."

"Why are you even talking to me? Just to humiliate me?"

"No," she said, "worse. To punish you." And as she said this she felt a surprising, sudden cold hard wave of arousal, like the injection of dye that floods your veins when you have an MRI and you are sliding into the machine, and she realized it to be true, that she was going to punish him and she would be aroused by this, and she would let herself go into hatred as if drunk and high.

A student girl was leaving a leaflet on every table. Gloria picked it up. It said, YOU CAN STOP IDEATION.

Gloria's phone buzzed. A text from Autumn: *Can you call me?*

She put it away.

He said, "Have I done anything to you?"

She thought about this. "Yes, you have. You make me scared to go outside alone. To be in the laundromat alone. You've done this to all women. It's a terrible thing."

"That's ridiculous." He was smiling. "That's just totally ridiculous. Look at me." He opened his palms upwards and smiled, and he was a pale, tall, thin boy with bad skin, smiling. "I've never hurt anyone."

She sighed. "What meds have you tried?"

"Excuse me?"

"I assume someone has told you at some point that you are depressed."

He shook his head. "No. I don't think so."

"Well, you are. If you hate yourself and women so much, equally, to be on those forums, you are really messed up. I know you are, I've been on there. I've never seen such sadness.

And all the symptoms of depression—social anxiety, never going out, too much time on the computer. You know there are amazing drugs these days. I can think of a couple myself that you should be on."

He scrunched his face. "Psychiatric drugs? No way. I don't . . ." He shook his head. "No way would I let someone give me a pill. I don't believe in them."

"Don't *believe* in them! You don't believe in science and medicine."

"Would you take them, if someone told you you were crazy, here take this pill, you don't know what's in it?"

She laughed. "I do take them. Everybody does."

His face betrayed such genuine shock she thought he might be acting in a charade. His mouth actually opened and his eyebrows went up.

"Oh come on," she said.

"You take those drugs, like antidepressants, whatever?"

"Antidepressants, yes, oh my god, I must be crazy!"

"Were you seriously crazy?"

"Oh my god. Crazy is, crazy is an idea that's not, that's not really . . ."

"Are you on them right now?"

"And besides, you shouldn't call women crazy. You know how common it is for men to call women crazy? It's one of the ways they—"

"Are you on them right now?"

She put her fingertips to her forehead. "Look, it's very common. They help people. A lot. I don't think I know a single person that's not on them."

He was shaking his head. "You see this is it. This is just it. They dole out these pills like they're candy, they tell everyone there's something wrong with you, it becomes normalized. You don't even think about it. Before you know it, it's in the water."

"Oh, right, of course, it's Big Government, poisoning us, like with fluoride."

He said gently, "That's not what I meant. I meant it starts showing up in lakes because it comes through the sewage systems. People excrete it."

She finished her kombucha. She looked at her watch. She had not meant to give him so much time. "Do you honestly mean you have never tried any medication for depression or anxiety or anything like that?"

"Nope."

"Wow. I don't think I've ever met anyone who can say that."

"And I don't think I've ever met anyone who assumes it's normal that everyone is taking pharmaceuticals for mental illnesses."

"Huh. I've never thought about that." She thought about it for a minute. "I guess I admire it. Trying hard to not treat yourself. Worth a try, I guess." But she was impressed. It was like meeting a priest or something.

"So, in what way did you think you were crazy?"

"No, no. I'm not telling you anything about myself." She stood up. She became conscious that if she left, he could follow her and then find out where she lived. She had not thought of this before. "I'm going to go now."

He stood up. "I'm really glad you talked to me. I'm glad to have met you." He held out his hand.

She hesitated, staring at him. She thought about it. "I'm not going to shake your hand."

He nodded.

"I have some people to meet. On campus. Some guy friends. I am not going home."

"Okay."

"Don't try to follow me."

"Okay." He smiled, did that palms-up gesture again. He wasn't going to follow her. "Can I see you again?"

"Of course not. And why would you want to? You think women are superficial and self-centred and they will only hurt you, why would you want to be close to creatures like that?"

He shook his head. "That stuff on the forums. It's all exaggerated. It's not real."

"Not real! Until someone gets in a van and—"

"No, no, that's not part of it, seriously, that's not what I—"

"Oh, give me a break."

"Look," he said, "you don't get it, I understand, and I don't want to be a part of it either, I hate it."

"You do?"

"Of course I do. We all do."

"No you *don't*." She picked up the empty bottle, but she couldn't leave.

"Ask me any questions you want," he said.

"Okay. I will. I could use this for a project. I will interview you."

He frowned. "For the media?"

"For a writing project."

"You're a writer?"

"Maybe I am. What you have to understand is you have no chance, ever, of getting with me, going on a date with me, nothing. Okay?"

He nodded. "I'm used to that."

"Oh, spare me. Bullshit. Anyway. I am going to go now, and you are going to wait here until I am well out of sight. If I find that you are following me, I will call the police."

He sat down and sprawled out his long legs. "Oh, relax. You know I wouldn't do that."

"I'll meet you back here in this spot tomorrow night at exactly the same time."

His face brightened. "Really? Sure. Sure. I'll be here."

"All right." She looked at her watch. "Eight o'clock."

"Thank you," he called after her.

She walked out into the night and knew she would have to go for a long walk now, as she had missed her chance to work out but was filled with energy. She walked very fast. She had no writing project, that was a lie, no writing project at all.

Her phone rang—Autumn—and she almost didn't answer it, but then she remembered the text from earlier.

"Hi," she said.

Autumn's voice was weak. "Hi. Gloria. I'm." There was a silence and some sniffling.

"Hey. What's wrong? I can't hear you."

"No." Autumn was clearly crying now, quietly.

"What is it?"

"I think I did something dumb. Really dumb."

"I can hardly hear you. Where are you?"

"Home."

Gloria stopped walking. "What is it? What did you do?"

"I took a bunch of pills and I'm going to take them all. I think I'm going to take them all. If I can."

"Oh." Gloria looked around. She was on the edge of a dark park. She knew she would have to find a subway now. "Which pills?" She said this calmly, as she had been through this before.

"All kinds. A whole bunch."

"Mostly your clonazepam?"

"Yeah. I haven't taken it yet. But I'm going to."

"Well," said Gloria, "then you need to call 911. You need to call 911 right away."

Autumn sobbed. She tried to say something, but it ended in a whine.

"I can't understand you. Listen, will you call 911?"

"Will you come home?" Autumn said. She was weeping and hiccupping.

"No, I don't want you to wait for me. I want you to call 911 right away."

"I haven't taken them. I won't if you come home."

"Oh. Jesus."

Autumn wailed. "Please come. Please just come home. Please."

WHEN GLORIA GOT TO THE apartment it was silent and there was no cooking smell. Autumn's bedroom door was open. Gloria took off her shoes and pushed it open.

The room was dark but there was a form under the bedclothes.

Gloria turned on a lamp and sat beside her. Autumn was rocking and sniffling. Gloria took her hand and quickly felt her temple. Autumn was sweaty but not too hot. There were no empty pill bottles beside the bed. "Okay," Gloria said. "You're okay now."

She went into the bathroom and confiscated as many of Autumn's medications from the shelves as she could. She put them in her gym bag. She went back to Autumn and sat with her.

"I'm sorry," Autumn was saying. "I'm sorry."

"So you didn't take anything? Not really?"

"I was going to."

"Right."

From then it was just a question of holding her hand and hearing what happened today (mostly stuff with her mom, and her family, which is just not getting any better, and school, and not finding any part-time work, and then there is the weight thing that has been coming again), and telling her she was beautiful and not a failure and that it was okay to stand up to her family. Gloria looked at her phone a couple of times as she did this; it was now nine o'clock and she could have Autumn asleep by ten. She wondered if Autumn had actually taken anything—she did seem groggy—and if it would be dangerous to just give her one more clonazepam, or a half, to get her quiet, and then Gloria could have an hour or so alone before sleep. In this shitty apartment with Autumn next door. She wished she was still out, just walking around campus.

"I'm sorry," Autumn kept saying. "I miss you, too, is part of it. You're always out and I'm always alone here."

"I'm sorry. I've been so busy with work."

Autumn's voice went high and thin again. "We used to spend so much time together."

Gloria looked at her phone. Nine fifteen. At ten she would go no matter what. Autumn was never going to take too many pills anyway.

5.

DARYN WAS WAITING FOR HER in the cafeteria. He was wearing the same clothes, or identical clothes, all black.

She said, "Do you have any other clothes?"

"Not really."

"I didn't mean to sound mean. It was an honest question."

He shrugged.

"It's weird, everything I say, I realize could sound exactly like the stereotype you have of mean girls."

"Well, it does, kind of."

"I'm just asking questions because I'm curious. And then even my curiosity confirms that I'm a bitch, right?"

He frowned. "I wouldn't have wanted to know you if I thought you were a bitch."

She had brought a notebook. She took it out. "Now," she said. "Tell me, um, something about your background?"

He lived with his mom. He didn't talk much with his dad. His dad lived in Alberta now. He hadn't actually seen him in a couple of years. He was taking software design at a community college in the suburbs and he worked part-time at Best

Buy. He didn't have a car but he'd love to have one. He'd had a Civic for a few years but he'd probably get a Subaru now.

"Have you ever had a girlfriend?"

"I don't feel comfortable answering that." He gave a little nervous smile.

She put down her pen. "Now isn't that interesting. Why wouldn't you answer that? Isn't it important?"

He scowled. "It's private."

She waited a second. "I need to know."

"Why? It's none of your business. Do I ask you about your private sex life?"

"You're not interviewing me. I'm interviewing you."

He was silent.

"Besides," she said, "That's different. Having a sex life isn't a big deal for me."

"Okay, so tell me about your sex life. Do you have a boyfriend?"

She hesitated only for a second. "Of course I do."

"So why are you talking to me?" He got up and his face told her he was really angry. He yanked his jacket from the back of the chair.

"Okay," she said. "Okay. Wait. I don't. I don't have a boyfriend."

He stood still. He was actually breathing hard.

She said, "Why are you so mad?"

"Why did you lie?"

"Sit down." She tried to smile and it worked. Slowly, he sat. "Here's why," she said. "And this is part of what you don't understand, I guess, and what you should understand. Are you ready to listen?"

He held out his hands, palms upwards.

"Okay. Women have to worry all the time, about men hurting them or bothering them, you get that, right? I guess you don't. We always have to be on our guard. And do you know what that's like? Do you have any idea what it's like to be always being careful?"

He sighed. "Whatever."

"Whatever? You think it's ridiculous?"

"Well, in my case." He laughed a little. "I think you can tell. Can't you tell, if a guy is weird or whatever?"

She shook her head hard. "No I cannot. Lots of guys get weird. And I don't know you. There is no reason at all for me to trust you."

"Okay," he said. "Okay."

"Okay."

They sat and sipped their drinks for a minute. He was drinking juice. He had been surprised that this cafeteria did not sell Coca-Cola. Gloria felt like a glass of wine but she had told herself there would be no alcohol around him, so that she would not relax. She could not imagine him in a bar anyway. He looked too young.

She couldn't stop thinking about the girlfriend thing. She couldn't drop it. "Just tell me, is it because you are embarrassed that you haven't had a girlfriend? Or embarrassed about how it ended? That you don't want to talk about it?"

"Not this again."

"What's the big deal?"

"Of course I've had a girlfriend."

"Oh. Okay." She felt hungry all of a sudden. She watched the line waiting at the food counter. There were pizza slices and hamburgers and all sorts of things she shouldn't eat. They might have some soup. She didn't know how to broach the subject of food with him. It might be too intimate. And she didn't know whether she should pay. If she was interviewing him. She said, "So it ended unhappily?"

"I don't want to talk about it."

She wondered if he was a virgin. She very much wanted to ask him, but she knew he would not like this and it would go badly. She watched someone pass with a plate of fried rice. "Do you want to get something to eat?"

He nodded. They got up and joined the line. He ordered the hot dog special. It came with a pile of potato chips and a pickle. He did not want the pickle. She waited for him to pay for his own food, and an orange drink that wasn't orange juice. She had the bean salad.

They sat and she wondered again if this was too much like a date. But she still really wanted to know what happened in his sex life. He had put ketchup on his hot dog.

"In the forums," she said, "you show a lot of disgust for women. For their bodies, especially. So, there's one thing most of us don't get. If women are so disgusting, why is it a problem if they won't date you?"

He shook his head, his mouth full of hot dog. In a moment he said, "The forums are all just, like, an act. Like, everyone is posing. It's just roles that everyone plays."

"Until they don't. Until someone who says he's going to murder girls gets in a van and then goes out and murders ten of them."

"Nope." He was waving his finger. "Nope, that doesn't happen. Any time anybody—"

"What do you mean it doesn't happen? What are you—"

"No, no, listen, just listen to me. The second anyone on those forums says anything about harming anyone or killing anyone he's kicked right off the forum, right away, no questions asked. No right to appeal even. They shut that down *now*."

"Oh, great. That's helpful."

"The stuff on the forums is not real. It's like a game. We've all been playing these character games all our lives, right? We have names and avatars."

"So it's kind of like a giant video game?"

He shrugged. "Sort of. Everything online is. Even your Facebook is."

She thought about that. "I'm not really on Facebook anymore. But I guess."

He said, "I'm saying we're just used to everything not being real."

"So that means that nothing you say online counts as real?"

"The forums give us a place to let our anger out. So, we all get to play an angry role. In everyday life I'm not angry. Well, not all the time. Sometimes. But not at girls. Look, it's like a loser club. If you feel like a loser, you join this club where everyone's a loser. So you're not alone and it's comforting to feel you're not alone in your loserdom. So everyone plays up their loserdom. You act it out. And some of the guys are funny. It's just an escape."

Gloria had heard much of this before, in the articles she had read about it, and so had stopped listening. She was disgusted by what he was eating. She wished there was at least a carrot beside it.

She said, "Do you all think you're ugly?"

"Well everyone else seems to. They treat us like we're ugly."

"Who does though? Who? Did the cafeteria lady treat you like you're ugly?"

He shrugged.

"You mean girls, right? Women? Who exactly has treated you like you're ugly?"

"I told you, I don't want to talk about that."

"Do you think you're ugly?"

"I don't know. I must be."

"You're not. You know that. You're not ugly. You could be good-looking."

"Could be? Thanks."

"Whoa!" she said. "Sensitive." He had reddened and she was smiling; she felt pleasure in this discomfort and then anxiety about this pleasure. Why was she doing this? "You are good-looking though. You're young, you're in good shape. Do you go to the gym? Or is that too normie?"

He revealed a tiny smile. "I have a weight set at home. And I ride my bike a lot."

"So, you know you're good-looking. You know you're good-looking, but—"

"I didn't say that."

"Well I'm saying it." She looked him in the eyes. "You are good-looking." He was bright red. "So now how can you go on saying you're a loser?"

"Because I'm not good-looking like you."

"Like me?" She laughed.

He stared at the table, his face on fire. "You are beautiful."

"Oh god." This had gone through her like a silver knife and given her a familiar warmth and then a familiar pain, a consciousness that she was not beautiful enough and must not think about that, for it was unhealthy and of course she was fine as she was, but it was a hole she could go down ever since her body had changed, swelled, just in these last two years, and this was something Daryn did not understand and would never understand, and no amount of reassurance would ever make this pain go away when some stupid guy said she was beautiful and she knew, and other women knew, that she was not. She felt troubled and angry. He looked pathetic. He was pathetic. "You are such a loser when you say that, you know?"

He looked up. His mouth was open and his eyes were shiny, as if she had slapped him. "What?"

"You become just a little dog, a little abject dog, when you're like that. And it's what you want, isn't it? It's what actually makes you comfortable, isn't it?"

He stood up. He picked up his jacket. "I just said something really nice to you."

"Nice, and complicated, yes." She sighed. "I'm sorry. Sit down. I was just kidding."

Slowly he sat down and then she really did want to be beautiful, to be even more beautiful, to be able to control him like this, it was undeniable, she wanted this. She said, "Do you eat like this every day?"

"Like what? We're in a cafeteria." Then some revelation crossed his face. "Are you a vegetarian?"

"Not exactly. I don't eat a lot of meat but no, that's not it. I do try to eat healthy. Does your mom cook for you?"

"Sometimes. Not always too healthy though. It's true I eat in the cafeteria a lot."

Gloria watched him finish the potato chips and she was horrified to realize she wanted to cook him a meal.

6.

GLORIA HAD TO GO TO the work party that Isabel had to go to; Gloria had to come with her because it was likely to be horrendous and all the tech bros were going to try to talk to Isabel one after another about whether she liked snowboarding or skiing, and if Gloria came they wouldn't have to stay long and they could go for sushi after.

Gloria was not curious about the tech bros, but she did want to wear a dress for once; she had a black one that was tight in the bust, the first dress she had worn in weeks and possibly months, and she was excited to be standing in the lobby of an office tower wearing it like a grown-up and about to be out with Isabel, a thing that was exciting in itself.

This feeling waned after fifteen minutes when Isabel was not there. There was nowhere to sit in the lobby, and the security guard had asked Gloria if he could help her.

Finally Isabel texted that she was already up there, in the restaurant on the thirty-fifth floor, and Gloria should just go up, which had definitely not been the plan.

Gloria did her breathing in the elevator. She counted all the buttons on the wall and named all the colours she saw—brown, beige, grey, and black, and a kind of dull silver, a nickel colour, possibly pewter, for the buttons. This got her to the top.

The restaurant was fancier than she had expected: the elevator opened directly onto an anteroom with black marble walls, water running down one like a terrible leak, and a lectern where two women younger than her in tighter black dresses were looking worried at a computer screen. They took just a second longer than they should have to look up from their screen. Then they smiled at her and said, "This way," and she followed them into the private dining room. This room was less fancy—it had beige walls and no windows, like a conference room in a hotel or the reception room in a funeral parlour. There was a bar tended by a guy in black who looked like Florian, and a long table with food. Another waitress in black was carrying around a tray of flutes of prosecco. About a dozen people, maybe fifteen, were talking in clusters. Nobody really looked at her when she came in.

In many ways in fact—the church-hall room and the caterers in black and everyone subdued—it was like a funeral.

Isabel slipped out from between two guys in dress pants and shirts with no jackets and came and gave her a hug. Gloria took a glass of prosecco. Isabel said, "Don, I want you to meet my wife, Gloria."

The guy Don's face changed to a kind of terror: his eyebrows actually went up and his mouth opened a little. "Oh," he said. "Wow."

Gloria held out her hand. "Not really," she said.

"Are you serious?" said Don. "Are you really married?"

"Does that shock you?" said Isabel.

"No. No," said Don. "Just didn't know. Holy! Nice to meet you."

"She's kidding," said Gloria.

"Oh," said Don. "Man, you are messing with me."

"I am not," said Isabel. "We're married." She was in what must have been her work clothes, a black turtleneck and a black blazer and a short skirt and flat little librarian shoes, very prim, and still she looked like a magazine.

"Okay," said Gloria, "we're married."

"You are totally messing with me. Anyway, nice to meet you."

"Isabel," said a lady who was behind her, "could you go in and see where the hot canapés are? They should have been here by now."

"Magda," said Isabel, "this is my friend Gloria."

"Nice to meet you." The woman was in her forties and had marvellous hair, all frizzy curls, and heavy glasses.

"Who do I ask?" said Isabel.

"I'm not sure," said the woman, smiling, and she turned away to talk to a tall man, the only man in an actual suit, but no tie, who did not look very old but whose hair was mostly grey. She stood on her toes to whisper something in his ear and put her hand on his lapel.

"*Vreeer*," said Isabel. "Be right back."

"Is that your boss?"

"Everyone here is my boss. I'm just the office manager. This is what I do."

As Isabel walked away, Gloria felt the eyes of the tech bro on her, so she walked briskly to the food table and stared intently at the cheese tray. A guy was standing next to her, then, and he asked her if she was a friend of Isabel's, which was great because Isabel was great, and he got along with Isabel really great.

"Do you snowboard?" said Gloria.

Isabel was back in a minute, and she handed Gloria another glass of prosecco and went to reassure Magda that the food was coming, and then the tall grey-haired guy was beside Gloria. His name was Don or John or David or Graham and he told her he was pleased she could come. He smelled nice. Then Isabel was back and he turned and walked away.

All this time Magda's eyes were on Gloria.

Then there was the VP of Customer Service to meet, a man in his thirties who seemed to be Isabel's actual direct boss. He had a red face and a giant silver watch with multiple dials on it. He shook her hand very firmly and told her she would be welcome at any of their events. Then there were more of the younger guys to meet, all friendly, who asked her and Isabel if they had any plans to get away this summer and told them about various boats and cottages and how long it took to reach these cottages depending on traffic. Only one of them was quite hot in a snowboardy kind of way and he was the only one who asked her, Gloria, what she did. Gloria was so startled by this that she couldn't answer. She never knew quite how to answer this anyway and so said "Communications" which always appeared to satisfy people like this, who nodded as if they knew exactly what she meant.

Aside from Isabel and this Magda there seemed to be only one other woman in the office and she was older so Gloria assumed she was a secretary. The men were more muscular than most of the guys she knew.

She went up to the bartender who looked like Florian with the intention of flirting with him but he turned out to be into fishing and he too seemed intent on imparting to her how long it took him, under varying traffic conditions, to get to the lake where he fished.

After only a few minutes of this Isabel told her that it was okay if they left now, and they left without saying good-bye to anyone including the grey-haired guy who was quite good-looking and may have been a boss of some kind. Magda was definitely a boss of some kind.

They walked to a sushi bar on Queen Street where Gloria felt overdressed, but Isabel never looked overdressed anywhere. Gloria said, "How is it, the work? I mean I don't really understand what you do, or what they do."

"It's work in an office. It's like every TV show about work in an office."

"So like there's a water cooler and a dumb boss and a cute shy guy who has a crush on you?"

"It's all guys, because it's a tech startup, and they all have crushes on me but none of them are cute, except one guy, you know the guy, the guy who is kind of muscly and dumb, you met him, I know, the one you think I mean, so dumb, I mean really, *zhooom*, dumb, but I find myself fantasizing about him. He is terrified around me and can't speak and also has a wife. But my boss is dumb, yes, and also a transphobe and a dickbox."

"A transphobe? There are trans people working in your office?"

Isabel shrieked. "No! It's a tech company! That would be *wheeee-ow, hooooh*."

"Then how do you know he's a transphobe?"

"Oh, he made the dumbest, stupidest joke, like a total dad joke, except offensive, and I really don't know if he knows it or not. He's like 'I self-identify as male,' with this smirk that meant he was expecting us to laugh and we didn't, me and this one other girl, who is, like, the receptionist, and it was so, oh, *eeeyeesh*. I was like *are you fucking serious right now, that is actually the most insensitive joke I have ever heard*."

Gloria sipped her sake, which she did not actually like. "It is a lame joke."

"But it's a mockery of a really serious problem, it's not a joke for people who are at a higher risk of suicide, who are constantly marginalized..."

"Yes, I know. Do they have wine here?"

"I know you know. I get so..." She pulled her hands back, palms outwards, and widened her eyes and showed her teeth. "So *yeeeeee* about this."

Gloria waved to the waitress. "I'm going to get some wine. So, you haven't had any interesting guys at all on this site?"

"Not really," said Isabel. "I've had some nice dinners. But you have to sit and listen. One guy took me to Chrism, which is, do you know it?"

Gloria shook her head.

"It's, like, you wait for six months to get a reservation, kind of thing. It was amazing."

"What did you eat? What do you eat in a place called Jism?"

"I had some kind of raw fish ceviche, that was good, and then I had pigeon, because he made me, he wanted me to try it, and I couldn't finish it, because it was bloody. It tasted like pain. It tasted like a wound."

"Great."

"And we had a wine that was like two hundred bucks. Fine with me. I can't really tell the difference."

"And then do you have any trouble because they expect something in return?"

"Of course they do. So you're always kind of declining, you know, afterwards, to go over and see his paintings or whatever."

"That sounds a little bit. A little bit ..." Gloria wondered how Isabel would phrase it. "A little bit *eeep*."

"A little *what*?"

"Do you think they have like carafes? Would you share a half litre?"

The waitress came and they ordered wine and edamame.

Gloria said, "I mean a little, you know, like harsh."

"Oh, like I'm a gold digger, kind of thing? You think that?"

"Well, what are you after, really?"

"Oh, look at you, all moral. And you've never done that, you've never let a guy take you out for dinner?"

"Well, I don't really meet those kinds of guys. I'm not looking online. I'm more the hockey pub guy talking about Jung kind of speed."

"What? Jung? What?"

Gloria laughed. "It was something you said. You said guys our age want to go to a pub and talk about Jung because of this one prof they have who's amazing. Jung and Joseph Campbell. Which is quite funny and true really, but I don't hate it." She was thinking of Daryn then, and how he wouldn't even be able to talk about Jung. She opened her mouth to tell Isabel and then didn't.

"I wouldn't mind it, I guess," said Isabel, "in nicer restaurants."

"Is that what men are for?"

"Oh, look, these guys are adults, they know exactly what they're doing, they can take care of themselves, it's not like I'm taking advantage of them."

"But you are, a little bit, aren't you? I mean if you don't really like them, and you just want an expensive meal at Chrism or Jism or Spermbank or whatever?"

"Whoa! What is this? Have you been going to church or what?" Isabel put all her fingertips together and arched one eyebrow. "Come come Mister Bond," she said in her English accent. "You enjoy killing just as much as I do."

Gloria gulped her wine. "What is this wine, is it apple juice or something?"

"It's fine by me. Quantity over quality. Are we going to eat anything?"

They ordered fried and crispy things, because Gloria also didn't, to be honest, really like sushi, even though she ate it frequently as it seemed healthy (just like the kombucha, which she also didn't really like a whole lot). The veggie curries she was always making were good, but her clothes had started to smell of curry.

She was drinking the wine quite quickly.

Isabel said, "So how are your boys?"

"What boys? I told you there are none." But she felt her face getting hot. She ate a crispy thing. "I suppose I could use someone who could take me to a nice restaurant."

Isabel looked away. "Yeah," she said faintly, "it's nice."

A shadow had come over her face, a fatigue, and Gloria asked her, "Is there something you're not telling me?"

Isabel looked at her once, sharply, and then away again. "No. No."

Gloria knew then that she should tell Isabel about the strange boy and ask her why she thought she was doing it, allowing him into her life like this, as she herself didn't really know why—Isabel would know, and perhaps would understand and perhaps would not, perhaps would get up on her own ideals and be shocked and angry. There was that risk but there was also the knowledge that if she talked about it, it would confirm that she was doing it, that it was a thing she was doing, and she wasn't really. It was not a thing. It wasn't a thing because she could not in any way justify it to Isabel, or to anyone she knew, and this made her feel lonely, and also guilty, as if she had betrayed everyone she knew.

7.

SHE DID NOT HAVE HIS phone number and he did not have hers. She had told him to meet her again in the cafeteria, but when he arrived she did not want to sit in the bright light and watch him eat another hot dog, so she said they were going to go for a walk and he put on his jacket obediently. She wasn't sure what she felt about being so totally in control of what they did. Other boys would have automatically resisted any suggestion she made—they would have said no, I'm hungry, let me grab something here or okay we can walk but we have to walk towards this building because Jonno and Bills and Frankie are meeting us there; nothing would ever have been this easy, as boys made their plans and then you made yours around theirs, and she was not sure that she could admire someone who did not even have plans, much less impose them. But perhaps it would be a good thing, to not have these decisions made, to make decisions, and perhaps this lack of distraction by other things he needed to do would mean that he would not be the kind of person who, like Florian, would stop texting her for about three months after each time they went out. It was something she could try on, anyway.

It was Sunday and there were few people on the campus. It was warm and the evening was long.

"What about your notes?" he said.

"Notes?"

"You're not taking notes this time. For your article."

"Oh yes." She had forgotten about the article. "I have a notebook in my bag. But right now this is more general stuff. Just want to get a general sense, you know."

"Of what?"

She did not say *of whether you are a virgin*. She said, "Of… of your movement and what you believe."

"I'm not really in a movement."

"You were in a demonstration! What was that about?"

He shrugged. "I thought I might meet some of the guys on the forums. Guys like me."

"Guys like you. I have a lot of questions about what that means. About what guys like you are, or what you think makes you an unusual kind of guy. I don't know. But let's put that aside for a minute. It was an anti-immigrant demonstration and there were a lot of neo-Nazi groups there. You know that. Do you hate immigrants?"

"No. I don't care. It just happened to be a thing that… where I…I don't know. I wasn't there for that part of it."

"That *part* of it? You were marching with racists, who had racist flags and white-power symbols."

"I don't know if they're racist, per se. They're just…"

Gloria waited but he did not finish.

"Look," he said, "I don't really know anything about politics. It's not about politics. And I would be scared to talk to you about politics anyway because you've studied it and you can, you can out-talk me, so I'm not interested."

Gloria blew out her cheeks. She could feel anger rising and knew this would not be helpful. "You were at a political demonstration."

"Sure, okay, go ahead, tell me how ridiculous it is, destroy me, make fun. This is why, this is exactly why..." He stopped talking again and they walked for some minutes.

Gloria held her tongue and waited. Whatever he would say then would be revealing, would reveal hatred or fear or whatever it was. But it didn't come.

They were at the big park now and would have to cross a busy road to get into it. She hesitated, as it might be romantic to walk in the park on such a warm evening. The trees were showing tiny bright green leaves. They were so bright as to be almost fluorescent. Waiting for the light, she decided to help him and said, "I'm not going to argue with you. I'm just asking questions. What is it you're angry about?"

He said, "We're going in the park, I presume?"

She drew a breath. "Sure. Okay."

They crossed and walked along a gravel path through the area that was most thick with tents. She had forgotten about the tents: it was not romantic, that was for sure. Most of the tents had junk piled around them, office chairs on wheels, wooden pallets in stacks, children's desks. There were signs, painted and hung between the tents, demanding to be left alone by police. BETTER THAN SUICIDE, read one sign.

There was shouting from just outside one tent as they passed. Gloria glanced over and saw a woman shouting at a child, a boy who was maybe eleven. The woman said, "Don't you fucking fuck with me," and he said, "Don't you fucking fuck with me either," in a surprisingly raspy voice and then he went into the tent where Gloria guessed they both lived.

"Jesus," she said.

"Epic," he said.

They kept walking till they were through the tents and in a clear area under a statue of a man on a horse. There were normal people walking quickly past, so they sat on a bench.

He said, "I'm not always angry. I'm angry sometimes because everything seems so fucked up."

"What is fucked up?"

"The same things you think are fucked up, I bet. Shit is fucked up. It's unfair. I'm a smart guy, my mom is smart, she works hard, and we live in a little apartment in the middle of nowhere. Kids at my school drive new cars. I don't get it. I don't get how they can. It's their parents, and it's not fair."

"So economic inequality. Okay. That is unfair. Is that the fault of immigrants?"

He looked puzzled. "I never said it was."

"But you were at the—okay. Never mind."

"I just think it's fucked up there are no more good jobs, no more job security, everyone has to be like their own business, I presume we'll never be able to buy a house, like never ever ever."

She nodded. "That's funny, because everybody I know is concerned about those things too. But we don't blame women for it and we don't join demonstrations against immigrants."

"Would you stop about the immigrants? I told you I don't—"

"Okay. Okay. How about this. Do you feel you should have certain privileges? I mean because you're white, you're male, you—"

He turned to her and his face was alight. "Oh, I do? I have privilege? What privilege? Where do you see it? I'm invisible. I would have been invisible to you, too, if I hadn't pissed you off."

"Okay, okay," she said, "but this thing isn't about economic disadvantage, though, is it? You could join a political party or an activist group or something if that was it. It's about girls, isn't it, mostly, and how they have rejected you, or how you think they've rejected you?"

He turned away and stared straight ahead for a moment.

She asked gently, "Who rejected you? The girlfriend? You said you had?"

He shrugged. "Sure. I guess."

"Can you tell me about her?"

He stared her in the eyes. "Is this for your article?"

Now she felt herself reddening. "Yes," she said at last. "It's all background." A wind blew and she shivered. He shivered too and pulled his jacket around him. He looked very thin. She looked at his hand lying flat on his thigh, on the black jeans, and it looked cold, and she imagined putting her hand over it.

"Nothing much to tell," he said. "I had a girlfriend in high school, or I thought I did, and I found out she was cheating on me, or whatever, she didn't think we were—she didn't think about relationships the same way I did."

"Maybe she never thought you were in an exclusive relationship."

"Maybe. But she did lie. And she didn't have to lie."

"Who did she—who did she cheat with?"

Daryn shook himself as if covered with bugs. "Guy I knew. Ashish. He's like Indian or something. There were a lot—there was a large community at my school. He was a popular guy. I knew him. His family had a big house, in one of those subdivisions that's all Indian. Or Pakistani. Whatever."

"What did she look like?"

"Nothing special. Redhead. Anyway."

"And you liked her a lot."

He nodded. He said, "I haven't eaten. So I'm going to have to go soon. I'm starving."

She said, "Did you guys ... did you have sex?"

He looked puzzled. "Sure."

"Oh!"

"Of course we did." He laughed. "You thought I'd be a virgin."

"Yes, I did. I guess I really don't get this whole thing."

"I don't believe in, like promiscuous sex though. I wanted a relationship, like a serious relationship. I don't think I could—I could only have like a monogamous relationship. With one person. I guess I'm romantic that way."

She laughed but she felt a curious sadness. Finally she said, "I think a lot of people are like that."

"Not women, apparently."

"Yes, women." She stood up. "What are you going to eat?"

He just shook his head. "No idea. Guess I'll go home."

"That's a long way." She was thinking of her place. Autumn was gone, back to her parents. "I'm going to make you something healthy," she said. "Come on". And she turned and walked quickly away before she could change her mind.

GLORIA KNEW HOW TO MAKE about five dishes, and even these she had not prepared for some time. The one she knew was healthy and voluminous was also the easiest—it was a lentil-and-cauliflower curry that you could make with curry paste, which she already had. They stopped at Kabul Farms near her house, after the subway and the bus, and got the cauliflower and a tin of lentils and a zucchini she thought she could throw in. She thought she had onions at home. Daryn watched these purchases with wide eyes. He seemed particularly alarmed by the cauliflower.

She watched him in the shop, waiting to see if he would react with any disdain or fear of the smells or the dark men behind the counter, but he was friendly to all of them. She said, "I guess you don't shop in places like these."

He said, "I live even farther out, remember. These are really the only grocery stores, where I live."

She felt a little nervous as they climbed the narrow stairs and entered her apartment. She began unpacking bags in the kitchen and he sat on one of the two chairs with his legs splayed out halfway across the floor. She had not realized how tiny the kitchen was. He seemed very tall in there.

She put the rice on. The smell of the onions was comforting. She wished she had bought some beer. She looked in the cupboard above the fridge and found a dusty bottle of a green liqueur and offered him some. He took hesitant sips. She took large ones. It was bitter and sticky.

It was very warm now, in the kitchen, with the cooking, and he had taken his hoodie off and his arms came out white and stick thin. He still smelled of his crisp cologne though. He had taken off his running shoes and she was glad of this, as he seemed nothing but vulnerable in his socks.

She took off her own sweater. She had a nice silky black blouse on underneath, but jeans, as she did not want to appear to have dressed up for him. The jeans were quite tight, though, and she was aware as she cooked that she was standing in front of him and bending over sometimes and he would be looking at her ass. She did not turn around to check if he was. She knew how round she was from behind, and she wondered if she had put these particular jeans on earlier with some kind of unconscious knowledge that she would be inviting him here. Because she had not planned it at all, indeed, not, as far as she knew, even thought of it until they were out at the cafeteria. If he were to touch her, she decided, she would be furious and lecture him and send him home.

"I don't really eat a lot of curry," he said, as the room filled with the smell.

"I'll make it really mild."

He looked frightened as she stirred in the cauliflower. She added some frozen peas. It looked convincing and she was pleased with it.

When he tasted it, she could tell he was trying to keep his face expressionless. "Interesting," he said.

"Maybe it needs salt," she said.

He covered his plate with salt and tried again. "It's good," he said, after a few silent mouthfuls. "I'll have some more later." He pushed his plate a way. He wiped his mouth politely with his paper napkin.

"You really don't like it?"

"It's good. It's good." He nodded vigorously. "I'm just not used to it. I have to get used to it."

The dish was a little fibrous, she had to admit. She ate half of hers and pushed it away too out of guilt for starving him. "I'll make you a sandwich," she said. "Trad wife."

"It's fine. I'm fine. I'm good."

She found some cheese slices in the fridge and made him a sandwich with white bread. He ate a little of this but did not finish it. She finished her glass of green-candy liqueur. It did not go well with the curry. He had not finished his.

She made some herbal tea. They had it in the living room on the sagging couch, side by side because there was no other chair. He turned off the overhead light and switched on lamps. He did not leap up to inspect the bookshelves as most boys she knew would. He stared for a while at Autumn's big, framed Frida Kahlo poster, but said nothing.

She remembered this was to be an interview so she went and got a notebook. She said, "So. Where were we." She flipped through pages. "What's your full name?"

"Daryn Boutilier."

"French!"

"Acadian. Way back. I guess. I don't really know the story."

She wrote this down. "And what handle do you use online?"

He scrunched up his nose. "Oh, I've used a bunch of them."

"So tell me one of them."

He sighed, then shook his head. "No. I don't want to...

look, whatever we say on there, it's not really me. It's just jokes. I've told you this."

"Tell me one handle you have used, so I can trust you."

"You can trust me."

"What sites do you frequent?"

"A bunch. Not important. Never mind."

"Of course it's important. Come on."

"No. I'm here. You have me right here. Ask away."

She tapped her pen on the blank page. "Okay. Tell me something else then. What's your favourite book?"

"Not a huge reader. I liked ... um ... in high school, the book about the fisherman?"

"Fisherman."

"Yeah, the old guy ... that's it, *The Old Man and the Sea*."

"Oh, yes. Okay. Anything else?"

"Jordan Peterson. Of course."

"Of course."

"But him, I mostly watched his videos."

"Okay. What's your favourite movie?"

He drummed his palms on his thighs. "Probably *The Dark Knight*."

"That's ..."

"It's a Batman. With Heath Ledger? It's the best Batman movie, anyway."

She blew out her cheeks. She wrote this down. "Okay. Moving on. Do you believe that women should be subservient to men?"

"Subservient? Of course not."

"A lot of your friends do. On the forums."

"I told you, the forums are just—anyway. No. If anything, the opposite."

"What?"

"I believe men should be providers for their partners and, you know, make sacrifices for them. And make them happy and comfortable and, you know. Do everything for them. Like a knight and a princess."

"The dark knight again."

He frowned. "Not dark."

Before she asked her next question, Gloria remembered to write this in her notebook. *Knight and princess*. "And what would she have to do for you? In return?"

"Nothing. Just be ... you know, like, love me."

"That's it?"

"Just love me and no one else."

"What about housework? Do you want her to do that? Or can she work, outside the home?"

He laughed. "Of course she can work. You have totally the wrong idea. Everybody has to work."

"Okay, but she must have to do something in return for this ... this princess treatment." Gloria cleared her throat. "What about sex?"

"What about it?"

"Does she have to be ..." Gloria stopped, as she didn't quite know what she was asking. "Does she have to be, like, make herself available? For you, all the time?"

Daryn frowned. "That is also insane. I think you have a very mean imagination."

"Oh, come on. There has to be some payoff, for you, right?"

He leaned forward, his elbows on his knees, and looked at her very intently. "The payoff is that I would find someone who loves me. For who I am. Even if I am going to have a shitty coding job and never going to own a house and never going to play, like, football. Because I'm not stupid and I'm a nice guy. And if she loves me then she wants to have sex with me, yes. Duh."

"A shitty coding job? That's funny. That would be a really good job, computer coding. Where I am, in life, anyway."

He sat back, his palms open. "Whatever."

Gloria was not quite able to understand the discomfort she felt—an anguish like jealousy, although she didn't know what to be jealous of. She was not envious of his life, or of his love. She could make him love her, she knew that, and it would not be a pleasant experience, because it would be a needy love, obviously, and exhausting, and then simply because he actually did belong to those forums and he actually did go to a march that was anti-immigrant and full of actual Nazis and he did actually wear the sad-face pin, which meant he was angry enough over god knows what to go out in public with it and get in fights over it; even saying *We respect rules, ma'am* was a sign of this police-state ideal they all had about women staying home and making babies and being princesses while men were knights, so he was genuinely weird no matter how polite he was, and she would always have to be nervous around him and she would have to change his mind about so many things. She was jealous of his imaginary girl, of any girl that would receive a love like that, not from Daryn, but from someone else, from Florian perhaps, who had been incapable of loving her? And perhaps Florian could love someone like that, but it wasn't her?

Or it was not jealousy perhaps so much as envy, envy of this girl she would never be who could love like that herself. Or perhaps she envied his idealism, for she knew the world would never be like what he wanted, but she wished it could be as well.

And there it was again—an anger, a desire to punish him, to make him see—what? His naivety? Or her own vulnerability, her pain, the fact that she could never be deserving of that kind of love from Florian or anyone like him—and she wasn't really thinking about Florian here, tall handsome Florian with his scarves and his rock climbing, she really wasn't, and actually she didn't love Florian either—was she angry that Daryn would never love a real person?

Was it Daryn she really wanted to punish because he believed in that fairy-tale stuff about men and women that made everybody so unhappy, or was it Florian and Mr LaRusso she wanted to punish for being such fucking dicks? Or maybe she just really wanted someone to fall in love with her, but the most likely candidate for this was this guy who said or who at least had friends who said they wanted to enslave or kill women, and even though he had shown no sign of saying this around her, she didn't want to be naked with a guy who could easily say these things because he could suddenly get weird on her. And yet she did, actually, want something, she liked this idea of devotion, and she liked this idea that she might, for once, be the one with power; not that she was going to dress up in some leather outfit with a police hat and build a plastic dungeon and call herself Mistress Icequeen Acantha Raven Metallica and talk about consent all the time—like, as Florian would say, one of the pronoun people—but there was this idea, an idea slowly congealing, and it was congealing around an image of Daryn being teased by her, just teased, on the verge of his pleasure the way she had seen Florian once when he had let her try this, maybe whimpering too, and her completely in control and him remembering her, always remembering her as this kind of supreme being who had given him this pleasure. This was really not healthy, she knew this, but she did not foresee any other way she might allow him to touch her.

She said, "Do you ever fantasize, though, about dominating a woman?"

His face flushed so quickly it was like a burn. He looked away. "You mean like sexually, I presume? No."

"Oh, come on. Of course you have. Everyone has."

"See, this is the kind of—I don't like talking about this kind of stuff. Sexual stuff."

"All right. Okay. Not sexually then."

"No, then. Not in any way." He drummed his hands on the sofa arm, and she knew he wanted to get away then. "Why? Is that what you want?"

"That's silly." She drew a breath here, conscious of lying, and wondered if he could hear it, tell that she was lying, that yes she used to get excited when Florian pinned her down and now she had this idea, this idea that she was trying to turn the conversation to, an idea that wasn't exactly about punishing him anymore, but maybe doing something for him, doing something that would make him love her more.

He said, "Well why don't you tell me about your love life, instead of grilling me about mine?"

"Would you ever let a girl dominate you? I mean a woman?"

He laughed. "I don't think any woman really wants that." His fingers drummed on the sofa. "Do you?"

"What if it were the only way to get a woman to trust you? To like you? Would you do it?"

"Why would any woman want that?" They were staring at each other now.

"To prove to her that you could be trusted."

"That's ridiculous."

"Do you want to have sex with me?"

He did not hesitate. He nodded yes. Then he closed his eyes and nodded again, his eyes closed.

She said, "What would happen to you, though, if you had sex with me? Wouldn't you ... like lose everything? Like you'd have to give up who you are?"

In a high voice, with his eyes closed, he said, "Fine with me." Then, almost moaning, he said, "I don't want to be who I am."

Gloria looked at his tall body, all vibrating wires, waiting there for her to take it, and she said, "All right. Do exactly what I say then."

8.

"STAND UP."

He stood.

"Take off your shirt."

He pulled it off. His chest was hairless, except for a trail on his belly. He did have some muscles outlined, and wide, bony shoulders. His abs were clearly defined.

"You do work out," she said.

He giggled and flexed a little. He said, "Where is this going?"

"You have to prove you respect me. And that I can trust you. Take your pants off."

He unbuckled his jeans and pulled them off. He wore grey knit cotton boxer briefs. They were quite tight. He did not have an erection.

"All right," she said. Her heart was beating too fast. She didn't know what she was going to do next. "All right. Go in the bedroom. Lie down on the bed and wait for me."

He did as he was told, looking quite serious. Gloria went to the bedroom and looked for her Ativan. She took a half milligram and then, after thinking, a second one.

She went into the bedroom. He lay looking straight up at the ceiling with his hands by his sides.

She sat on the bed at his side. She wished she had taken the Ativan earlier. She was too warm. She leaned over and placed a hand on his chest, and he quivered. His skin was cool.

She was aware that she felt no arousal. But this wasn't the point—perhaps the arousal would come later.

She had had a boyfriend once, a guy from Fort Erie who was a hockey player, who had shown her a porn video that he had said would turn her on: it was a man tied up and masturbated by a woman in high leather boots who was insulting him, and he, the boy, Kyle was his name, had been excited by this and wanted her to do this to him, and she had done it, but without the insults, and it wasn't exactly arousing for her but she had at length become aroused by his arousal.

But this wasn't the point, here, really; the point was to see, just to see, really, whether Daryn would be nice or not if they were undressed, without any risk to her. And also, she supposed, to start to make him think differently about what sex was, and what women were, if it was true that he believed all the alpha-male, sigma-male, cuckboy stuff he was reading on his forums.

She tried to remember what had so excited Florian when she had made him lie still that one time. It was probably not powerlessness but just the stroking, to be honest.

Daryn reached out and put a hand on her knee, and this tiny confidence of his gave her a tiny flicker of alarm, of fright, something almost like fear. She pushed it off. "You may not touch me," she said. "Put your hands over your head." He did so. "If I had something to tie you up with, I would." She stroked his chest and ran her hand down over his abs, which were very firm. She glanced at his shorts and saw him hardening. She stroked his nipples and pulled on them a little and he twitched. He gave a little whimper, but did not reach out for her again. "All right," she said. She straightened and undid three buttons of her blouse. She watched his eyes fix on her chest. She pulled her hair out of its ponytail and shook it loose. Then she leaned over him and let her hair feather his face. He lifted his head up to kiss her and she pulled away. "Nope," she said. "Nope, nope. Do that again and I'll stop."

He nodded.

She teased him with her hair again and then let her hair brush over his chest and belly. She leaned close over him so that her shirt fell more open and he could see her whole bra, a plain bra with some padding, so it wasn't that sexy, but still his mouth was open and he was breathing harder. She glanced down and saw that he was aroused. She pulled on his nipples, lightly, and he quivered and moaned again. "You like that," she said.

He nodded.

"Good to know that I can control you," she said. Finally, she was not unaroused, herself. "Do you like it?"

"Yes," he breathed.

"Okay," she said. She sat back. "Take off your shorts."

He closed his eyes. He shook his head.

"Okay, I'll stop then."

He sighed. "Okay." He pulled them down and his cock sprang up. It was a good size, larger than average but not huge, uncircumcised, very hard.

"I'm not going to touch it," she said. "You are."

"I can't do that."

"Then I'll get dressed."

"Okay." He closed his eyes and began stroking it, with his left hand, she noticed, first just pushing his palm up and down along it, and then gripping it quite hard with a fist, and jerking up and down right over the head. He began to breathe hard.

Gloria unbuttoned her shirt completely, and he opened his eyes and stared hard at her chest. She pulled off her blouse so that he could see her bra. The concentration in his eyes was a quick shock of pleasure for her, the unrecallable quiver you have when your name is called out as the winner.

"Take it off," he murmured.

She shook her head. The room shifted slightly and she knew it was the Ativan coming on. She yawned a little, but he didn't see it. She knew she would have to lie down soon.

He was panting and the head of his cock was very shiny, slightly wet, and bright pink. She thought he might come any moment, so she said, "Okay, that's enough. Stop."

"Oh." He threw his hands to his sides and his head back. "God." His cock throbbed and flailed a little on his belly as it subsided.

Gloria put on her shirt and buttoned it up. "Very good," she said. "It's a start."

"A start?"

"You can get dressed now."

"Oh, I get it," he said. "It's just to torture me."

"A little, yes. But don't you enjoy that?"

He sat up and looked around for his shorts. "Is it to humiliate me? Is that the idea?"

She said, "Did you enjoy it? Or not?"

"Yes, I did."

"Well that's okay, then, isn't it?"

He was silent as he dressed. She stood up. She said, "You are going to go now, but we'll do it again if you're good."

Finally he smiled. Then he said, "How about you?"

"What about me?"

"Did you enjoy it?"

For a second she considered lying, but knew she had put him through enough. "Yes, I did. And now I know…"

"What? You know what?"

"I know I can trust you."

He said, "How long is your roommate away?"

"I don't know. She could be back any time. I'd say we have a couple days."

He put on his jacket and shoes and thanked her for the meal. He was red-faced and smiling a little, slightly more confident, as if he was not ashamed but proud. He even tried to kiss her at the door but she refused. "It's not like that," she said, "yet."

"Yet," he said.

From the bottom of the stairs he looked up at her, suddenly miserable, his face full of pain, and said, "I'll do anything you want." Then he closed the door quietly and left.

He was not attractive like this and she felt the sudden heavy weight of regret and shame for everything that had happened. But she was sleepy and a little dizzy. She left the dishes and got undressed and into bed. She started touching herself but gave up again and fell asleep.

9.

ARTICLE TOPICS:

- *"Don't be afraid to ask for help!" (includes updated list of mental health resources)*
- *"Asking for intimacy" (how to be honest with your partner about your emotional needs—will have interview with Dr Satz who we used for piece on trauma memory)*
- *Spirulina turmeric smoothie recipe*
- *"Could your trauma be your creativity?" (interview with Deborah Cornwall who runs the Breakthrough creativity workshops)*
- *Five easy yoga stretches for posture (public domain images are up at Health Network site)*
- *"Accepting trauma" (can use quotes from Dev Brahmin on how to forgive yourself if your trauma is blocking your creativity—will run on another week from article above)*
- *"Eating for mental health" (talk to Dr Wong of Mindful Wellness about links between gluten, dairy*

and GMO food with depression and anxiety. Also letting go of anger for immune system.)

- *Are you dating a narcissist? A checklist.*

Gloria hit send on these, to Surinder at The Hype Report. Now she had to wait for him to approve them.

She busied herself compiling some of the motivational quotes that had to decorate the site as well. At first she had found these by googling combinations of words like "collective" and "love" and "childhood" and "dream," but now she found she could make them up herself just as well. She wrote, "If trauma occurs in childhood, we are the children of our trauma." Then, "The feeling is the healing." She worried for a moment that she had heard this somewhere and should find its source, but Surinder didn't seem to mind about attribution for these. She could go on with you-create-your-own-reality ones for a while. She wrote, "You deserve to hear that you are loved." She had done a few variations of "Know that you are loved" and would do so until Surinder noticed. She could do more around *joy*, and *knowing you are joy*, too, but that was enough for now.

She was frustrated that she couldn't work until Surinder responded. It seemed to be warm out, from the slice of tree she could see from her room. It was still and had tiny buds on it. She wanted to go out and walk and perhaps get fit by doing so, and be desired more, which was what she was enjoying at the moment.

There was a discomfort in her body. She needed movement, and she needed something else.

She closed the laptop and lay down and pulled down her sweatpants and masturbated, which she tried to do sometimes, although she hadn't come since she had begun combining the Latuda and the Pristiq, replacing the Wellbutrin, a year ago, at least a year ago, maybe a year and a half ago, which was troubling to contemplate. That must mean that she had started sleeping with Florian, on and off, a good two years ago, which was even more disheartening. She came close to coming, quite close, as she often did, and then she felt numb and gave up. She knew she was aroused by the sight of Daryn's cock and she was troubled by this too.

She went to her desk and googled "Daryn Boutilier." There was an optometrist in Yarmouth, Nova Scotia, by that name. And a client-care service manager in Louisiana. An Instagram account with the name had one photograph posted, about two years before, of a Christmas tree. There was no caption.

She went to the Reddit incel threads, and then to the websites, and began looking for handles like Darkknight, but there were quite a few variants on that.

An email from Surinder came in: all her ideas were great but they couldn't use Dr Satz anymore after this one, and she needed to find some mental-health recipes, things like the anxiety-busting vegetable broth they had done last week. Perhaps, he said, she could include some of the pumpkin-seed and sweet-potato recipes that *Kids Can Cook!* was promoting, as it was advertising a lot on the site. He added a row of happy faces after this.

Autumn emailed that she was doing much better and really looking forward to coming back to the apartment and hanging out again. She was so grateful for true rock supportive friends like Gloria, with whom she felt a bond deeper than anything anyone who had not experienced female friendship could explain. Gloria put off answering this till the afternoon.

Isabel wrote to say, *Having a bad day. Suicide?*

Gloria replied, *Call me.* She very much wanted to tell her about Daryn and knew she couldn't. Also, it was odd for Isabel to say she was having a bad day. Isabel was not supposed to have bad days; that was not the point of Isabel.

Daryn would be working at the electronics store. She did not know where it was. She wanted to know if he was obsessing over her. She was sure he would be, and she was a little regretful that she had still refused to give him her phone number, for she would have liked to know for sure. Nor did she have his. He did know where she lived, now, which was, she knew, a bad thing, a terrible thing, really, an idiotic thing, and she should not have done what she did, any of it.

IN THE AFTERNOON SHE TOOK the bus and the subway downtown to the university gym and got dressed in her running leggings and tank top and got on the treadmill for a few minutes, but she couldn't commit to it. Really she was there to go to the cafeteria afterwards, where she knew he would show up, for they had an agreement now, she supposed, or at least a pattern.

She showered and conditioned her hair and took some pleasure in putting on makeup and even a spray of the perfume her mother had given her. And then she went to the cafeteria and waited.

He did not come. She drank two kombuchas and had a salad. She called Isabel, who did not answer. Isabel had been strangely monosyllabic all day, insisting she was fine and didn't want to talk. Autumn emailed her to invite her to a Sharing Circle that she was going to come downtown for. Gloria did not answer this as she had no excuse in mind for not attending and would either have to make up a very good one or else go, she supposed, as she should give these things a chance.

By nine the cafeteria was empty and the staff were cleaning up, and she felt nothing for Daryn but a clear fine hatred, the hatred that comes of humiliation.

Gloria got up, and on the sidewalk outside she saw Daryn walking towards her very fast.

"Hey," he said, breathing hard. "Hey. Are you leaving? Man. I ran."

He bent over, with his hands on his knees, and panted. He was shiny with sweat.

"It's okay," she said. "Relax. Chill."

"I had to close the shop," he said. "Adnan. The manager. He was sick. So I was the only guy. Man. I knew you were waiting. I'm sorry."

"It's okay. It's okay."

"Are they closed? Is it too late?" He looked so genuinely panicked she almost laughed. The anger had not dissipated; it prickled. In another mood she would find his being so pathetic rather sweet.

"They are. But let's go to the park."

He looked around wildly, so she took his arm and led him.

They went into the centre of the park and sat on a bench. The tents were just dark shapes, and figures moved around them in darkness. There was the usual shouting, sometimes close and sometimes distant. A siren passed a block away. He had stopped his heavy breathing. He kept saying, "Man. I made it. I ran for that bus like, like I don't know. Man."

"What did you bring me?" she said.

"Bring you?" His face wrenched again. "What did you want me to bring you?"

"A present, I don't know. A gentleman brings a gift for a lady."

"A present? What kind of present?" There was panic in his voice again.

"I'm kidding. I don't want a present."

"What?"

"I'm just teasing you. Because I know you would never bring a present." She said this too quickly and then was conscious of its cruelty.

"What?"

"No, seriously, just forget it. I'm just messing with you. That came out too mean. I meant no guys think of bringing presents." This was true. Florian would never have brought her a present of any kind. He had not given her a single present in two years. And she did not expect presents from anybody. But she had, she supposed, been aware that Daryn did not have a lot of experience with dating and it would not ever occur to him to try to impress a woman with any material luxury, and that he could not even if he wanted to because of his limited resources, which was fine; she did not want the rich dudes and tech bros who tried to take Isabel out;

still, she had been aware of a kind of immaturity there and it had come out. She did not want to mock him. "You should drink some water."

"I'm fine."

"Well," she said, "I was on my way home."

"You don't want to like, hang out?"

She pretended to think about this. "I really have to go."

"Man."

There was a silence and then he said, "I'm fucking stupid."

"What?"

"Stupid to be running after you. Stupid." He stood up and slapped himself in the face, so hard it made a wooden sound.

"Hey," she said, "Jesus, stop that."

He slapped himself twice more. "Stupid. Cuck."

"Okay, stop it. Stop it. That's enough." She tried to grab his hand, and instead he grabbed hers and held it very tightly, staring at it.

"Ouch." She held still. She stared at his face; it had the blank look she had seen before, when men were angry at themselves. It wasn't to do with her. She could defuse it. She wasn't going to be frightened by it. "Okay. Chill. Just chill. Everything's okay. Let's walk."

He moved her hand towards her face and slapped her with her own hand, not hard. It happened too fast for her to pull back. When she tried to pull away, he held her fast.

"What are you doing?" she said evenly.

He dropped her hand and sighed and stared at the ground.

She rubbed her wrist. "You are a little tightly wound, right?"

"No *fucking* kidding."

"Okay. All over now. Relax."

He nodded and his breathing was slower.

"Let's just walk. Walk with me for a bit. To the subway." She walked quickly and he followed. It was a bit like having a dog.

Behind her, he said, "I wanted you to hit me. Not yourself."

She considered this and decided it was likely true.

When they got to the subway she just said, "Come on. Let's go."

He said, "What?"

She said, "You can come to my place. But you have to do everything I say. Like before."

He nodded and gave a little smile and she found the smile pathetic.

WHEN SHE LET HIM IN, he took off his shoes and she made him drink some water. He stood close to her and put his hands on her hips and leaned towards her. She pushed his hands away. "You can't touch me," she said. Then she walked into the bedroom and stood beside the bed. "Lie down," she said.

"Not this again."

"Oh, you don't have to. Do you want to leave?"

He smiled and lay down. She stood over him a moment, unsure what she was going to do. She should have researched this. She should have looked up "femdomme teasing" or "what do boys like when they are tied up." What would Mistress Amethyst Draconia do? She didn't even have any red lipstick. You needed at least red lipstick.

She took the chair from her makeup table and pulled it over to the bed. She took off her sweatshirt and sat. He stared at her shoulders. The straps of her sports bra were visible under the tank top. "Okay," she said.

"Okay," he said.

"Take off your shirt."

He did this and then she made him take off his jeans and socks. He had tight white boxer briefs on and he was hard.

She took off her tank top and shook her hair out over her shoulders. He stared at her bra with his mouth slightly open, as if he were seeing a suspenseful action scene in a movie.

"Come lie with me," he said, his voice high and faint.

She shook her head. She was not aroused, exactly, but there was pleasure in seeing him quivering there. "Take them off."

He closed his eyes and pulled off the shorts. He was breathing a little faster and his cock was very stiff.

"You can touch yourself," she said. "Touch yourself like you do when you're alone. Pretend I'm not here."

"Ha."

"No, really. I want to see what it looks like. How you do it."

He took his cock with his right fist and began stroking, quite roughly, she thought. The head became shiny and purple. His body gradually tensed.

She stood up and pulled her leggings down. She was wearing rather demure black underwear. She sat beside him on the bed. His eyes went up and down her. She reached over and stroked his chest, and he trembled. She flicked at each of his nipples, then pulled on each one. He gasped and then whimpered.

"You like that?"

"Yes."

"Hard like that?"

"Yes. Oh."

"Is it going to make you come?"

"Yes."

"Don't come. Don't come. Stop." She released his nipples, then pushed his hand away from his cock. "Stop."

He lay there breathing hard, his hands at his sides. "Come on," he said. "Lie down with me." He reached for her breasts, and she pushed him away again.

"Stop that. Do that one more time and I will stop everything. Okay? Understand?" She pushed his head back onto the pillow and held it there. "You are not going to be allowed to control me in any way," she said. "That's the only way I can do this." She let him go and pulled off her bra. She leaned over him and brushed her breasts in his face. He licked her nipple and then she shoved it right into his mouth and let him suck on it.

She reached down and stroked his cock lightly and it quivered in her hand. She began rubbing it with the flat of her hand, just the underside, and it was very stiff and full. There was a drop at the tip. She smeared it all over the head and stroked it. Then she put her fingertips just under the base of the head and began to pull up and down. She knew this to be very effective.

He began to breathe very hard and moan, and she said, "You can only come for me when I tell you. Do you want to come now?"

"No," he said, "I want to touch you. Please. Please."

"No. Not yet. Come for me first. Are you ready?"

She squeezed a little harder and increased her pace. She let him suck on her nipple and her hair fell over his face and neck. She was aroused. She supposed it was his arousal that did this, not the idea of controlling him. For a second she wished it was him controlling her. She would like to come under someone's hand this way too. She whispered in his ear, "Come for me now, it's okay. Do it. Come."

He tensed and squirted onto her hand and his belly. There were several jets. He made almost no sound.

"Very good," she said. "Very good." She stood up and went to get a cloth. She threw it at him and then put on her clothes, her back to him. Then she relented, because she was really quite excited, and she lay down beside him. She let him take her hand. "Well," she said. "I guess I'll have to give you my phone number now."

He turned to her and looked her in the eyes.

She said, "Did you like that?"

"My god, yes. It was ... You are strange. You are so mean but so kind to me."

"Kind?"

"Generous."

"Oh. Yes, I am."

"Like what do you get out of it?"

"Not a lot," she said, "except to show you that you don't have to dominate and control women."

"I never ever wanted that."

"Sure. And also I get to test you, see if you are safe. And can be trusted. Before I get to know you better."

"You are so beautiful," he said, and his voice had that hint of the plaintive about it that she hated.

"Oh, stop that."

"I love you," he said more clearly.

Something burned inside her and she said, sharply, "No you don't." She sat up. She needed to get away from this. But she had felt, immediately, a warm rush like some kind of liquid, like his burst of sperm itself, but inside her, an astounding pleasure, when he said it, and she knew this was very dangerous and idiotic and hated herself for it.

"I do."

"Okay, enough of that." She left the room, and she called, "You'd best be going."

She listened from the kitchen and heard him putting on his clothes. Her phone was flashing. She wanted him to go before she looked at it.

He came out and she held the door open. He asked her when he would see her again and she said she didn't know; she expected trouble but he was quite docile. He tried to kiss her, and she pushed him away. He thanked her many times. He reminded her about her phone number, and she gave it to him. And he left calmly.

On her phone were texts. One was from her mother: *Are you safe?*

She replied, *Yes, why.*

Her mother wrote, *There's been an incident on campus. Some sicko trying to kill girls.*

10.

ISABEL KNEW ALL ABOUT IT already, of course.

On FaceTime, she said, "It's completely *woow* overexaggerated. It was one accident and no one is going around trying to kill girls." Her face filled the screen so Gloria couldn't tell where she was. She appeared to be wearing no makeup and had a fleck of something white in the corner of her mouth. "I know there's been a lot of school shootings and people writing manifestoes and whatever *meern-meern* stuff, but it isn't that, it was one dickbox guy who had a fight with his girlfriend, and I know her, too, it's that Samantha Ingebrecht who was in that Decolonizing Narrative course that Oakley taught and then she went all student politicky and student union and everything."

"You have something on your mouth," said Gloria. "No, other side."

"Did I get it?" Isabel shook her head and Gloria saw her hair was hanging flat again as if it needed a wash. There was a mirror and black wall behind her, as if she was in a hotel-bar bathroom or something.

"Yes. Where are you?"

"You know her? Samantha? She was with this guy in a car and he was driving and he was jealous or something and he was screaming he was going to kill them both and he was driving all over the place and he tried to drive into a tree or something, and she grabs the steering wheel and he like, *snerk*, just swerves and he hits this other girl on the sidewalk instead. It's this Asian girl, Soon Li or something."

"Jesus Christ. And she died?"

"No, Jesus, she's fine, she got a broken leg, she's not dead."

"How do you know this?" Gloria held her phone with her neck and searched on her computer. The local-news TV station had a short article about a pedestrian struck on a street in the middle of the downtown campus by a car driving erratically. It didn't mention any names. "When was this?"

"Earlier today. Everyone is posting about it like crazy. Samantha was living with this girl Francesca who I know from when I worked at Shakers, and she's basically going *whoo-whoo* online about how she knew this guy was an abuser and everything."

"Is Samantha okay?"

"Yes, she's fine. The guy ran away and left the car then they caught him. This girl Soon is already out of the hospital."

Gloria was searching for the names on the news sites but they weren't coming up. She went to her socials and the comments were starting to take a political tack. Two more women victims of male rage. Troubling echo of the Toronto incel van attack of a few years ago. Men weaponize their cars, are we surprised? Toxic masculinity. If you are in an abusive relationship there are resources. Vigil for Soon Li. Then there was a news report of an arrest made: Ernesto Santiago, 24. Reckless endangerment. "How does my mother know about this?"

"Thing on the radio this afternoon," said Isabel. "Someone from the student union was interviewed about how this guy was some kind of incel or something because he was targeting women in his car, but that really isn't what happened. Francesca says he was really *grrr-grrr* possessive and was telling her what to wear and all that shit, so maybe kind of stalkery, and with that kind of guy it's bound to happen, something like that, once they start telling you you can't go out with your friends and stuff you know he's going to get scary. It's her own fucking fault."

"Is that what he was telling her?"

"I don't know but Francesca is saying stuff like that. So now it's this whole toxic-masculinity thing and femicide and all that."

"Well, it kind of is all that."

"He didn't leave any manifestoes or anything. You know the way they usually do if they really want to kill women, they record videos and everything. This guy was just an ordure sac."

"Wow. That's all so awful."

"I have to go," said Isabel. She was holding her phone away from her face as if she was reading something on another screen.

Gloria looked at her watch. It was eleven o'clock at night. "Where do you have to go? Do you have a date?"

"You'd better calm your mom down," said Isabel. "It's all getting blown out of proportion."

Gloria checked her roommate Autumn's feed. Autumn had already heard about a march against male violence that was going to happen on campus the next day. "Are you going to go to this march?"

Isabel made a hissing sound. "No. That would be just. *Lecchh*. If you're too stupid, if you're so stupid you stay with a guy like that, like the first second he gets jealous and weird you should be out of there. Actually we should all be out of there. Like with all guys. I don't know why we bother. They should all be sent to an island, like a penal colony or something."

"Okay. Well that doesn't really help—"

"You know who should get the blame here? Samantha. Fucking Samantha. She's the idiot. You invite a guy like that into your life, like there would have been a million red flags, you know why? Because you're vain and stupid and dependent. If you need to associate, if you need these insecure thugs, then you should be sent to the island too. God knows I should be on the island."

"Wow. Isabel, this does not sound like you. That's—"

"And it's a real pity about Soon Li because it was Samantha who put her in danger, and any other girl walking on the street that day. It's Samantha who deserved to have her leg broken, not Soon Li."

"Isabel," said Gloria. "you're not making any sense. You sound like you're mad about something—" Gloria's phone was vibrating with an incoming call. It was her dad, her dad in Thunder Bay. "I have to go. My dad is calling. But you don't really think any of that."

"Go," said Isabel. "Say hi to your dad."

"Are you really going out?"

But she had hung up.

HER FATHER HAD BEEN IN touch with her mother and felt she was maybe getting too upset over this one psycho nutbar. He hoped Gloria wasn't too upset. Her mother certainly was.

Mostly he wanted to talk about gun control. "You see how dumb it is?" he said. "If you want to hurt someone you're going to hurt someone. You don't need a gun. Gun, knife, car, whatever. You can use a piano if you want. If you're a criminal type. And if the guy had wanted a gun, you think he would have gone and applied for a licence and done the training course and the waiting period or whatever? You think he wouldn't have just bought one on the black market? The guns that are used for crimes are illegal anyway. Anyway. Glad you're okay."

"I'm fine. The woman who was hit is going to be fine too."

"And they got the guy, the driver?"

"I think so, yes."

"You don't hear anyone asking for a ban on cars since you can kill someone with a car, now do you?"

"Yeah," said Gloria. "You do need to register cars though. And have a licence."

"I'll tell you something else for free," said her dad. "This is the kind of thing they're going to say is a mental-health crisis. Send in the social workers. Like you think a crisis-management person maybe should have stood in front of the car? South of the border they would have just shot him, *blam*, no questions asked. And he'll probably be out on bail by morning. Ready to start all over again. They won't even lock these guys up. Throw away the frigging key, excuse me."

"Send them to an island," said Gloria.

"That's what they'd do in Russia. Siberia. No girls to bully there."

"I think I'll be heading to bed now."

"You do that, sweetheart. Sorry to talk your ear off."

11.

THE NEXT TWO DAYS THERE were a lot of phone calls and typing. People were setting up a crowdsourced fund for Soon Li, and there were a couple of open letters to the university administration about safety for women on campus. Gloria talked to her mother and explained to her that she didn't live even remotely close to the campus anymore.

Her phone rang and she answered it without thinking.

"Hi," said Daryn.

"Oh."

"Hello?"

"Daryn," she said at length. She was trying not to feel angry at him. He had not driven into anyone or threatened anyone, except possibly himself, and yet he had, in a sense, because that's what all the stupid slapping himself and all the stupid talk of suicide on the stupid blogs was about, it was about making everyone afraid of upsetting them, so he was part of it, really, although he couldn't even know that.

"Have you ever heard," she said, "of BPD?"

"No," he said. "Are you—"

"It's a personality disorder," she said. "Borderline Personality Disorder."

"No. I guess. Yeah. Why?"

"I'm in a really bad mood," she said. "And I don't want to take it out on you. So, I don't think we should talk right now. I'm sorry."

"What? Why? What's wrong? What's going on?"

"I'm serious. Don't freak out. I'll call you later."

"No," he said, and his voice was getting high. "You can't do that. You can't just be all weird and mysterious and I have no freaking—"

"Okay. Okay. Chill out. Calm down. See this, this is what—"

"What is? What are you even saying?"

"Okay. Okay. You're right. I should—be calm though, okay?"

"Just what the fucking what?"

"Okay," she said. "Did you hear about this accident on campus? Yesterday?"

"No. What? Are you okay?"

"I'm fine. It's not important. Or it is, I guess, I don't know. Some guy got mad at his girlfriend and tried to kill them both and ended up driving his car, with her in it, into a tree and he hit another girl who had nothing to do with it and broke her leg."

"Wow. That's. Okay."

"The guy was being jealous and possessive, and he ends up almost killing someone."

"Okay. Well that guy is just a cuck."

"You think?"

"I don't know. I don't know the whole story. Was she—like did he have a reason? To be mad?"

"Did he have a *reason*? To try to kill her? You think anything—"

"I don't know. I'm just saying I don't know the whole story. There's always two sides. And if someone gets pushed, like pushed to the—"

"I was really afraid you were going to say something like that. See, that's why I didn't want to talk. You understand I'm really upset about this, right?"

"Yes. Of course. I do. But—okay. I won't say anything."

Gloria breathed deeply.

He said, "Why did you say that thing about BPD or whatever?"

"Well," she said. "That behaviour, the guy who feels he might be being rejected or ignored or whatever, and he gets hysterical and starts threatening to hurt himself, like this guy with the car. Those are symptoms of BPD. I write about this stuff."

"Okay," he said, and there was a silence. Then he said, "What are you saying? You think I have that?"

"It's something to think about," she said.

"Oh, here we go," he said. "Everything's a disease. Nobody's ever just a fucking jerk. Everybody's mentally ill and they just need a social worker and some pills and then nobody would ever get angry ever again."

Gloria laughed. "You sound like my dad."

"No, seriously. Don't ever call me mentally ill." His voice was hard now.

"Did I call you mentally ill?"

"That's where you're—listen, this guy may or may not be mentally ill, I have no fucking clue. I don't know anything about it. But if someone acts, like, dangerous, then you get the cops and you arrest him and you lock him up. It doesn't fucking matter if he's mentally ill or not. Fucking shoot the guy."

"Okay. Okay. Never mind."

"Don't you ever fucking dare call me that again, okay?"

"Whoa." Gloria sat up straight. Her heart had sped up. "Okay, you need to calm down."

"I'm sorry."

"This conversation is not working for me. I'm not enjoying it and neither are you and I'm going to go. We're going to take a little break."

"No," he said. "No, wait. I didn't mean it. I'm sorry."

"I'm going to go now. Okay?"

"No no no. Just—"

"I don't want to hang up on you, okay?" Gloria did, in fact, want to hang up on him, but she did not want to enrage him to the point where he would get all abject and stupid again, and she was aware that this tactic, this caution, this trying to avoid enraging him was exactly what she had been trying to talk to him about, and that in fact he was getting exactly what he wanted. "So, let's say goodbye politely and then we'll talk later, okay?"

"No. No no no no no."

"Daryn, I have to go. I don't want to hang up on you. Goodbye."

She heard him sighing. Then: "When will you call me?"

"I don't know. I don't know. I'm going now. Okay? Okay? Bye-bye."

There was a long silence then and she did hang up. It was a kind of compromise, she supposed.

She took her computer to a coffee shop. She would get more work done there, and it was good to walk a bit. But it was also better to not be at her apartment in case he was mad and came there.

AT LUNCHTIME SHE WAS SHAKING from coffee and wanted to go home.

A number of texts had come in through the morning from Daryn. He was really sorry and he understood why she was mad and he hoped she understood why he got so tense. He was just kind of in shock that she was so upset and being so weird.

She had a Breakfast Wrap from the coffee shop for lunch. The egg was runny and there was some kind of mayonnaisy sauce that was too sweet, like Big Mac sauce. She did not finish it and then had a cookie, which was a dumb thing to have for lunch.

She went home with the idea that she would have a nap. Her apartment was cold. She texted Daryn, *Okay we donlt nee dto talk about it aby more.*

He replied *When can I see you.*

She did not reply.

She lay down and tried to masturbate with no success. She wondered whether she should try one of the huge wand vibrators that cost two hundred bucks. If she were a true sex expert who knew how to play these games with Daryn she would have one. Mistress Jessamyn Morgana would certainly have one.

She got up and paced around and made coffee. She had no plans for the evening. Perhaps she had been too hard on Daryn who really didn't have any clue about anything she was thinking, and why would he?

She texted him, *This evening.*

She spent the afternoon pacing the apartment and almost told him not to come several times. She fantasized about slapping him across the face when she saw him. But she knew it was not him she wanted to slap. She did not want to slap anyone. She went out to buy a bottle of wine and opened it.

When he arrived he was carrying flowers. She let him come into the kitchen and put them down, because she had told herself she really was going to slap him, but he looked so concerned, and also tall, that she could not. He tried to give her a hug, but she pushed him away and said, "I hate everyone so much."

He nodded and said, "I read about the accident. Car thing, whatever. On campus. The guy wasn't part of anything. I'd never heard of him. He was never on the—"

"Oh, stop it, Shut up. It's meaningless, it doesn't matter. And besides, you would never know, right, who he was? He could have been Rapechicks-four-one-six for all you know, you could have been talking to him for, oh, for fuck's sake, forget it. You know you are under surveillance right now, don't you, the police have every right now, under the new laws, the terrorism law, to hack you and follow you and read your emails."

He shrugged. "They already had that right," he said. "We all knew that. I never do anything to worry about. Anyway. I'm sorry that thing happened and I'm sorry I flipped out or whatever."

"Okay." Gloria was surprised to find that she was about to cry. She turned away but he came behind her and put his hands on her shoulders. She let him hold her then, and she put her face tight against his neck and felt him breathing. She very much did not want him to know that she had cried a little because she didn't know why she had. But he must have felt her face was wet. He was warm and she put her arms around him and held him too for a moment. It felt delicious, terrible, corrupt, as if she were taking flowers from the psycho car guy himself and enjoying it. She felt his crotch swelling against her and she pushed him away again.

"You are one confusing guy," she said, wiping her eyes. "Put those in water. There's a thing down in that cupboard. Under there."

He got a vase and water and put the flowers in, following her instructions. She asked him if he wanted some wine and he said, "Sure, I'll try it." He sipped at it very tentatively. He said, "I don't drink a lot of wine."

"What do you drink?"

"Beer, I guess. If I go out. But I don't go out."

"The flowers are nice. Thank you."

They went into the living room and sat down and she let him stroke her knee for a moment. She thought of not being able to come this afternoon. She would like to be able to come some time. She had to confess she was not unexcited by his presence. She had been naked with him before and so as far as people one could safely get naked with went, he was just as dangerous as anyone new. If they had sex, it would more likely make him nicer rather than meaner. It was true she wanted to have sex as well, just because she hadn't now for several days, and it would get her out of her head. But she could not allow this to happen on his terms. He kept asking her if she was okay and how she was dealing with the tragedy and he would not argue with her in any way. "I let you hug me," she said, "because I really needed to touch someone. But it's not you I wanted to hug. It could have been anyone."

"Okay," he said.

"What do you think of the wine?"

He had had a half a glass. "It's very nice. Very good."

"You don't like it."

"Sure I do. I'm just not used to it."

"You know when I talk about . . ." She was about to say *mental illness*. "When I talk about people having conditions, like psychological states, it's not an insult. Everyone is different in their own little way, right?"

"Oh no. Here we go again."

"If someone tries to help someone—I don't mean you, I mean anyone—because they're acting a little weird, and they say, hey, maybe a specialist could help you with that, would it make sense to treat that as an insult?"

He gave a short laugh. "If you're trying to say I'm weird then just come out and say that."

"I know a lot of people who are proud of being weird."

"I bet you do."

He was not angry now so she felt she could go further. "You're a little spectrummy, aren't you?"

"I don't know what that means."

"Yes you do. You've heard it. You're like on the spectrum."

"Like I'm autistic?" He laughed. "I don't think so."

"Have you ever been tested? Seriously."

He sighed. "I didn't grow up with stuff like that. Psychiatrists and testing. And learning disabilities. It would never have occurred to my parents. And now I wouldn't do it because I just wouldn't."

"Because you don't believe in psychiatry?"

"No, I guess I don't."

"Do you think the guy who got so mad at his girlfriend he tried to kill them both could maybe have benefited from some psychiatry?"

"I guess. I don't know. Is there a pill for that?"

"Yeah. It's a black pill."

He smiled. "Ha ha. That's pretty good actually. No, but I don't know. I doubt it really. Do you know the pill that could do that?"

"I don't know," she said, "I'm not a psychiatrist. But there would be more to it than that. There would be therapy, I don't know, counselling, the person would—"

"Counselling? You're going to sit a guy like that down and tell him maybe not to murder someone? You're going to say it in a really gentle voice? Do you think that would help?"

"Well, maybe, yes, in fact."

He made a puffing sound. "There's no helping a psychopath. You just have to have a gun ready for when he goes off."

"Jesus. What a world you live in."

He held his palms upwards. "It's a tough world. It's true."

She finished her wine. "And you like it tough."

"No, I don't. Not really."

Gloria felt her face growing hot: she had supposed she had been trying to find some suggestive way to become Mistress Lucretia Pronoun whatever again, and he hadn't bitten. He wasn't into it, not really, and she still wasn't sure whether she wanted him to be submissive or not. But she did not like admitting she wanted to have sex with him. "You do like it when *I'm* tough with you, a little, though, don't you?"

"Um. Maybe. If that's what it takes. I mean if that's what you like."

She laughed and leaned back. Perhaps he would lean towards her and kiss her. But he didn't. He was sitting stiff and nervous.

"Okay then," she said. She stood up, then stood in front of him, then lowered herself onto his knees, facing him. Her skirt rode up and he clutched her thighs. She said, "Unbutton my shirt."

He did so, and she unhooked her bra and let him lick her breasts. She told him to take off his shirt and he did. She pulled on his nipples and felt him harden beneath her.

She led him by the hand into the bedroom. She said, "Undress me," and she stood as he unzipped her skirt and let it fall. She stopped him from taking off her underpants. "Now yourself," she said. She stood with her hands on her hips and watched as he stepped out of his pants and then struggled a bit with his socks. "Everything," she said. He took off his shorts and she pushed him back on the bed. "Lie still."

She went to a drawer and found a ribbon. She made a loop with it and flicked his cock a few times with it, enough to make it sting. He flinched but did not move. "You like that?" He didn't answer. "You do. You do like that. Look at how hard you are. Now close your eyes."

He did as he was told and she slipped out of her underwear. She straddled his chest and then moved up, on her knees, so her crotch was over his face. He lifted his head up to lick her.

He was too hard and fast at first and she had to slow him down. She said, "Gently, gently," until she began to feel herself get warm and slick. She moved back and forth over his tongue to show him the rhythm.

She got off him to let him breathe then said, "Open the drawer in the bedside table."

He did so and found the condoms and held one out to her. She tore it open with her teeth. "I'm not on any birth control. Do you know how to put it on?"

He took it and tried, but fumbled, and she helped him. She slid it down the length of his cock and even this appeared to excite him greatly. "Don't come yet," she said, and he whimpered.

She straddled him again and lowered herself onto his cock. He was quite big, and she had to do it slowly. She was very excited by this, and surprised by the excitement. He didn't dare thrust in her, he held perfectly still, a stick inside her. She leaned forward and let him suck her nipples, then without knowing why she put her hand around his throat. His eyes went wide. She squeezed. "Don't come," she said. He nodded, staring at her. He gritted his teeth. She rode him, slowly at first, and then began bucking a bit as she found herself breathing hard.

"I can't," he said, "I can't," and she squeezed his throat tighter. She knew you could do this quite hard without hurting someone, as it had been done to her. It was a little scary to do, but she had a feeling it was what he wanted, or perhaps it was what she wanted, which was unfathomable, but perhaps she was a little bit excited at frightening, really frightening him just a little. His face was red. "I can't."

She felt him spasm and thrust inside her and she knew he had come. She got off him and his cock was still hard in its tight bag filled with slime. She slapped the cock lightly with her palm and he yelped, and she slapped it again, a little harder. "Pathetic," she said, but she laughed a little as she said it, and he giggled a bit too, and she did feel excited and indeed euphoric, thrilled, in love with his helpless desire for her and this hot liquid feeling it gave her. She remembered what it was like to come, and she wanted to do it again, and thought that perhaps one day she could teach him how to work on her, to help her push through the numbness of the pills, do it for her, but not yet.

She lay down beside him and he turned to her, his eyes all shiny and doleful, and she let him kiss her on the lips. They kissed for a minute and she let herself go into it, allowed herself to feel the pleasure of kissing and of his hand on her waist and her breast. She had not kissed anyone since Scott, and he had not ever wanted to kiss much, so they had rarely kissed. It was dizzying. He did not try to grope her further, probably because he didn't even know he was supposed to try to make her come now, and she wasn't going to tell him.

She wanted to ask him about what he had felt when she had choked him but she was afraid to talk about it, as she couldn't really say why she had thought of doing that or wanted to do it, except that she remembered it being done to her and being excited by it. When Florian had done it to her early on, before she had increased her meds, she had come once, and quickly, and she remembered asking Florian for it. She had not really, in the end, enjoyed choking Daryn, but had wanted to try it and see what he would do. The fact that it seemed to arouse him was not entirely reassuring to think about, though; if he was truly masochistic, she would not be able to keep up with this, would not be able to whip him or whatever. But perhaps at this point it was just that he wanted to please her, and she was happy with that, if that's what it was.

It had felt almost like squeezing the very spunk out of him, it had been that fast, and she had to admit it had been exciting, very exciting, so exciting she wanted him to penetrate her again now.

They lay together for a moment until she felt afraid of losing her dignity and she got up and told him to dress.

He went to the bathroom, and she saw his phone lying on her floor.

She picked it up and touched the screen.

It was not password-protected, and the screen came to life. Of course it was not password-protected, because of course a boy with no girlfriend had no need to hide what was on his phone. She was alarmed by the sweetness of this and almost put it down again.

She jabbed at the email icon and a bunch of messages scrolled by. The email address he was using was Gentlemanwhiner at something.

His text messages were mostly from someone called Jeb. The last one from Jeb said, *Let me know when you fuck one in the ass*.

She did not see a reply.

She put the phone down before the bathroom door opened. She was pulling on her bathrobe when he came in.

He dressed in silence. At the door he turned to her and tried to kiss her, but she stopped him and said, "Okay, okay, see you later." She was afraid he was about to tell her that he loved her. "No talking. Goodbye."

After he had left, she wrote down *Gentlemanwhiner.*

12.

The choking trend—healthy s/m play or dangerous misogyny?

Sarah*, 26, says the first time her boyfriend clasped a hand around her throat in the middle of sex it was a turn-on. "Oh, for sure, it was very exciting," she says in an email correspondence. "I liked how he was asserting himself, trying something new. I wanted to seem game."

But then she realized he wanted to do it every time they had sex. "It was the same every single time. It was like he couldn't do it [sex] without that part of it." Sarah began to wonder if this was innocent s/m play or reflected some real hostility towards her. "I started asking myself if he really wanted to hurt me."

"Choking has become increasingly normalized sex play," says Dr Raina Chowdhuri, sexologist and author of the popular blog on healing and relationships Trauma Times. "And we think it comes from pornography. Young men who come of sexual age on a steady diet of porn have seen this act, along with a number of aggressive behaviours such as slapping or degrading talk, so many times that it starts to seem like something to expect. We saw this in the last decade with anal sex—it was simply not an expected part of everyday sex until about 20 years ago, and now young women feel pressured into participating in this act. We fear that the same thing is happening with choking. Sarah's experience is actually quite common." Dr Chowdhuri suggests that women talk immediately to their partners about these expectations, before it becomes an established pattern.

Sarah says she did not confront her boyfriend about the choking. "I didn't want to come across like a boring girlfriend. I didn't want him to look somewhere else for a girl who was more daring than me." She put up with the behaviour, but in the end it was the boyfriend who ended the relationship.

Jennifer*, 25, says her boyfriend likes to choke her too but she enjoys the practice. "It makes me feel really feminine to be dominated," she said. She agrees that more of her partners seem to enjoy the practice than ever before. "I like porn," she says, "so I get it."

Dickbox fucknugget douchenozzle ordure sack

GLORIA DELETED THAT LAST LINE and then read the whole thing over; she was getting close to the maximum word count for one post. She would wrap it up with an anti-porn message and another quote from the sexologist about making your boundaries clear from the start. She knew she could get her to say that communication was key in any successful relationship and that was always a useful ending. In case anyone asked for her sources later she had got Autumn to agree to be Sarah, and she could easily get Isabel to repeat Jennifer's lines; she really didn't even have to call her. Nobody was ever going to fact-check this anyway.

Surinder was going to be resistant to the anal-sex line. He wasn't going to let her be that explicit. But maybe he would just skim it and she would get it through.

She closed her window blind and turned her computer screen away from her bedroom door and opened three porn sites on three tabs. She searched "femdom" and "mistress" and "male slave" and skimmed through several videos. She didn't know what she thought, exactly: she wasn't aroused, but she did like seeing the ejaculations.

She texted Isabel, *Have you ever used a cock ring on a guy?* Isabel did not respond.

She went to a message board called Blackpill and scanned through several forums, searching for the username Gentlemanwhiner. She did the same on a message board called PUAChat and then one called Sub/incels. She did the same at Toronto Beta Males and there she found it: a user named Gentlemanwhiner had contributed to a thread called "We Are Ugly." She could not read the full thread unless she was a member, so she registered as Cunthater88. Her password was *darynboutilier.*

This took some time, and she was aware of the afternoon passing, and aware of her waist and thighs lying immobile, spilling outwards like a pudding as she sat longer and longer in her chair, with her shoulders hunched and her neck craned forward over this little screen exactly as it was not supposed to do—she could visualize a little cartoon graphic every time she felt a spark of pain in her neck, a stick figure in the wrong position, inside a red circle with a red line through it, with a little red lightning bolt flashing over the neck—and it was unbelievably stupid, doing this, as she really did not want to know what he was writing on here, and she did believe him, actually, when he said that he didn't mean what he wrote on it, but still she knew she was going to sit there for as long as it was going to take to read every single thing he had ever posted.

Gentlemanwhiner had written, *If you have a small dick like me—like many of us, I presume—you are just never going to be confident enough to be able to approach a girl, which is hilarious, because you know she can't see it, but you're always aware of it.*

Gloria sat and reread this a few times. It was of course possible that Gentlemanwhiner was not Daryn. But there was that *I presume* that she had heard before.

Other commenters had responded with things like *Staceys always claim they don't care about dick size but reality proves they are lying.*

And Gentlemanwhiner had responded, *The society teaches them to only value material things.*

And then the thread just ended with no more comments. Most of the threads seemed to end suddenly that way, after two or three exchanges.

She went through five more forums—on video games, sports, pickup lines, depression/anxiety, school problems—

searching for his handle. She found it again in a forum called Jokes.

> *What's the difference between women and Kleenex?*
> *Kleenex doesn't follow you around after you use it.*

There had been no response to this.

She found him again in General Philosophy. The thread was "What do you dislike about women?"

> Gentlemanwhiner: *That they have all the power all the time. They control dating and sex. They control the whole world's attention. the society gives them all the power all the time because the society values beauty more than hard work, it's a superficial society. And because they will cheat on you in a second if given the chance.*

Gloria exhaled and stood up. She stretched her neck and shoulders. She felt physically bad. Although she was still not certain that this was Daryn. It probably wasn't. She resolved not to think about him or see him for a long time, possibly ever, *certainly* ever, if she could do it.

Her phone pinged. It wasn't Isabel. It was a text from Florian, of all people. It said, *Just checking in to see how you are doing. Stressful times. Miss u.*

She wrote back, *That's nice of you. Have you just broken up with somebody?*

There was a pause before he wrote. *Why would u say that?*

G: *I figure you must be horny*

F: *I see u are still mad @ me*

G: *No, not really. How are you?*

F: *The whole car crash thing got me down. When will it end?*

G: *You are very sensitive, I know.*

F: *Wow u are still mad*

G: *Nope.*

F: *I texted to check in on you.*

G: *I am very well, thank you.*

F: *I am so glad. I worry about you sometimes.*

Gloria laughed out loud at this. She put her phone aside. But a minute later she could not resist picking it up again. Florian had written a long text about how women must be feeling so nervous right now and how it was the job of all men to take responsibility for what had happened.

She wrote, *So what are you going to do to change the world?*

F: *I think the best thing men can do right now is just listen.*

G: *Sweet.*

F: *What are you up to these days?*

G: *Super busy.*

F: *That's good.*

She waited for a bit after this; she expected him to ask if she wanted to get together, but she wasn't going to make it easy for him. And when he did—*Are you up to hang out some time?*—she made herself wait and think about it. There was no reason, no reason whatever to meet with Florian except to sleep with him, which would make her sad, and meeting with him without having sex with him might make her sad too. But she was curious to see what it would be like, how she might be with him with a little more confidence in her. She was not excited to see him but wondered if she would be excited when she saw him. She wondered if she could be indifferent to him, in his presence. And if perhaps he would no longer be indifferent to her.

THEY MET THAT EVENING, at Piñata, where they used to go when it was called Shave Your Head. It looked the same, very dark, with red lights, but now it served tacos of sorts and beer in jugs. Florian had a loose V-neck T-shirt that plunged down a little too low, she thought. His beard was trimmed, and he had a cotton scarf knotted around his neck as well, which was a little silly as it was almost summer. His hair had grown long and he had pinned it up in a bun.

"If you don't need a sweater," she said, "why do you need a scarf?"

He shrugged, smiling. "Do you ever wear scarves?"

"You mean like for fashion?" She thought about this. "I don't think I do. No. I wear them in winter. Maybe I should wear scarves. I would have to wear big, floppy straw hats if I did that though, and change my name to Miriam, or Clothilde."

"Annabelle. Henrietta. We could get you a big bicycle, with a basket in front and you could put flowers in it."

"Right. And a sundress. And I would ride over to people's houses and deliver them bread that I baked."

"Why is it, do you think," he asked, "that those girls' bikes have to be so big? I mean they are always just these huge heavy thick things like tanks. With all the fenders and baskets and bells. Is it to make the women seem kind of frail in comparison? Je me demande."

"If you speak one more word of French I will fucking leave."

"And they have to be white or yellow or pink. If you have a straw hat, you are not going to ride a black bike, it's a rule, at bike stores they won't sell you one." Florian's eyes flickered away from her, following something, and she turned to see the waitress behind her, the very tiny one in a very tiny skirt and a crop top. Gloria turned back to him, and he was still far away, following the waitress's legs as she walked away.

Her phone vibrated and she looked at it in her lap. A text from Daryn: *Am I not seeing you tonight?*

She thumbed, *No, have plans tonight.* She put the phone in her purse.

Florian never minded her texting while she was with him and in fact texted a great deal himself. He hadn't even noticed her texting, perhaps because he was staring at women.

"Hi there," she said. She waved at him.

"Hi."

"Well. What's up?"

"I guess I wanted to see you, we need to see people we love when all this weird shit is happening."

"What weird shit?"

"Well," he said, "these loser lunatics running down women because they can't get laid."

"Oh, that guy. I think that guy was getting laid, actually."

"And they think women owe them or something. It's a hard time and I know everyone is kind of scared and I wanted to just be there, you know, I don't know, be an ally or something."

"Oh, okay. Well what do you think you can do about it?"

"Well, I guess we can be mindful, I guess, would be a start, all of us, I mean men, or male-identified, we could just make more of an effort to be mindful of what we do or don't do, consciously or not, what we say or how we behave, consciously or not, that's part of a system that creates this, or tolerates it or even encourages it."

"Well, how would you educate a guy like that?"

"Guys like that," said Florian, "just need . . . we need a whole different education system. Maybe one that doesn't teach that sex is just all power and domination in one direction or another."

"Are you still doing your dissertation."

"Sure. In theory. Yes."

"How is it going?"

"Okay I guess. It's hard when you're working." He was picking at the label on his beer bottle.

"Where are you working?"

He looked surprised. "At the writing centre. On campus. Same as before."

"Oh right. But is that full time?"

"Well, no, but it's really hard to work around. It cuts into your hours, it's distracting . . . It's hard to get down to research when you have like two hours free in an afternoon."

"Right. Well, how far are you along?"

"In the thesis? I don't know. Tough question. Not my favourite question, to be honest. Kind of my least-favourite question."

"Okay. Sorry. I forgot."

"It's okay. How about you? How is your—"

"It's so funny to me, though," she said, "no, it's weird, it really is, that people doing grad school can always say this, and they always do, and no one doing any other job in the world can. I mean if my boss asked me, how is that piece on whatever coming, I would love to just say to him, *I hate that question, you* know *I hate that question*. And he would say, *oh, sorry, sorry, I know it's delicate, I won't bring it up again*."

Florian laughed. "I know. But I don't have a boss. And it's not really a job because I don't get paid for it."

"Sure you do. You get funded by grants and by the university. You get paid by taxes. And I pay taxes. So I'm your boss."

"Okay, boss. I'm happy to work for you."

"Okay so what are you writing for me in your thesis that I am funding? Is that really so hard a question?"

"Do you really pay taxes? I would think you get a refund every year."

"Oh whatever." She sat back, suddenly tired, and had an urge to check her phone again.

"I have to say you are looking really great," said Florian. "Really healthy, like fit, and summery. You look hot."

"That may be like one of those unconscious things that you need to be mindful of saying, but whatever, thank you. What is your thesis about, anyway?"

"Did I not tell you all about it? In the past?"

"You did but you have to update me."

"What do you remember about it?"

"Umm." She reached for her purse. "I need a hair elastic." She rummaged a bit so that she could look at her phone.

There were four new texts. She found an elastic and began pulling her hair back with the elastic in her teeth. "It's about education?"

"That's right. And?"

"Education and race?"

"That's right." He sighed. "It's hardly the Gesamtkunstwerk. But."

"German," she said, "is not less pretentious than French."

"It's about education and race and privilege and new approaches to marginalization in education." He sighed and looked away again.

"Tell me about it again."

He began to tell her about it, at first as if very tired and bored by it, and then he warmed up, and told her about the prof he was working with who had done research in schools in the North, and about paradigms and institutionalized racism, and she remembered he had indeed told her about this prof before and this research and there seemed to have been no new research done since he had last explained this. As she listened she reached back into the purse as if to find something else for her hair and flipped over the phone, inside the bag, and managed to read the first text. It said, *Are you on a date?*

"You see," said Florian. "You're not interested."

"No, I am. I'm remembering it now. It sounds like very valuable work."

"I hope it is. I don't believe academic work should exist in some kind of intellectual... anyway. Do you want another beer? Or do you want to go?"

"Go where?"

"Anywhere you want to go. Do you have any beer at your place?"

"My place."

"You don't want me at your place?" Florian reached up and took out his own bun and shook his hair loose. It was thick and dark brown and wavy. He stared at her for a second and then looked away, back at the room and its legs and midriffs. His fingers drummed lightly on the table.

Gloria just sat for a minute. She felt hot, hot with some kind of emotion—annoyance, or something stronger, something that felt like pain. She tried to sit with it, as her therapist used to say, sit with it and accept it and analyze it and figure out where it was coming from before she just ordered a shot of Jack, which she used to do while with Florian quite often. It was anger, anger really, at his expectation, anger at herself for allowing this expectation to develop in him, anger at her past self for always saying *sure, let's go to my place*, and then being sad for three weeks or until whenever he texted again.

"I don't think that's a good idea," she said, as calmly as she could.

He raised his eyebrows at her with a little smile. "Are you dating someone?"

"Nope."

"You are. You totally are."

"You think that would be the only reason I might think it was a bad idea to go home with you? You have a high opinion of yourself, then."

"Hey. Hey." He said this in his gentle voice and reached over the table and took her hand in both of his. "I'm not so bad. You know this."

She shook her head.

He leaned close, as if to whisper something, and she couldn't help leaning closer, too. "And you know I can make you feel good. I can make you feel very good."

Her body reacted to his and the memory of him, and it felt nice to have his hands on hers. She closed her eyes for a second and allowed this to happen. She could lean into him, and it would be very pleasant. Then she let go of his hands and pulled back. "Okay," she said. "No."

He reached farther and stroked her wrist. "You worry too much."

"And you don't worry at all. About me."

"What's that supposed to—do you want me to worry about you?"

"I don't want to be a booty call."

"Oh, come on. What is this, 1955? Do you really think like that?"

"I don't want someone to text me when he's single or lonely or just whenever he feels like it. I want to be the ... the most special person to someone. You told me yourself you were incapable of having a relationship. Those were the words you used. Incapable."

"I am," he said with a big smile. "But we still have a lot of fun together."

She pulled her arm away from his fingertips which were soft and delicious. "You don't treat me with... I want to be like someone's princess." She was aware as she said this that she was using Daryn's words and suddenly her face was hot.

"Now that is sweet."

She grabbed her bag, "I'm going to the bathroom."

DOWNSTAIRS, OUTSIDE THE TOILETS, she pulled out her phone.

Are you with a guy?

What are you up to?

Why won't you answer?

She typed: *What makes you think you have the right to ask me that?*

Immediately came back: *I don't have the right to ask you what you are up to?*

Very quickly, she typed, *It would be nice if you were really asking how I was. Do you care? Or do you just care if I am with someone?*

Then, *Who do you think you are?*

Then, *You have no rights on me at all. Now leave me alone.*

She waited a minute to see if he would reply to this flurry and he didn't, so she went back upstairs.

Florian was thumbing on his phone. He was laughing at something he had read. When Gloria sat down and stared at it, he put it away very slowly. Then he reached and took her hands again. "Well," he said dreamily.

"Well what?"

"What do you think?"

"About what?"

"About going to your place."

"Oh my god. Did we not just have this conversation?"

He looked puzzled, but nodded. "Okay." Then he raised his eyebrows as if remembering something. "You have to meet your guy."

"There is no guy."

"Is it someone I know?"

"There is no guy."

"Are you back with Scott?"

"Oh my god. No."

"Then who?"

"There are some people you don't know, you know." Gloria looked around at the tables in the red light, at all the boys exactly Florian's age with exactly his beard and glasses, and at all the girls with their bellies exposed or their shoulders exposed or with the nipples visible, and at their jumpsuits and their tank tops and their glasses and their tattoos. A girl she knew called Clarita was sitting in the corner; she had shaved one side of her head. Damien the bartender was passing; he had grown a moustache. "There are people beyond this street and this row of bars, you know, and even beyond College Street and Queen Street as well. And they all have lives and jobs and there are even schools out there, and colleges, and towns with their own law courts and everything, and they are actually real people inhabiting them."

"Fascinating," he said, nodding. "Thank you. It is fascinating to think about. All these places with these little people in them with their little houses and their own little dishwashers and refrigerators that look just like ours, in little houses that look just like ours, like little play cities. It's very cute. I know.

I have heard about this. It's very sweet, really. It's like play life but they take it just as seriously."

"There you go."

"So it's someone I don't know then. Where would you meet someone I don't know? I know you don't use dating apps. You're like the only person I know, possibly the only person left in the whole world who doesn't. Is it some kind of power guy, like a lawyer or something? Like a finance guy? Did you go on a sugar-daddy site?"

"That's it, yes, that's it exactly. I have a powerful sugar daddy and he's waiting for me in a Lamborghini right now."

"I knew it. I knew you could do that. No, seriously, is he a lawyer?"

She nodded. "Uh-huh. A lawyer."

He frowned. "Lawyer like law school or is he a real lawyer, like practicing?"

"What do you care?"

"Are you going to go on a vacation to, like, Costa Rica with him?"

"Why Costa Rica?"

He screwed up his face. "It's where guys like that take sensitive women. To eco-resorts with like yoga retreats."

"Oh, right. Okay."

"I bet he has a small dick though."

"Thanks for the drinks," she said. "It was great to see you."

SHE DIDN'T GO STRAIGHT HOME. It was a warm night and she wandered into a park. She sat on a bench and checked her phone. The only new message was from Isabel: *No one should spend any time with men again ever.*

She was a little surprised that Daryn hadn't replied. She felt a little empty, after rejecting both Florian and Daryn, and she wondered if she had been too harsh with Daryn. He was uncivilized only because he was unsocialized and his lack of socialization was what had made him so hateful, or maybe just sad, in the first place. He was like a wild animal, perhaps, and he couldn't be blamed for not knowing how grown-ups behaved. And indeed, it was nicer that he was desperately jealous than not thinking of her at all.

She texted, *If I did see anyone else, would you call me a slut?*

There was a long pause, and he wrote back, *I would want to know.*

She sent, *Would you have to kill me?*

There was an even longer pause. She put away her phone and was getting up when it buzzed again. It said, *Had to help my mom with groceries. Are you still out?*

G: *That's sweet.*

D: *I'm done now. Do you want to get together?*

G: *Not tonight. Maybe tomorrow.*

And she switched her phone off feeling a little better.

13.

SHE TOLD HIM TO COME to the cafeteria on campus. She didn't want him to start expecting to be invited to her place even if she might invite him to her place. It would be a kind of reset to go back to the cafeteria. They could start again from there.

He showed up wearing a real shirt, a fitted navy dress shirt, untucked, and he looked almost grown-up. And he had blue jeans instead of the black ones. He still had some kind of running shoes on instead of real shoes, but still, he could pass for at least a commerce student, or even as somebody who did not live with his parents. He had a silver chain around his neck, though.

"Was that a gift?" she said.

"What?"

"The necklace."

"Yeah. From my mom."

"Oh. That's nice of her. I guess that means I can't ask you to take it off then."

"Why? Why would you ask that?"

"Because it…it's just. I don't know. It doesn't…" She was hesitating because she didn't want to tell him it was tacky and looked suburban, because she didn't want to be rude about his mother and because she knew that this was about class and class was something she didn't want to underline, in principle class was not an issue to her, and also they were probably just going to go straight home and have sex, so it didn't matter what he wore, but perhaps it was a bad idea to take him home this evening because he would then come to expect sex every time he saw her, and so there was actually an idea, a terrible idea most likely, flickering somewhere in her, that she might actually take him somewhere, like somewhere *out*.

"It's not up to your high standards?" he said.

"No, you look fine. I like your shirt."

"You look beautiful," he said.

"I don't really like it when you say that," said Gloria. "I can't really explain why, but it makes me uncomfortable."

"Compliments make you uncomfortable? I'm kind of like that too, to tell you the truth."

"Not all compliments. Just that one."

"You don't think you're beautiful?"

"Okay, we are not going to continue that conversation, right? I just told you."

"Okay. Okay."

They sat at the table for a moment and both looked around. The place was full of teenagers, foreign high-school students who were there for some kind of summer language school. They had just finished their classes and were sprawled everywhere and gathered in loud knots. Most of them seemed to be speaking Spanish but there were other languages Gloria did not recognize, possibly Hebrew or Portuguese. They were obviously rich kids because they were all beautiful and had linen sundresses and bright white running shoes. The boys all looked like Brazilian soccer players. They had glossy black hair. And the girls all had long hair—all of them, every single one, long straight hair, black or dyed, hanging over their bare shoulders and backs, that they kept swinging out of their faces or finding a reason to play with in one way or another. They all seemed very happy and chatty and they kissed each other on the cheek when they greeted each other.

Gloria said, “Beautiful kids.”

“Uh-huh.” He quickly glanced around and turned back to her. It was as if he was trying hard not to look at them.

“What do you think of them?”

He shrugged. “Nothing.”

“Do they make you uncomfortable?”

“I guess. Yeah.” There was a silence, then he said, “Now you’re going to ask me why.”

“That is how conversation works. Among grown-ups.”

“Conversation is about putting me on the spot and making me feel uncomfortable?”

“You were already uncomfortable.”

“Yup.” He nodded and looked at the table. He drummed his palms on his thighs. “Are we going to get something to drink? Are we staying here?”

“What is it about them? The way they look? Their languages? What?”

"Okay. All of those things, yes. They are obviously the kind of people I ... I was never a part of."

"Were there people like this in your high school?"

"I guess. Yes. Not quite as rich looking. But there were popular kids, yes."

Gloria was watching a girl with big glasses flip her hair around as she talked to the boys. She was wearing a loose cotton dress with bare shoulders, and she looked as light as breeze. "They make me uncomfortable too," she said. "They have privilege that we don't have."

"Tell me about it."

"So, these are the girls you hate, right? And the boys too? These are the Staceys and the Chads. Who do you hate more, the boys or the girls?"

"I'd have to think about that." He looked around, frowning. "I think the boys. Definitely the boys."

"Huh."

"They just look so incredibly dumb. And they don't even know it."

"They do look a little dumb," she said. "The girls have more taste and seem more mature. I don't like them either. The boys. And I would never have been sent to a foreign country to learn a language for a summer holiday when I was in high school, so I am resentful about that, that there are people who get to do that, yeah."

"They come here and it's like a holiday resort. It's like a third-world country."

"Ah. It annoys you that they're foreigners as well?"

"I don't know. I guess."

"So, do you want to murder them?"

"Of course not."

"'Of course not'? Really? Is that what you say on the forums? Aren't these the people who have to die to teach them a lesson?"

"Oh, shut up."

They watched the teenagers in silence.

She said, "It does bug you that they're so beautiful, right?"

Quickly and forcefully, he said, "Fucking right it does."

"Aha. Here we go."

"Oh, come on," he said. "You get it, of course you get it. We're surrounded by these girls all the time who want to be attractive, right, that want to be looked at, and then they say they don't."

"Well," she said, "it's a bit more—wow. First of all I don't know if they want to be looked at. They want to be attractive, sure. I don't know if they want to be looked at by you specifically."

"No, of course they don't want to be looked at by me. That part I get. They make that very clear."

"And you have a problem with that."

"Don't pretend you don't understand what I'm saying."

"I don't, I genuinely don't."

"Okay." He stood up. He was stiff. "You win. Make me look stupid. This is dumb. You think I want to sit here and argue with you?"

"I'm sorry."

"I told you. I already told you. I don't know how to argue. I didn't get to take gender studies or whatever. Go ahead and call me stupid, I don't care. I'm not here to win an argument with you."

"Sit down."

"I'm leaving."

"I'm sorry. I don't want to argue with you either. I'm just trying to understand."

He looked around. His fists were clenched.

"Sit down," she said. "I'm sorry."

"And you do understand what I'm saying. Don't tell me you don't."

"Yes. Okay. Yes. I do understand."

Daryn sat down. He folded his arms and looked away from her.

"I understand," she said, "that you feel they're teasing you specifically, but they're not. Maybe they're just dressing for their friends."

"Oh right. For their girlfriends maybe."

"Yes! Why not? In fact they most likely are dressing for their girlfriends."

"Give me a break," he said.

"Let me try to explain. When you say you think they're dressing specifically to make you—to get you all riled up, just to tease you and then reject you or whatever, you make it sound as if . . ." Gloria faltered here, for she really didn't know what her argument was. It was something she could feel and not explain. "You make it seem like they owe you something. Like if they dress sexy then they're making you some kind of promise, like you have a right to them."

Daryn exhaled and when he spoke again his voice was lower. "It's not them, themselves. They're not telling me anything. But everyone else is."

Gloria relaxed and leaned towards him. To keep him talking she wanted to put a hand on his. She laid one forefinger on his thigh. "Who? What do you mean by that?"

"It's not me saying that," he said, "it's every single thing around us, it's every movie we go to and every TV show, right? In every movie there's a guy who meets a girl, a woman, a beautiful woman, and about a third of the way through the movie they fall into bed together and they have crazy fantastic sex. Right? It's just normal life. In movies. In movies it's easy, it doesn't even take long. Sometimes they have sex right after they meet. It's all so easy. So, they're telling you that's what's supposed to happen and if it doesn't happen to you then you're abnormal. And that drives you crazy, a little, because in real life it's not so easy." He slapped a palm down on the table and it made a girl at the next table glance over.

"Huh," she said. She looked at the teenage boys at the next table who were watching a video on a phone and snorting about it and the girls were ignoring them. She knew that not all these boys were having sex with all these girls. "Have you tried, though?"

"Tried what?"

"Having sex with women."

"I tried with you. Didn't I? And look where it got me. You called me a stalker."

"I'm not sure that's exactly what I said, but anyway. We did actually ... whatever. But the point is, you don't think anything else in movies is real, though, do you? I mean you know you can't drive your car off a bridge and have it turn into a submarine or whatever, right?"

"Yeah but—"

"Everyone knows that's not real."

"Huh. Movies aren't real. What do you know."

She thought for a moment that he was ending the conversation and was relieved herself. She wondered if they would have sex now.

Then he said, "Funny though. About movies not being real. Because people are always saying they affect people. Like make people believe the things they see in movies are things they should have. Like give them unrealistic expectations."

"What do you mean?"

"Like body types. In movies or whatever. Don't you like to talk about that a lot? How come they're always talking about unrealistic body standards. Right? I thought that was, like, a feminist talking point. That movies put pressure on you and give you unrealistic expectations. Isn't that the same?"

"Hmm. So movies put pressure on you to have women sleep with you."

"Of course they do. And so does this. All these girls showing off around you all the time. Put them all in burkas, I say."

"Right. Okay."

"No seriously. Girls, women, walk around in less and less, and you can see their bodies all the time, in yoga pants all the time, you can see every outline, you can see a camel toe, they show their belly buttons and their nipples, no bras, of course it drives you crazy, and it's your fault, I mean our fault, guys' fault, if you feel something, like you're turned on, of course, and that's something that's bad, it's terrible, you shouldn't even look at them, you're a sick pervert if you look at them because it makes them feel uncomfortable, of course they're not dressing for *you*—we heard this in high school all the time, right, of course we're not dressing to turn *you* on, don't be disgusting, don't be a sick perv, it has nothing to do with you, just leave us alone, just look and feel sick and that's your problem. And by the way you're making me uncomfortable by looking at me or even thinking about me in that way, you little cuck. See, we're just disgusting in every way. I'm disgusting you even now."

"Wow." Gloria tried to sit still and calm her breathing and not answer right away. "There is lots to say about that, and lots I think you are not understanding, so let me just think about it for a while."

"Don't bother."

"Burkas it is then." She breathed out and breathed in. "Are you still on the forums?" She could still see, flashing before her, the texts she had read. *Let me know when you fuck one in the ass*.

He shook his head. "No. Sometimes."

"No or sometimes?"

He took a deep breath. "There's been stuff going on. On this one forum. It's kind of important."

"So you are. You're still reading and writing this vile and disgusting stuff and hanging out with me. That is so, so—"

"Listen. Just listen."

"What is it? Is the next massacre being planned?"

"Nope. But two guys have offed themselves in the last two weeks."

Gloria closed her mouth. She stared at his face.

"One of them did it live. Online."

"Did you watch it?"

He shook his head. "I missed it. I mean I didn't see it. I wasn't... I need something to drink."

Gloria didn't move. She looked around at the beautiful young people he hated so much and she hated a little, too, and she hated them a little less. She did know, however, that there were ugly kids in their schools, or poor ones, who had not come on this trip. And that they were at home writing in their diaries.

Daryn said, "You know guys are always talking about it. And there are rules, on the forums, the mods will shut it down. But it's hard because it's kind of a joke and everybody does it. It's like it's part of..."

"Part of the culture. Death is part of the culture."

He nodded. "Sure. But talking about it takes the edge off it, you know?"

"That is called catharsis."

"Okay."

"It doesn't work. Catharsis."

"Okay."

"Do you do that? Do you talk about it?"

He shrugged and grimaced as if he had a pain. "I guess. Sure."

"So how can you tell when anyone is being serious?"

"Oh, you can tell, I think. You can tell when someone ... they will say like specific things. Like, *this evening is going to be the time, by eight o'clock I won't be here anymore*. Or whatever. Or they'll say *I have saved this much Vicodin and this much Percocet and I have my mom's Dilaudid* and if you add up all the amounts you know it's, you know, serious. Or they just take Tylenol. You know how easy it is to do with Tylenol? It's sick how easy."

"Yes," said Gloria, "I do know this."

"Anyway. One guy, last week, he was talking like this and there were a bunch of jokes and stuff and people called him a cuck or whatever for talking about it and not doing it, like, *you soyboy, just do it*, before anyone started talking about calling 911. Of course, no one knew where he was."

"You mean people were encouraging him?"

He shifted in his seat. "I am so thirsty."

Gloria was thirsty, too, and almost left it alone. She was not enjoying berating him. For a second she wished for total forgiveness for everyone for every stupid idea they had ever had. She wished she could just have a boyfriend, and they would be nice to each other. She wondered whether she was making him uncomfortable because she felt she should, in case she had to report this conversation to some imaginary committee of girlfriends later. But it was too important to drop. "Like they egg him on," she said. "You do."

"There have been cases like that, yes. You know there have been. I would never do anything like that."

"Did you call 911?"

"Girls do it too, you know. On their sites."

Gloria was surprised he knew this. "How do you know this?"

"Huh?"

"Anyway. Did you call 911?"

"I wasn't there for that. I had been talking to the guy before. Trying to talk him down. I was online with him for about four hours. Trying to get info, like where he was, where his parents were. Didn't do any good."

"Wow. Why would you do that?"

He scrunched up his eyes. "What do you mean why would I do that?"

"I don't know why I said that. I mean I know why you would do that. I guess I just don't know you very well."

"What a vote of confidence."

"Anyway."

"Anyway. Then when one of those things happens, and we all knew it really happened because his sister or someone came on and took over his account and made an announcement, and then it came on the news, where he was, someone found it, it was like in Texas or something, and then you kind of have to brace yourself because then someone else is going to do it for sure. It's suifuel."

"It's what?"

"Suifuel. Fuel for ... Like you might have a spike. Copycats. Like there's gasoline everywhere and that one thing is a match."

"And sure enough."

"And sure enough, the next guy has to go one further and do it live. Like I said, I didn't see it. But I watched some of the video yesterday."

"They *posted* the *video*?"

He shrugged. “It was up for an hour or so before the mods got it, yes. Hey, you’d watch it too.”

A girl in a canary-yellow dress laughed and bent over a table. The front of the dress dipped and Gloria could see the tops of her breasts. The boys at her table didn’t even look. They were so used to beautiful breasts all around them. “Yes, I would watch it too.”

“By the time he was passing out people were trying to take action and track down his username and so on. There are some pretty serious computer guys on there and they can do that. It’s not too hard. But anyway, it was too late.”

“I feel a little sick.” She really wanted a glass of wine. The light in the cafeteria was too bright. “That’s so horrifying.” A knot of boys burst into laughter and one chased another out of the room. Some of the girls applauded. Gloria said, “What did he use?”

Daryn frowned. “You’re not supposed to ask that. You know that.”

“Yes, yes, I know that. What did he use?”

“Thinking of doing it?”

She shook her head. “Not in the slightest. What did he use?”

His voice went low. “His own insulin. Just shot up a whole month’s supply. Went pretty fast.”

She nodded. “Smart.” He nodded back and they both smiled a little. She said, “Couple of professionals here.”

“Ha.”

“And then,” she said, “I suppose he’s a hero, right, a martyr?”

“Yup.” There was a pause. “And you know the sad girls’ sites are just the same.”

"No, no they are not actually. I have done some research on this. I wrote an article about those sites. They don't succeed nearly as often."

"Yay! Guys are better at something."

"Oh my god." But she had giggled a little. She looked at him and he did look pinched and pale and quite sad. "That must have been a tough time for you."

He looked surprised to hear this. "Yes it was. It is kind of tough."

"Does it make you want to do it?"

"No. It's dumb."

"Yes, it is dumb. Okay." She stood up. "Let's go out."

He didn't move. He was staring at the floor and biting his lip.

"What? Don't you want to?"

He shook his head. "I did try it. Once."

She sat down again.

He took a deep breath. "Well, I didn't actually do it. But I planned to and everything. And then I announced online, in one of the chatrooms, that I was going to. And that felt really good. It was exciting."

Gloria was quiet. If she said anything she might stop him talking.

"So then. After I said I was going to, I got a lot of comments and messages, and it was weird. It wasn't exactly what I expected. I thought everyone would say, *sure go for it, good plan, you're ugly anyway, you don't have a chance, go on, show us how it's done* kind of thing."

She couldn't help herself; she asked, "What were you going to do? Like how?"

"Oh. Jump. Tall building."

"Did you have one in mind?"

"Oh yeah. Near where my mom works. I found a way up to the roof. There was a service elevator and then a staircase. I went up there many times."

"Wow. Jumping is so ... violent."

"Yeah, I guess that was part of it. People would have to clean me up and that would be part of it, like my revenge or something I guess. Nice and gruesome."

"What about your mom?"

"Yeah, I didn't like that part. I didn't like thinking about it."

"Women almost never jump, you know," she said. "They take pills. They don't like the idea of the mess. Men seem to love it. Maybe it's about having a servant, even after your death. I don't know."

"Is that true?"

"I don't know. I read it somewhere. Anyway. What happened."

"Well. So a lot of guys did say *go for it*, you know, like *congratulations for having the guts*. But a lot of guys got kind of concerned, and I started getting direct messages, like *where are you, you should call 911*, and long letters about how I shouldn't do it, and they were including distress lines and psychiatric hospitals, which is kind of hilarious because I thought we didn't believe in that stuff. But some of the stuff they wrote was really personal, like heartfelt, and they kind of made me feel sad, especially about my mom. So I never did it."

She thought for a moment. "So why did you want to do it?"

He frowned. "For the same reasons I was there in the first place. That's the whole point of it. You have to hate yourself to be there."

"I still don't get it. Why did you hate yourself?"

"Because I'm a loser. I'm ugly and I'm poor and I'll never get anywhere."

"You're not ugly." She paused. "But I know how it is when you can't realize that. You know girls have that a lot."

He sneered. "So you're saying I'm girly too. Well that about adds up."

Quietly, she said, "You are more like a girl than you think." She braced for his getting up and storming out, but he just sat there looking flat and tired. She stood up again. "Okay. I'm going to take you out."

He blinked. "Out? Where out?

"We'll get a glass of wine." She stood up and waited for him to stand up too.

"You talk like you own me," he said.

"What?"

"It's like you're civilizing me. You think I need civilizing."

"Well, maybe. Why not?"

"Okay," he said, and stood up. "Civilize me."

THEY WALKED WEST ALONG COLLEGE Street, away from the campus, and there were more people on the sidewalk. The cafés had begun to put tables on their patios, but it was still too cool to be crowded. She stopped outside a place

Florian had taken her to. It was a tequila bar, with dark wood inside and bartenders with beards. There were four or five people in a line outside. Florian had known the architect and so his name had been on a list. "Here," she said.

There was a guy at the door with a headset. He was on his phone and ignoring the people in line. Gloria had met the guy through Florian. He had an odd name. Elton or Alton. She walked up to him and Daryn held back. "Good evening," said the guy without moving.

"Hey," said Gloria, and she shook her hair out over her shoulders. "Alton?"

The guy looked up, frowning. "Yes?"

"I'm Gloria, Florian's friend."

The guy looked her up and down. He nodded "Right," he said. "How you doing. Two?"

She nodded, and he stepped back and opened the door and Daryn followed her in.

"Sick," he said.

The bar was loud. Instead of tables, there were barrels with tabletops on them and you had to stand around them, but all the barrels were taken. The crowd was two deep at the bar. Daryn looked a little bewildered and Gloria pushed forward. He followed behind. The bartender looked like Florian. In fact most of the guys here did. She asked Daryn what he wanted, and he said something she didn't understand, and the bartender had to lean forward and ask him to repeat it. He brought them a glass of white wine and some kind of vodka cooler in a can. Gloria waited until Daryn pulled out his wallet. He paid with one twenty and she saw there was only one other twenty in the wallet.

They moved away from the bar, but there was nowhere to stand except against the wall, near the stairs down to the toilets, where servers had to keep pushing past them. They were jammed against two guys who were a little older, maybe in their thirties, who were also against the wall. One of the guys was shouting to the other, "I can't imagine it. I can't imagine it. Not at my age."

Gloria didn't say anything mean about the vodka cooler. "This sucks," she said. "I was hoping we could sit down."

"Okay," he said. "Let's go somewhere else." This was very different from what Florian would have said; he would have said, "It's cool, relax," and because she would have known that he would say that, she never would have expressed her discomfort in the first place. She had spent a lot of time in loud bars with Florian.

"It just really doesn't sound like fun," yelled the guy beside her. He was really right in her ear. "Like, I get it, a relationship, sounds like a good idea, support and all that, like, I like the idea in theory."

The music was bassy hip hop. The song playing seemed to be repeating the words *what the shop she in, what the shop she in.*

"In principle," yelled the other guy.

"In principle, right. But in practice it means I'm stuck, like, no options."

"Like you're never going to get laid with anyone else ever again."

"Right? Like can you imagine that?"

"Oh my god," said Gloria, "I'm going to kill someone."

"What?" said Daryn.

"Nothing."

Across the room standing at one of the barrels with two tall boys was the girl she knew called Kayleigh, who had long red hair and a tight top with a low scoop that showed a lot of firm breast. "Shit," said Gloria. "I know that girl."

"What?" Daryn was almost shouting.

What the stop doin', what the stop doin', sang the speakers.

"I know that girl."

"So what?"

"She was in Leibovitz's class. And she was in my Decolonizing Fiction class."

"I don't even know what that means."

"Maybe when I'm like forty-five," the guy next to her was yelling. "But right now, like, it's Friday night, and there's a party, and I can't go because a girl I fucked yesterday says I can't? Like, can you fucking imagine?"

"What about kids?" yelled the other guy.

"That does not sound like fun. That, to me, is not a party, my guy. Not my kind of thing."

"I don't want to talk to her," said Gloria.

"Why not?"

"Shit." Kayleigh had seen her, and then Daryn, and then raised her eyes wide and opened her mouth as if she was opening a Christmas present in a Tiffany box—she pushed through the crowd towards them with her eyes wide.

"Eeeeee!" she said, and Gloria had to embrace her. "Hey! Oh my god! Look at you! You look so gorgeous!"

Kayleigh had pushed the two yelling guys to one side and made space along the wall for herself. Gloria assured Kayleigh that she looked gorgeous, too, and this went on for some time. Kayleigh turned and smiled full force on Daryn, and so Gloria had to introduce him. She was relieved that he shook her hand properly, if a little weakly. Daryn had to say his name three times before Kayleigh heard it properly.

"So what are you guys up to this evening?" said Kayleigh. "Just chilling? Do you know Vincent and Justin? Were you in Marginal Writing with Richardson? No? I thought you loved her, took every course! Vincent was in it but I met Justin in Gender. Daryn, were you at the school at the same time as us? No, I would remember you. So." All this time she was looking at Daryn and smiling and playing with her hair and this made Gloria look at him too. She tried to see him as Kayleigh would and she saw a tall and quiet boy who was almost handsome. She thought about him thinking he was ugly and was meanly, momentarily, glad that he thought this. He was looking back and forth between Gloria and Kayleigh and nodding as if listening closely. Perhaps he even was. What she saw was a mysterious possible boyfriend who wore running shoes to a bar, perhaps a handyman or a drug dealer.

"So," said Kayleigh. "How did you guys meet?"

Not a prob-a-lem, not a prob-a-alem, sang the speakers.

"We're just friends," said Gloria.

"We met online," said Daryn.

"No shame in that," said Kayleigh, beaming. "Never had any luck with it, myself. It's the Wild West out there. Like so many retrograde beings. It's like the primeval swamp. You are so lucky to have found someone civilized."

Behind Kayleigh, one of the two older guys was yelling, "It would be like a prison, am I right? Like who wants to go to jail?"

"You guys on your way somewhere?" said Gloria.

"We were hoping to get into Fridge," said Kayleigh. "Justin knows the guys. You guys want to come?"

"Sure," said Daryn. He drank from his cooler and looked around the room.

Gloria looked at him. This was the first confident thing she had ever seen him do. Aside from stalking her. She said, "You want to go to Fridge?"

He laughed. "I don't know what it is."

"You want to go anyway."

"Sounds sick. I'm up for anything."

"Are you now?" Gloria watched him and saw that he was looking quickly at Kayleigh's chest and then away again. He was smiling.

"He's a keeper," said Kayleigh.

Stop the sufferin', stop the sufferin', sang the speakers.

"What is this song?" said Gloria. "It sounds like they're saying *Götterdämmerung, Götterdämmerung*."

"Which one is your boyfriend?" said Daryn, pointing his can at Vincent and Justin.

"Oh, them!" said Kayleigh. "Neither. Believe me."

"Why not?" said Daryn. "They seem like fine fellows."

Kayleigh laughed and put her fingers on her collarbone as she did so.

"Listen," said Gloria. "We have to get going." She put her glass down on a ledge behind her. "We should catch up some other time."

"I would totally love that," said Kayleigh. "Don't let me keep you. It was really nice to meet you. Is it Derek?"

"Daryn."

Gloria took his hand and began moving to the door. At the door he said, "Let me finish this."

"Not now. I'll get you another one. I really want to go."

On the street he said, "What was that?"

She walked quickly away from him and he caught up. "Did I do something wrong?"

"No. You did nothing wrong. In fact you were surprisingly fine. Confident. Like you had no problem hanging around in bars and talking to girls."

"Ah. Oh, well, I do. I mean I don't do that."

"You seemed very convincing to me. You were a total Chad in there."

"Okay. Wow."

She walked very quickly and he scampered a few steps behind. A light rain began to fall, and she stopped under an awning. People were holding their jackets over their heads and trying to flag taxis. Big bass boomed from cars with darkened windows, and the street began to shine.

He stood next to her. "It's going to pour, I think."

"I'm sorry," she said. "I shouldn't order you around. I'm not sure why I had to leave, all of a sudden."

"You didn't like me talking to that girl," he said. "I get it. I'm your boyfriend. You got jealous."

"Oh my god."

"Well?"

Gloria knew if she said *You're not my boyfriend* he would get whiny again and she couldn't face that on a night out so she didn't.

"I think that's perfectly normal," he said. "I wouldn't like it if you were talking…I mean too interested in a guy. I like it. It makes me happy."

"What makes you happy?"

"That you would feel like you didn't want me talking to girls. That's cool. I understand it."

Gloria thought about this and felt a rush of anger because she was embarrassed because he was right. "No," she said. "Of course I don't want to stop you from talking to women."

"Yes you do. Yes you totally do."

"It's not quite as simple as that. I was uncomfortable with the whole conversation. I'm not really keen on that girl. That woman. She makes me uncomfortable. It wasn't you."

"It's okay," he said. "It's totally okay. You got jealous. You got jealous."

He didn't look happy though. His face was tight and he was flicking his hand back and forth as if trying to get something off his fingertip.

"It is kind of interesting," she said. "I think what she found so fascinating about you, aside from the fact that you were with me and she was just curious because everything in life is a big competition to her and she has to know if she's winning or not—aside from that, what she found interesting is that you seemed to be listening to her and you didn't talk over her. That's a really useful trait."

"Yeah, no. I don't think women like that."

"Well, see here's where all your theories may be wrong. Frankly you don't know anything about what women want."

"That is true."

"And you see, it is a lot easier than you think to talk to women."

"I didn't want to talk to her," he said in a slightly higher pitch, a pitch that approached a whine. "I just wanted to talk to you. I didn't even want to go there."

"Okay, okay. Don't start crying or anything."

"I am totally happy to just be alone with you."

"And you are okay with me saying that we have to go, then?"

"Yes. Yes of course."

The rain started to come down and drum on the awning now. Women were squealing as they rushed by. Cars splashed the sidewalk and men yelled at them. It was all so cinematic it was slightly erotic.

Gloria shivered. She said, "Like if I tell you what to do in bed. You like that too."

"I like whatever you like."

This was actually nice to hear. And it was nice too, she had to admit, that Kayleigh had found him worthy of flirting with. "I suppose we're going to end up back at my place," she said. "It's the only safe place." She stepped into a sheet of water and raised her hand and a taxi squealed its brakes.

14.

SHE HAD HIM LYING DOWN with his hands over his head, his underwear was off and he was hard, and she wished she had some kind of ropes or cuffs or something to make sure he stayed still, but he was being very obedient so far and not grabbing at her. She undressed in front of him, down to her panties and then straddled his face and tried smothering him a little with her crotch. She felt his tongue trying to lick her through the cotton and she raised herself off and slapped his face lightly and told him to stop. "Just let me smother you," she said. She did this on and off for a few minutes and looked over her shoulder to see that he was still hard and he was, very hard.

She got off him and tore open a condom with her teeth and rolled it onto him. Then she took off her panties and straddled his face again and allowed him to lick her. When she was wet enough she slid down and sat on his cock. He was very still while she lowered herself. She was breathing hard and wondered if she might come this time. She pinched and twisted his nipples, and he gasped and thrust upwards in her. "Don't come," she said. She began rocking, rubbing against his pubic bone, feeling the warmth build up. "You're going to make me come," she said.

She did this for some time and she could not come. He was staring at her with wide eyes and saying, "Yes, yes."

"Be quiet. Don't look at me. Close your eyes."

She rocked and rocked on him and felt herself getting almost close and then it receded, and then it would come again and recede, and then she felt the arousal fleeing altogether.

"I can't hold it much longer," he whispered.

"Shhh. I told you." She closed her eyes and tried to concentrate. This was reminding her of sex with Florian, when he used to say, "Come on, come for me," and it would go on forever. He was so disappointed when she wouldn't come and afterwards he would ask her to talk about why she hadn't been able to come. A part of her had always felt that if she had been able to come more he would have been more committed, and she wondered if every other woman he was with had multiple orgasms every time. And when she closed her eyes and pictured Florian she felt such a rush of fury through her that she slapped Daryn again.

"Don't," he said.

"Will it stop you from coming if I do that?"

"Maybe. Yes."

She slapped him again. "You like it when I domme you? Right?"

He nodded, his eyes closed, whimpering.

"Because you think you don't deserve me, right? Right?" She twisted his nipples hard, rocking hard against him. "Well you don't. You little loser, you don't. You don't deserve this. You don't deserve anything."

She was breathing hard and wet but not any closer to coming. She also realized she was crying. "You think you're god's gift to women, you self-centered little prick."

Daryn's eyes were wide and frightened. "Me?"

"You think your dick is so big. All you can ever do is perform, perform." She was weeping now and she stopped thrusting.

"Oh god," said Daryn, his back arching, "Oh god," and he tensed and pumped into her and grunted and she felt his penis flexing.

"You little wimp," she said, "you came," and she rolled off him and put her hands to her face and cried.

"I'm sorry," said Daryn, "I'm sorry, I couldn't help it. What's wrong? What's wrong?"

"Nothing," she said, and cried a little longer. Her face was soaked and she couldn't stop.

He turned and pressed himself close to her and stroked her hair and said, "Tell me. Tell me what it is."

She stopped crying and used a sheet to dry her face. "It's nothing," she said. "It's nothing. Sometimes I get frustrated when I can't come. It's just the meds I'm on."

"Why do you take them?"

"I won't," she said. "I'm going to stop." And then she felt very tired and much calmer and even drifted off to sleep for a minute.

When she awoke he was still there, naked beside her, and he was dozing, as well, and she was angry at herself for letting this happen as she didn't want to let him spend the night there.

She got up and went to her computer. She went to the Toronto Blackpills forum and searched his handle again.

There was a new post by Gentlemanwhiner, on a thread called "Examples of Misandry."

> Gentlemanwhiner: *It's the constant barrage of hate against men that wears you down. Just this constant scorn, like you're personally responsible for every evil in history and you're just by your nature a kind of violent neanderthal and you should spend your life apologizing for having a sex drive. We've just realized we don't need to apologize and be silent about who we really are. The society hates you. It's a misandrist society. The way we are constantly told we are inferior beings—the way every time you open any screen or newspaper you're reading that men are hateful monsters and idiotic is bound to make you hate yourself, and you have to stop hating yourself. I don't believe that women should be harmed or prosecuted in any way. But we don't have to elevate feminine values to dominate the whole society. We are naturally dominant, and so it's unnatural that women should be artificially given so much power over us and unnatural that we have to feminize our values and the values of the whole society.*
>
> MrRodger1997: *Are you naturally dominant? That sounds kind of like Chad talk. If we were naturally dominant would we be here?*
>
> Pokéboy: *I wish I were naturally dominant*
>
> Gentlemanwhiner: *We have had our natural dominance erased from us by fear.*

She could have woken him then and asked him if this was really him, and if it was, why he had felt the need to post this just the day before, but she could not, because she did not want it to be him, and because he was sleeping.

She closed her eyes and tried to sleep without taking any of her pills.

After a while he turned towards her and his eyes were open. "So," he said, "this sleep thing. The way it's supposed to work is you close your eyes and then, what. You just fall asleep?"

"I've heard it described this way."

"Okay," he said. He lay on his back and looked at the ceiling. He pulled both arms out from the covers and laid them stiffly by his side. "Here we go. I'm doing it. I'm ready."

"Sure," she said, "if you want to just slavishly follow the injunctions of Big Sleep."

"I am not in the pocket of Big Sleep. Wake up, sheeple. Fight Big Sleep."

Gloria did the same with her arms. They lay together staring at the ceiling. "I am totally about to sleep."

"Yup."

"I've got myself a ticket to dreamland."

He laughed out loud at this. "First-class ticket to dreamland. Dreamland here we come. Dreamland Express."

She giggled too and there it was again, the nauseating feeling that they could somehow be friends and that this was nice, however silly.

The light in her room was silver from the street lamp. It must have been after midnight.

"I won't make you go home now," she said.

"I would hope not," he said.

"I don't hate you, you know."

He was silent for a moment. "Okay."

He put a hand on her breast and she did not push it off.

"You know," she said, "I don't really enjoy dominating you. It doesn't come naturally to me."

"Okay."

"It doesn't really turn me on. And I feel I'm kind of...acting or something. It was a decision I made because I was angry. Angry and kind of scared, because you can be scary, you know, and you have these scary ideas. And because I didn't want you to feel that you had any power over me, and I guess I wanted to punish you for your ideas, and also maybe because you can be so..." She wanted to say *abject* but did not. "So down on yourself, so self-hating, and so passive, which is, it makes no sense, I know, since I wanted you to be passive. I don't know what I want. But I feel very strongly that I shouldn't like you, and I don't like you, to be clear, when you say idiotic things about being ugly or about women wanting to destroy men or—"

"When did I say that?"

"Oh." She realized he had never said that to her and that she had read it in someone else's text, and she couldn't tell him that. "Well we don't want to destroy men." She thought of Isabel, who sometimes did. "Well some of us do. Anyway."

He waited.

"I think," she said, "that I am not doing you any good with this and I, really, actually I only want a relationship, I can't see myself being a mistress in some latex outfit, you know, with some Dungeons and Dragons name. In some plastic dungeon room. It's not me."

"You want a relationship with me?"

She turned away from him. She could not look at him. She didn't know what she wanted. "I don't see how that could work," she said. "I feel that I shouldn't like you and ... and, but I also don't think you have ever had a loving relationship, and you have no idea what it should be like."

She waited for him to ask her if she had ever had a loving relationship, herself, a question which she would not be able to answer, but he did not.

"Yeah, well," he said, "I guess I don't, but how would I ... I mean you talk about loving relationships, but that would mean, that would mean you trusting me."

"Right."

Gloria was silent then because he was right. She did not trust him and that would forever prevent anything normal from happening between them and if she wanted anything normal then she would have to trust him, at least provisionally, maybe as an exercise, and perhaps trust would be a good thing for him too; perhaps she was a good influence, or could be. *Trust is always a leap*, one of her therapists had said. Autumn liked to say this, too. *Trust is a leap of faith*.

"We're not going to have any more hate sex," she said, "or s/m games, whatever."

"I was only doing it because I thought you liked it."

"Right. Okay." She turned to face him. "Okay, we are going to try regular vanilla sex and it's going to be gentle and nice."

"Okay."

"So, you start," she said, "by kissing me."

He kissed her on the lips. His eyes were open.

"Try closing your eyes. Also, try kissing me not on the lips. Like on my forehead."

He did this and she closed her eyes too. She took his hand and enlaced her fingers with his. This action seemed clichéd and embarrassed her, and she almost withdrew but stuck with it. It seemed more intimate than anything they had done.

He kissed her neck and her ears and her chest. He pushed his body against hers and he was aroused again. She put her hands around his neck and pulled his mouth tighter to hers.

She twisted onto her back and pulled him on top of her. He kissed her everywhere, then, especially her neck and breasts. He lifted her arms up and kissed her underarms. He slid down and licked her between the legs. He did everything normal.

She had to slow him down from time to time. She tried to let herself relax, but she couldn't come. It was pleasant though. She let herself let out sounds. She knew he would like this. She let herself be loud.

When he rose up and kissed her, his mouth was slick and she tasted herself on his tongue.

When he tried to penetrate her, she took his cock in her hand and said, "Wait, wait." She pulled out from underneath him and then tried to take his cock in her mouth.

He said, "No," but she said, "It's okay. It's okay. Stay still."

He let her do that then, lying back and trembling, and she was careful not to let him come.

"All right," she said. "All right." And she lay back and opened her legs for him.

He pushed inside her and she said, "Slow, slow."

She pulled back her knees to let him go as deep as he could. He was hard and it felt good.

He would accelerate his thrusting and then slow, as if trying to calm himself down, which was good. He was breathing hard and whimpering a little, so she twisted so he would pull out. They faced each other so she could stroke his cock. She kissed him deeply and stroked him until he came in her hand and against her belly, and it was only at this point that she felt she was aroused enough to come, but it was all right, it was over, and she probably wouldn't anyway.

"Oh," he said, "that was so beautiful. I love you so much."

"It was nice," she said.

"I will take care of you forever."

"Okay. Sure."

"I'm serious."

"Sure." She let her breathing slow, and she let him nuzzle against her, and she let him fall asleep.

She knew she should take her meds before she fell asleep but it would have been an effort and also she didn't want to take them anymore.

15.

Is all sex labour? Hear from the activists who think you should be paid for your intimacy

"Anything that adds value is labour," says sex-work and trans activist Skye Winters (they/them). "And for centuries women and femmes have been providing an unpaid service while providing many other unpaid domestic services at the same time." Winters—who used to write a sex-advice column for *Next* magazine as Mandi La Bomba—is glad that this thesis is gaining ground among mainstream sex and gender theorists and will be outlining its impact in their online seminar "Unpaid Labour and the Future of Sex" (streaming this Saturday at 7 p.m. ET; click here for tickets). "Unpaid sex," says Winters, "whether consensual or not, no matter if it's in a monogamous, exclusive relationship, is a form of essential care work that is dominated and exploited to serve the rich and powerful."

Indeed, it's especially in marriages where unpaid sex is most likely expected or coerced. According to researcher Kathleen Basile, "76% of the general public believe husbands use force to make their wives have sex and 80% believe it occurs often or somewhat often."

Winters believes that as interest rises in the compensation of women-identified domestic roles, such as child care and emotional labour, sexual intimacy will also come to be seen as essential care. "The history of sexual coercion and unpaid labour—especially emotional labour—are inextricably linked. Women taking control of sexual oppression by demanding compensation for this labour is implicitly antipatriarchal."

What do you think? Is all sex labour? Take our survey.

FOR THIS LABOUR, WHICH HAD taken all morning—to set up the interview with Jessica, her friend from the Women's Centre who was now also Skye Winters—and all afternoon—for writing and setting up the links to sources—Gloria would be paid seventy-five dollars. She was finding she was writing more and more about labour these days, especially as *labour* and *work* were words that could be usefully used in any Daily Self Care piece. "Do the hard work of . . ." would never get her into any trouble. Surinder would get antsy, one day or another, about too much sex in these pieces, and this one in particular he might find too radical, but he might allow it because there would be a reader survey, which tended to shoot the metrics up. Anyway, a conversation with him about what her own labour was worth would, right now, only provoke the usual puzzlement. The budget was the budget, he would say; he had nothing to do with it. It would be like asking him if he thought daylight saving time could be eliminated for her.

Gloria still had to write the survey questions and then send them to the coder they used to set these things up. She suspected the coder was paid the most of anyone in the organization, even more than Surinder. It was almost five and she was to meet Isabel downtown at six and she was nervous about it, she didn't know why, nervous that she would be unable to please Isabel, as Isabel had seemed so down and mysterious lately, nervous about the possibility that Isabel was keeping something from her, which would mean Isabel no longer considered her as close as she had, nervous too that she would want to tell Isabel, very much, about this boy Daryn, and nervous that she would, and unhappy that she couldn't.

She was nervous about Daryn too, if she admitted it, because he probably expected to see her this evening and she was probably guilty of leading him into this expectation, which she really didn't want, and now she had got herself into this, so it would be imperative that she not text him to say that she would be busy, not check in, as that would set future expectations of daily check-ins. He had no right to expect this.

She knew what would have happened had she texted Florian every day to wonder what he was doing. He would have blocked her.

It wasn't until she was on the bus downtown that she got the first text from him. *What u up to tonite.*

She hesitated: even if she answered *out with a friend* she would be capitulating, in a way, agreeing that she had to check in and explain where she was; and yet it seemed cruel, and might upset him, to ignore it. She was in a bind.

She typed, *out with a friend.*

Immediately: *what friend.*

She sighed and almost shut her phone right off. This was exactly what she had been afraid of. She thought for a minute before writing, *Do I have to tell you again? You know that's none of your business.*

Then: *I am not comfortable about having to check in with you. I am not your girlfriend.*

The bus was approaching the subway station, where there were concrete-covered bus bays, and always a jam of buses nosing their way in and out, snorting and huffing. When each bus got to its own slot it sighed and settled and disgorged its people into the greenish light of the station fluorescents. It always made her think of pigs jostling to a trough, but she also liked the bus bays, with their crowds, as she could see what people wore and carried, which was always interesting. There were a few seconds of outdoor time, too, waiting for the crowd to filter itself into the escalators leading them down to the underworld, and she could see beyond the highway a strip of sky that was a warm pink, and it felt like summer for a moment.

Her phone: *it was just a question.*

Then she was underground.

WHEN SHE EMERGED DOWNTOWN there was a message from Isabel. She couldn't make it and was very sorry but she was Tray Tray Fatty Gay.

Gloria typed that she was already downtown, and it was a shame Isabel couldn't have let her know earlier, and Isabel replied that she was really really sorry. Gloria did not reply to this. She wasn't going to let Isabel be dramatic and self-absorbed anymore.

She walked through the business district past bars and restaurants with men in suits and women in heels, all drinking and laughing in the windows in orange light. She would have loved, for once, to be in one of them, with Isabel, being looked at by the men in suits, and failing Isabel she would have wanted to be with one of the men in suits, or even with Daryn, actually, to be honest, so that they could laugh together at the men in suits. She had not had a date in a while. She didn't count the time she had gone out with Daryn.

She took out her phone and typed, *I am free now if you would like to get together.*

He answered right away, *ok where.*

She hesitated. He could not afford to go to one of these bars, and he would likely be wearing running shoes, but she didn't want to go straight home. She would have to pay for a drink for the two of them and then he would expect to go home with her and that wasn't really what she wanted, unless the drink went well and he was able to talk like a person, which was possibly worth a try. She would also have to wait alone somewhere until he got there.

She typed, *my place*.

Then she went into a hotel with chandeliers in the lobby and sat at the bar and ordered a glass of white wine that cost twenty-two dollars. Some businessmen sitting on the sofas looked at her but then looked away.

IN THE UNDERGROUND MAZE SHE had to enter to get to the subway, there was a liquor store, about to close, and she bought a bottle of white wine.

Daryn made it to her apartment before she did. He was waiting outside and he had a small bunch of flowers. This was at once moving and embarrassing.

The last flowers he had brought her were still in the vase and drooping. She threw them out. The new flowers were pink carnations.

She opened the wine and then tried to remember how one might behave with a friend or a boyfriend, so she asked him how his day was.

"Good I guess," he said.

"Did you work?"

"Sure."

"So, what happened at work?"

"Not much."

"Okay then."

There was a silence while they drank wine and then he said, "How was your day?"

"Well, thank you for asking. My day was pretty shitty, actually. I was on my way to meet my best friend, and I kept getting harassed by someone who was being possessive and insecure, which is a real turnoff, you know? It is not hot."

"Your best friend? Who's your best friend?"

"My best friend is a girl called Isabel."

"That's who you were meeting?"

"You see?" she said. "That's what you've got to stop. You can't obsess over who I'm meeting. That's not the point. The point is..." She had finished her wine. "I forget what the point is. No, the point is to ask how I'm doing and if I'm okay and not obsess over owning me."

Daryn frowned and looked at her and then at his wine.

"No," she said, "that's not the point, there is no point, you don't have to ask how I'm doing, you don't have to care."

"Of course I care," he said. "But."

"Yes, okay, but. But what?"

"Well, I'm really not allowed to ask who you're with? It's normal to ask that. You can ask me that any time."

She thought about that.

"I mean we've had sex, right? We've been having sex. It's normal for me to know if you're seeing other people. Right? Wouldn't you want to know that?"

"I guess." Gloria got up to get the bottle. "Yes. Okay. I guess." She poured them both more wine. "So, I guess that is what we're doing."

"It certainly looks that way. I mean to an outsider it would look that way."

"Right." She took off her shoes and folded her legs under her and thought how normal this could be, to be sitting beside someone on a Friday night and drinking wine at home, because you were going to have sex later and then probably get food together. It wasn't really the sex she wanted, although that was fine. The idea of this thing was nice, and he would certainly want to do that, in fact, long to do that, and to give in to it would be easy but very silly, not because it would be like giving in to Florian. Who always made her feel for brief moments that such a thing might be possible and then instantly left her alone and embarrassed, this was almost the opposite problem, in a way she couldn't work out.

"I'm just a normal guy," he said finally.

"Oh you are so totally not. Okay. Okay. But listen you just can't be possessive, okay? It creeps me out and it's a turnoff."

"Okay," he said, "so make me not possessive. Like make me feel relaxed. Like I don't have anything to worry about."

Gloria puffed out her cheeks. "Jesus. Tall order."

"My day was kind of shitty, to be honest," he said.

"Okay, why."

"Because I spent seven and a half hours standing up and walking around inside a store with fluorescent lights and no windows, and most of the time I was trying to avoid a guy called Rashid who wants to get me onside to complain about the scheduling, which he does every day, and he's starting to have a fight with this guy Arash who is the manager, sort of manager guy. And Rashid also likes to talk a lot about phones, like *a lot* a lot. I like phones too but."

"Wow," she said, "this is almost like a normal conversation."

"Have you had supper?"

"Oh. No. I forgot. I'm sorry, I always forget to have food for you."

"That's okay. I'll ... that's okay."

"I really have no food here," she said.

"It's okay. I'll eat later."

"Later? After what?"

He smiled and then frowned and shrugged and said, "Okay. I never really know what's going on."

"Nothing is going on."

"Okay."

He looked unhappy then, sitting on the couch, and she took pity on him. She got up and straddled him. She put her hands on his shoulders and held her face close to his.

He flinched and stiffened.

"No," she said. "Nothing is going to happen to you. Remember?"

Now he smiled. "Okay."

"Maybe that will make you nicer."

"Okay."

"Okay so now you kiss me."

"Oh." He kissed her gently on the lips. Neither of them closed their eyes.

"Did you know," she said, "that if you stare into somebody's eyes for forty seconds without looking away, it will make you fall in love with them? There was a study." She was feeling nervous, she didn't know why. "Or maybe it was sixty seconds or four minutes. Something like that."

She tried kissing him again with her eyes closed. When she opened them, he was still staring at her. "Wow, this isn't going to be easy."

"What?"

"Nothing." She pulled his T-shirt up and he lifted his arms up like a child to have it removed. They kissed some more on the couch but he was still reluctant to touch her, so she moved him into the bedroom. There he took off his clothes at the side of the bed, facing away from her, and she started to do the same but then waited till he had finished. He turned to her and she said, "You can take my clothes off."

This worked, and he began to be more passionate. He kissed her neck and her breasts as he undressed her.

She pulled the duvet back and they got into the bed and embraced. She was giggling a little. He was fully aroused and she was enjoying being kissed. But the pleasure was of a sickening kind, like eating ice cream made of frogs or glass in a dream. She had a feeling of doing wrong, as if she were teaching him to commit a crime.

She taught him how to touch her and how to lick her. He spent a long time on her nipples but was gentle with them. She guided him into her and made him go slowly. She was aware that she was still controlling the way it went, but it was better than giving him orders like a schoolmistress.

She let him try for a while to make her come, but not too long, as she knew she was not going to. He was good, when he penetrated her; he was slow and steady and he did not get overexcited. She felt close to coming but not close enough. It was pleasant.

When he was about to come he pulled out and shot on her belly. And then he held her very tightly, nuzzling her neck and kissing her. He was almost more passionate afterwards than during. He kept his face hidden in her neck and she was afraid he might be crying. Eventually she had to pull away.

"That was very nice," she said.

"That was beautiful," he said, "so beautiful."

He was not crying at least. But she knew that at this stage she could not ask him to leave, that he would be staying the night. She did not, admittedly, want him to leave, but there it was again, the feeling of unhealth, of abandon and indulgence, that dream of drinking a whole bottle of vodka or having sex with one's English teacher, the dream of having consumed poison.

THE NEXT NIGHT, ISABEL WAS waiting outside the sushi place but she looked different. It had only been about a week since Gloria had seen her last, but Isabel gave the impression of being even thinner. Her hair looked flat. "I can't go in here," she said. "I can't afford it."

"You can't?"

Isabel was looking up and down the street. She had a pale foundation on and the skin was taut around her cheekbones. She wore a short skirt and tights and her legs looked frail and bony. "I don't want to be on this street."

"Okay."

"We have to go somewhere really like *shhhhhhm.*" She flattened the air in front of her as if smoothing a bedspread.

"Like chill?"

"Like cheap. And away from here." She turned and began walking.

"This is cheap," said Gloria, following.

"I don't want to see anyone on this street. I don't want to see anyone."

"What's going on?"

"Nothing. Nothing new. In fact, nothing at all is going on, which is the problem. I lost my job, by the way. Okay, don't get all upset. This is exactly what I don't want to—Okay, no, stop it." She pushed away Gloria's arm.

"Stop. Stop. Talk to me."

"We'll stop when we find some *weirk-weirk* like *spoochy* dive bar where I won't know anyone from the douchebag office, and where every drink isn't like twenty bucks."

Gloria half-ran to keep up with her. "When."

"When what."

"When did you lose your job. How long ago?"

"A week."

"A week! Why didn't you tell me?" Gloria felt her voice quivering and there were tears in her eyes. She was going to cry right here on the sidewalk and she shouldn't.

"I was embarrassed. And I didn't want you to make a big all-my-sisters-support-me thing, like some Instagram girl. Oh great, now you're crying."

Gloria was, without sobbing, just letting the liquid pour from her face. She felt a pure irradiating pain like a searing light. It was everywhere through her. It was astonishing. It was a feeling of emptiness, as if Isabel had reached into her and pulled out a plug and everything that made her herself had vanished; she was worthless, she had nothing.

She followed doggedly until Isabel stopped outside some chain pub with screens inside.

"Here," said Isabel. "They'll have pitchers."

Inside, the smell of fried food was like a curtain. Men were sitting on high stools and at the bar watching baseball. They found a corner booth and a waitress in jeans and a rugby shirt with the name of the place on it left them laminated menus.

The booth next to them held two men and two women, maybe in their late twenties, actually one of them was older, maybe forty, and they were all taking notes on notepads and the older one, who wore a golf shirt and one of those puffy vests, had a laptop open, and he was talking, so maybe it was a business meeting. Gloria was distracted by what an awful place this would be to hold a business meeting, and so she stopped crying.

She could get a closer look at Isabel as Isabel glared at the menu. "Did you quit?"

"First of all," said the guy leading the business meeting, just behind Gloria, "I want to talk about the rewards program and how it's going."

"No I didn't quit. There are a lot of layoffs going on. But I was...I wasn't doing well. I was going to get let go anyway."

Gloria felt her purse vibrating on her lap: her phone. "Why? Why? I thought they loved you."

"Just lately." She put the menu away. "I don't want to eat anything."

"You need to. I'll pay."

"Are we calling it a rewards program," said one of the women next to her, "or a points program?"

"How about loyalty points," said one of the guys.

"What like fried grease in batter?" said Isabel. "This is food for like the end of the world. This place is like the end of the world."

"You chose this place."

There was a shout from the men at the bar as something happened in the baseball and Gloria turned to look to see if someone's head had exploded but Isabel stared straight ahead, as if looking over Gloria's shoulder.

Isabel's makeup made her face whiter than it usually was. It was white with faint blue veins under her chin. She said, "I was seeing this guy. And he works there. At the office."

Gloria was silent, stunned again and hollowed, feeling cold inside. For how long? How could she, Gloria, have been excluded from this?

"He was the lawyer," said Isabel, "the company's lawyer. And he was married. Is."

"For how long?"

Isabel shrugged. In a very small voice she said, "A year. Year and a half."

Gloria nodded and felt tears again.

"I couldn't tell you," said Isabel, still very quiet, "because I knew it was so dumb, and I knew it was terrible, and I knew it would end like *neeearr...smuck*." She turned her hands horizontal and smacked her palms together as if killing a flying insect. "And I knew you would know that and say that, and I was just really scared, and I couldn't stop."

"Oh." Gloria was only then aware that the same might be said of her. How could she blame Isabel? "Tell me about him."

"Oh he's like super *whoo-hoo*, hotshot douche dude. He's like thirty-eight and like very hot, quite hot really, and fancy car and squash and skiing and all the stuff I hate."

And then the waitress was on them and Gloria ordered a cider and Isabel ordered a double vodka soda.

Gloria waited until she had gone and said, "And he's married?"

"This was kind of the bad part. Because she works at the office too. She's the VP marketing."

"So she was your boss?"

"Kind of, yes, not directly. But yes."

"Wait a second," said Gloria. "Was he there? At the office thing I went to?"

"Yes."

"He was the tall guy with like silver hair."

"Yup," said Isabel.

"He didn't even talk to you."

"Yup. He was very careful not to."

"He acted like you weren't even there."

"Yup."

"That was the guy?"

"Yes, okay?"

"And the woman who told you to go get food, that was his wife? Oh my god. That's awful."

Isabel frowned and stared at Gloria.

"I mean it's awful for you. I mean that must have been so weird for you."

Isabel looked away. "She's just like that. She treats everyone that way. Me maybe more because she didn't want any women in that office, really."

Gloria said, "And she found out?"

When Isabel looked back her eyes were large and glassy wet. "No, god, not yet. She watched me. Like close. But no, I don't think she knows. I am so terrified of that."

"So what happened?"

She shook her head, blinking. "I guess I just asked for too much. I was kind of a bit jealous I guess. And he said he got nervous and he couldn't like jeopardize all his *bleeahh*, whatever." She wiped her eyes and let out one quick sob. Then she shook her head, and Gloria knew she was telling her that that was all she would cry, there was to be no more crying from either of them, it was over.

"Izz. Why couldn't you tell me?"

"That's not what this is about. Does it have to be about that?"

"No, no, of course not. It isn't. I'm glad you're telling me now. I'm sorry. It sucks. Did you... did you love him?"

Isabel shook her head. "Sure. Yes. No. I don't know. I have no idea. I had a lot of fun with him and he was a total dick and I kind of liked that too because he was, you know, kind of dominant, and then I became kind of desperate. Then when he broke it off I went a little crazy and I started to fuck up."

"Fuck up how?"

"I didn't do much work at the office and then I missed a lot of work and when I did come in I was kind of out of it. I was doing a lot of day drinking and then sometimes a lot of Adderall. And then I just didn't show up for a few days."

"Wow."

"They should have offered to send me to rehab. I could have made a complaint, like a grievance. They are supposed to accommodate. But I didn't want to. I just didn't want to be there."

Gloria reached out and Isabel let her take her hand. "So what are you doing now?"

"I'm doing this. I'm doing absolutely nothing."

Gloria was trying to remember the silver-haired man from Isabel's office. "Where did you... where did you get together?"

"All over. My place. Hotels, mostly. In the storeroom. In the bathroom at Acedia. In the bathroom at Cut. In the bathroom at Sonar."

Gloria's purse buzzed again.

Isabel said, "He has a bunch of pictures of me."

"Oh."

"He liked to take them in the hotel rooms. And, like, videos."

"Oh. Well, everyone has those. You don't trust him?"

"No, yeah, I do. I asked him to delete them all and he said he would, but of course they never do. It's not that, though. It's just that I don't want him to have them. I don't want him to look at them because I don't want him to have me anymore and look at me any time he wants. It feels like he's in my underwear drawer. Like spying on me. I withdraw my permission." Isabel bit her nail, something Gloria had never seen her do.

Gloria's phone buzzed. "Someone is trying to text me, one second."

Her phone read, *Are you lying to me?*

Isabel was waving for the waitress.

Gloria said, "We really should eat something."

"Another round?" said the waitress.

"And some fries," said Gloria, "and, what, wings? Would you eat wings?"

Isabel shook her head and the waitress left.

Gloria glanced back at her phone. *Are you fucking someone?*

These were all the texts that had been coming in.

Why would you lie to me?

Do you believe women should be sluts?

I thought you were different

She powered down her phone.

"Are you seeing someone?" said Isabel.

"No. I'm. No."

"Really? Who is texting you."

"Oh, Autumn, as usual. My mom."

"Autumn is the one who tried to off herself?"

"Well, she didn't really try, but yes. My roommate."

"Did she move out?"

"No, she's supposed to come back any day, I don't know when, really. She keeps delaying it."

Isabel drank the last of her drink quickly. "Are you really not seeing anybody?"

Gloria took a breath. "I was fooling around with someone I met, like online. But it didn't work out."

The people in the booth behind them all started clapping their hands. "Sarah!" they were saying.

Gloria looked around and saw whoever must be Sarah smiling and looking down. The boss guy said, "You deserve it, you totally deserve it. The loyalty program has been the key to engagement here."

"Winner, gagnant," said Gloria.

Isabel screwed up her eye. "Why wouldn't you tell me that?"

"I was a little embarrassed, I guess. He's not—"

"No, not about the guy, about going online. You would never do that. You said you hated that."

"Oh. Okay. Well, I don't know."

"Weird," said Isabel, watching her.

"Well, anyway, I only saw him a few times and he was kind of boring because he had just a normal job." She was aware as she said this that it wasn't really true; she had nothing against normal jobs and in fact often wished she had one. She had said it to amuse Isabel and Isabel did not react. "I just mean he's not like a university guy. Not that there's anything wrong with that."

"Go on."

"Okay, and it's getting, it got a little weird." Gloria's face was hot. "The sex got a little weird, to be honest."

"Was he a lawyer?"

"Why does everybody always think I'm dating lawyers? I don't know any lawyers."

"Who else thinks you're dating lawyers?"

"Oh. Florian did. Anyway. Not a lawyer."

"Because," said Isabel, as if explaining to a child, "you are smart and you like smart guys and lawyers are smart. And kind of dominating. In my experience."

"I'm not really into dominating. I mean being dominated."

"Aha," said Isabel. "So did he try that? Is that why you don't, you didn't . . . they all do that, at some point. They always want to choke you or something at some point."

Gloria laughed. She gulped her drink. "Yeah, that was it."

"You don't have to do that. If you don't want to."

"I know."

Another thing had happened in the baseball game and the commentators were shouting, so there was a silence between them as they both looked at the big screens.

The guy at the next booth said, "So the thing is going to be—and Jen and I, we're going to offline about this further—but basically the thing with the loyalty program is there has to be a call to action, a call to use those points, basically at every point of the purchase."

"I really don't know why we would bother dating anyone," said Gloria.

"Men have too much choice, is the problem." Isabel was almost finished her second drink. "They're drowning in options. There's always the next person to swipe on. And we keep on letting them. They can do whatever they want and there are always more girls."

"Well, don't we have the same options."

Isabel rolled her eyes. "Of course we do. But we don't want them." She slammed down the empty glass.

"Wait until we eat some food before you have another one."

Isabel had turned to look for the waitress.

"Izz," said Gloria.

"Yes."

"This guy, this hotshot. He's not. He's not such a hotshot. You're worth way more than he is. You are smarter and cooler, and you are going to go farther."

"Oh right."

"You can't let these guys have this kind of power in your life. And you are normally so tough on men!" And as she said this she remembered the high-school teacher and stopped.

"Tell me about it," said Isabel.

"Do you think that you do this because, because of..."

"Because of Mr LaRusso. Sure. Everything is that. Everything is some trauma you had in your past. No, I'm just a dick."

"But seriously, it's kind of like the same thing, isn't it? Here's a guy with power and you can't have him."

Tears came quickly into Isabel's eyes and they dripped down her face but she didn't sob or flinch or try to wipe them. They just flowed quickly down her face. "I'm just a cliché I guess. I'm like the girl in some YA novel. So I just go and do the exact same thing all over again. Now you see why I hate myself so much?"

"I do. I do see that."

"Because me, me of all people, I should never have let that happen. I should be the one who tells other people not to do that."

"But that's totally understandable," said Gloria. "Patterns repeat themselves. You can't hate yourself for it. It's not your fault."

"Oh stop. What is this, Instagram? You should put all these sentences over a photo of like a sunset or a butterfly."

Gloria picked up the menu. "How about something nicer than fries, too. There's one of these bean bowls."

"No. I'd better go anyway. I'm just going to get sloppy and sad, and I don't want to."

Isabel was staring at Gloria in a glazed way, towards the wall, and Gloria even looked around to see if there was anything there. "Isabel? What do you want to do? You should eat. Stay with me."

Slowly turning her gaze back, Isabel reached out with both hands and took Gloria's. Her hands were cold. "I love you," she said.

"Oh, don't do that," Gloria said, looking Isabel right in the eyes.

"Do what?"

"Don't get all portentous and ... like you're going to do something."

"Do what."

"Something bad. I live with Autumn, right. And she's telling me she's going to off herself all the time. And she's always writing notes that say she's always loved people or whatever. And even—" She stopped herself for she was about to say *Daryn*. But it was Daryn she was thinking of, with his threats and his hysterias. "If you are really in a bad place, Izz, then you need to tell me straight out, and I'll help you in every way I can. But the dramatic stuff, I'm just, I can't anymore. And it's so not you."

Isabel laughed and nodded. Then she closed her eyes and shook her head. "I so totally agree with you."

"So what's going on, really? We need to get you help or not?"

"No. No. *Ssshwhink.*" Isabel brushed aside the air in front of her. "God, I hate that, too. One way you can be sure someone's not going to off themselves is if they talk about offing themselves."

"Right? This I-love-you-goodbye shit. It's for people who are imagining themselves in a scene in a movie. It's not real."

"Okay well I don't love you then. At all."

"That's better."

"I'm just sorry I've been . . ." Then she stared off at the baseball game. "I'm fine," she said. "I'm fine." She stood up. "I'm really going to go. I'll take a Klonopin and I'll sleep. It's what I need."

"Don't go. You are not allowed to hate yourself for something that other people did. Stay with me. Please."

"I'm sorry. I can't tonight. I'm really sorry. We'll catch up later. I'm fine. You're going to be okay."

Gloria held on to her hand. "Honestly, I am so sick of self-dramatizing moments. If you really need me, if things are so bad, you'd tell me, right? I mean, I do understand if you really just want to be alone." Although she did not understand that, and the thought made her a little sad and a little angry.

Isabel smiled and it was a warm smile, it was a fine smile. "I'm totally fine. I'm Fatty Gay. Very very Fatty Gay."

"Okay. Bye Fatty Gay."

Gloria watched Isabel set off quickly down the street.

She was afraid to check her phone but she did.

Are you sucking a cock? It's disgusting and it hurts.

Then the last one, from just a minute ago: *You fucking slut.*

The phone was hot in her hand.

16.

GLORIA WANDERED A BIT AS she had not planned to be home so early. And Autumn might be already at her place. She tried to make herself go into several bars, the cute or unthreatening ones, to have a drink alone but she hadn't the courage. So she got on a fluorescent-lit streetcar feeling forlorn.

She was going, she had decided, to end it with Daryn sternly and curtly by text, with no possibility of discussion, and perhaps even the threat of something, what, a restraining order, calling the police, something. But she would not do this now when he was in a rage. He would have to receive it tomorrow.

There was a figure outside her apartment building and she hung back to see who it was.

It was him, of course, thin and agitated. He sat on the curb and then stood up and checked his phone, then sat again.

Gloria watched from behind a car. She could leave, but she was exhausted by the buses and trains. She felt that she should be afraid, that his hatred was dangerous, but she couldn't feel it. She couldn't feel frightened. What she felt was rage. She was angry that she was prevented from entering her own house. She was angry that she had to worry about him at all.

He put his head in his hands and shook it a little. He was probably crying.

She stepped out and walked towards him. "Get up," she said sharply. "You're pathetic."

She walked past him and took out her keys with a jangle. She opened the building's front door.

"Wait," he said.

She slammed the door behind her. In the brightly lit glass vestibule she looked at him through the square pane in the steel door. The glass of the pane was reinforced with wire and thick and so she could mostly see her own reflection—frizzy-haired, bags under her eyes—overlaid on his face on the other side, tear streaked, speaking. He mouthed "*Please*" and she shook her head *No*.

She took out her phone and pointed at it. He nodded, fumbled with his and pressed buttons on it, frowning. His fingers were shaking. He wasn't wearing a jacket, only a T-shirt.

She answered. "Yes."

"I just want to talk."

"No you don't. You want to threaten and insult me."

"I'm sorry," he said.

"That's better."

"Where were you?"

"What is *wrong* with you?" She jabbed at her phone and threw it in her purse. She turned and went through the second door and up the narrow stairs.

Inside her apartment, she locked the door to the stairs. Her phone was buzzing.

There was no sign of Autumn.

She answered her phone, kicking off her shoes, and said, "I think you should go home."

"I will," he said, "I will. I just need to know. Just tell me and I'll leave and I'll never come back. I'll never bother you again."

"Oh for god's sake."

"Look," he said. His voice was high and shaky. "I have nothing in my life except for you, okay? Nothing."

"Oh for." She tried to calm her breathing. It wouldn't help to scream at him that he was a baby. "Well if that's true," she said, "then you'd better not call me a slut, right? Or anything else."

"Yes, right. I know. I'm sorry. I'm so sorry. Just tell me. Tell me and I'll—"

"Tell you *what*?"

"Where were you?"

She took a deep breath. "I have told you a dozen, a hundred times I don't have to tell you that. You have no right to know where I am at any given time and you shouldn't expect it. Who do you think you are?"

"Okay," came his thin voice. "Okay. I'm leaving. I'll go."

"Do you know how fucking crazy you are? Do you know how fucking psycho you are to be so fucking crude and scary? Do you know how scary? Do you hate me?"

"I love you," he said.

"No you don't. No you do not. That is not what love looks like." And now she felt her own tears coming again, seeing Isabel and hearing Isabel tell her her secrets.

"If you don't tell me," he said, "this is it, I will never see you again."

"That is totally fine with me."

"No, I mean nobody will. This will be it for me."

"Oh, not this shit again."

"Goodbye."

"Fine, go kill yourself. "

Her phone went dead and she threw it on the sofa. She sat and wept for a moment, then the crying stopped and she dried her face.

She knew he wasn't going to hurt himself but she shouldn't have said what she said. You weren't supposed to. You were supposed to take every threat seriously. No one would know that she had said that. No one had been listening to this phone call. No one had heard her tell him to go kill himself. But if you told someone in distress to kill themselves you could end up in trouble.

She got up and went downstairs and opened the doors. He was sitting on the curb.

She held the door open. He got up and came in without saying anything.

She sat on the sofa and he stood. She said, "I was out with my friend Isabel. You idiot. My best friend."

He stared at her, his mouth slightly open.

"What, you don't believe me?"

"I don't know. No, I do. Why wouldn't you just tell me?"

"I am too tired of explaining this to you. And don't you dare threaten suicide again. It's idiotic. And we all know it doesn't mean anything." She got up and went into the kitchen to put the kettle on. He followed her. She said, "Aren't you freezing?"

He shrugged. "Were you really with her?"

"If you ask me that one more time I will kick you out. I mean it."

He was shivering visibly now. His face had no colour. She pushed past him and went to her bedroom to get him a sweater.

He looked at it very doubtfully, as if she were handing him a dress, but he put it on when her voice went stern. She made tea and a peanut butter sandwich.

"We are not going to have sex," she said.

He nodded, his mouth full.

She dialled Isabel's number and Isabel didn't answer.

"I'm worried about my friend," she said.

Daryn got up, the sandwich in his hand, and went to the window. He pulled the curtain back a foot and stared out. The street was dark and quiet. "Listen," he said, "some strange things have been going on."

"No kidding."

"No, I mean with me." Daryn made a show of looking up and down the street and half hiding himself behind the curtain. "There were a bunch of arrests yesterday. In the US."

"Okay."

"That's all."

"Okay. I don't know what you're talking about. Are you in trouble?"

He shrugged, let the curtain fall. "Not me, no. But I got, like, private emails from people on the, people I used to talk with, not anymore, you know, that were like, all paranoid."

"Who got arrested? Friends of yours?"

"No. I didn't know them. But they were guys who posted on this one message board and some of them cross-posted on, you know, ones that I was, like, I told you, sometimes, sometimes only, when I was doing that."

"If you're not doing it anymore then how did you find out about it?"

He looked at her. "I told you. Someone was sending around these warnings."

"Yeah but. Never mind. So who was arrested and why?"

"Oh god knows." He sank onto the sofa next to her and it sagged dramatically. "Down there guys are saying crazy stuff all the time and threatening stuff that's total bullshit, but still, they don't fuck around down there. You make one dumb joke on some stupid forum and there's a SWAT team bursting down your door and they've got like flash bangs and they're holding machine guns to your head. I've seen videos. It's bananas."

"What kind of joke? Like an *I'm-going-to-shoot-up-a-school* kind of joke?"

"Yeah, dumb shit like that. Whatever."

"So what does it have to do with you?"

He had stopped shivering and she could smell him now; no cologne, but sweat and laundry soap. She could feel his warmth close to her. "Nothing, but they have a lot more surveillance of message boards now, there's a lot more resources on it now, because it's called terrorism now, and it's a whole different set of charges, it's like you're in ISIS or something, and they start tracking you if you've ever made like a single comment anywhere. And they can track people now, even with completely fake email addresses, VPNs, whatever, they can track you. And it's so stupid, all these resources, like guys with PhDs using all this counterintelligence hacking software to monitor a bunch of nerds with a masturbation problem."

"So you think the FBI is watching you?" She tried to laugh but it came out a snort.

"It wouldn't be the FBI," he said solemnly. "More like the NSA. They do the hacking stuff."

"Okay, whatever, but is that what you think? You're like a wanted man? How glamorous for you. No seriously, like they would follow you?"

"They wouldn't follow me. In real life. Online they might. I don't know. I have had some weird messages. Like guys on the forum whose handles I don't know and they want to talk to me. I don't trust them so I don't answer."

Gloria thought about this for a minute. They both stared at the door as if a SWAT team was about to burst in. "So now I'm on a watch list too," she said. "Great. Terrific."

"I doubt it," he said. "But I can show you some basic security measures. You can get a ghost email address that's pretty secure."

"Oh my god. This is ridiculous. Why did I even let you in." Suddenly she didn't want to be in the apartment with him anymore. She got up. "I'm going out. Let's go."

THEY WALKED TO THE MAIN road near her house, which was pretty much a highway. There was a dedicated streetcar lane in the middle of it, with concrete barriers separating it, which made it very wide. There were condo buildings and car dealerships and parking lots on this road, and some low strip malls with massage parlours and electronics repair shops, and some restaurants. The restaurants were mostly chain franchises, surrounded by their own parking lots. Gloria had never been to any of them, but she picked the Western-desert-y one with steer horns on the sign and a name like Dakota or Corral. "I have no idea why deserts are supposed to be so romantic," she called to Daryn, who was slightly behind her as she was walking so fast.

"What?'

"I have no urge to go to a desert. Like there's nothing there and it's really uncomfortable and you could die. And the people you'd find there are all completely like, I don't know, I picture them all ex-cons, you know, guys who drive pick-ups and have guns and I guess that's it, that's exactly it, that's romantic, we all want to be super-poor criminals because they have guns, I guess, I don't know. And the food … like all barbecue cow all the time, I guess people like that."

"Why are you talking about the desert?"

"We're going in there."

"Oh. Is that place—"

"Because this is a kind of desert, where we are, this highway, this total desert, like, look, there's an Ikea in the distance, like an oasis, and so I guess a real desert, or some kind of fantasy of a desert, with steer horns and like cow skulls, is preferable, because even a real desert, with no water, is preferable to this?" They were almost at the parking lot. They could hear country music playing from speakers onto the lot, presumably so you wouldn't be without country music on your fifteen-second walk from your car to the glass doors of the restaurant. "Oh I am so glad they have music in the parking lot!" she said.

Daryn was hanging back. "Have you been here before? I wonder if it's kind of pricey, this place."

"Oh you don't have any money, of course. Don't you have a job? You make more than I do."

"You must make very little then."

"You've seen my apartment, what do you think?"

She pushed through the glass doors, and they were in a kind of vestibule with a lectern and a sign that told them to wait to be seated. There was a strong smell of barbecuing meat and french fries, which was troublingly enticing, and loud country music. A girl in a black dress greeted them overenthusiastically and gave them menus in heavy black bindings and took them to a booth under a TV screen. Every booth was under a TV screen. There was baseball playing on the screens.

"The desert theme kind of disappears once you get inside," said Gloria as she sat down. "It's weird. Like the waitresses don't have to dress as cowgirls or anything, they just have to have tight dresses like everywhere else. Do you hate them?"

Daryn looked confused to the point of being frightened as he glanced around. "What? Would you stop with that?"

"I thought you might hate them because they are sexy."

"They have nothing to do with me."

"But aren't they actively rejecting you every single second? Aren't they all sluts?"

"Stop. Please stop. I said I was sorry. I really am sorry. What are we doing here?"

Gloria picked up the heavy menu. She was suddenly hungry, and she knew she was going to eat meat, some kind of meat, and fuck it. She had been hungry a lot since she had stopped taking her meds, which had been only two days ago. She was sleepy and hungry, which was a great way to put on a lot of weight, eating and sleeping. "I wonder how fat I would have to get," she said, "to stop being a Stacey."

"Please."

He ordered a beer and she ordered a glass of red wine and was left with the massive menu again. She couldn't afford any of the steaks, and hamburgers were always disgusting and greasy. She settled on some sizzling shrimp dish. She had seen it pass by to another table with some ceremony.

"This whole thing about steaks being from the desert," she said. "Deserts are poor. People who live there eat like corn and cactus. I don't know what they eat really. They make tequila out of cactus anyway. There are no steaks. Steaks are for cars and parking lots. This image of the desert, we are familiar with it from *these* places really, places beside highways in cold countries. Right? There is no real desert. There is only like this kind of cartoon of the desert. There is a word for this in philosophy." She felt sadness remembering who always used to talk like this, who taught her this word from his stupid courses: Florian. She was talking as Florian now.

"They have to walk that sizzling dish all around the restaurant before they serve it," said Daryn, watching it make its rounds again. "Did you know that? Every time someone orders it you have to walk it all around so everyone hears it and smells it and wants one."

"How do you know that?"

He blew out his cheeks. "I knew someone who worked here."

"A girl?"

"Yes, a girl."

"*The* girl? The girl from high school? Your girlfriend?"

"If that's what she was. I guess she was."

Gloria thought about the plate held high, bubbling with butter and garlic. "I guess it worked on me."

He kept glancing up at the TV screen.

She said, "Do you watch baseball?"

"Yes. Yes I do. Is that bad?"

She thought about this. She could not think of a reason for its being bad although she very much wanted to. In some way it was even good, as it was the kind of thing Florian would have no interest in and know nothing about. If she learned something about baseball it would be a kind of independence.

When the waitress came to take their order, Daryn said he wasn't hungry. Gloria was embarrassed about the shrimp dish now—she didn't want to be so simple as to have succumbed to Daryn's ex-girlfriend's sizzle—so she ordered some vegan bowl with quinoa and avocado that was twenty-three dollars. She had already finished her wine and ordered more.

There was an enormously fat man at the bar, a young man with a fan of red beard and skin like plaster, and he kept saying things that made his two friends laugh. He had the sides of his head shaved, and the kind of tongue of hair in the middle. It exposed rolls in his neck. The two other guys were skinny and wearing baseball caps and hoodies. The laughs were so explosive they made Gloria turn her head. Daryn was staring at them.

"Don't pick a fight," said Gloria.

Daryn screwed up his nose. "Shit."

"What?"

"Can we go somewhere else?"

"Why? What is it?"

"I really want to go. Let's go." He stood up.

She grabbed his hand. "We can't just leave. We've ordered. It would be rude." He sat down. "What is it? Do you know those guys?"

He nodded. "One of them." He shifted in his seat to angle away from them and look Gloria palely in the face. "I don't want to see him."

"Oh, I see. I get it. He's one of them."

Daryn shook his head. "I don't know. I mean yeah, I guess."

Gloria sipped her wine quickly. "Which one. The fat one?"

"No, the other one. Taller one. With the Raptors jacket. Don't stare, please."

"I'm not afraid of them," said Gloria, and stared. The guy was something like Daryn; a little rougher, perhaps, less well shaven, with workboots of the kind many of the men she knew wore when they bartended or served coffee, but these boots were dusty so it looked as if he might actually be a workman. He gave yelping bursts of laughter and people down the bar were turning to stare. "How could you meet him," said Gloria, "if everything is online?"

"He was the guy who got us all to go to that demonstration. Where I met you. So I met a couple of them when I got there. And we all kind of hung out before. We had a couple of beers."

"Wow. A real Nazi. Right in front of me. Do his friends know?"

"Let's just go. I'll leave money for the bill."

She looked at him. "He can't see you with a Stacey, right? What will happen? Do you get executed on the spot or do you just get your name ripped apart in the forums?"

"It's not that. We're... they're supposed to *try* to date, you know. You don't have to give up."

"But you have to leave the group if you succeed."

"That's never really stated. You're just not allowed to boast about it, online."

"So, what are you afraid of?" Gloria turned and smiled over towards the group at the bar. She was hoping one would see her. "Are you ashamed of me?"

"It's not that. I just don't feel like chatting. Come on. Please."

The fat man was the first to see her and he smiled back, quite easily. His friends saw where he was looking and stared.

"Oh good," said Gloria.

Daryn sank in his seat.

It occurred to Gloria, at this point, that she was not being nice to Daryn, and that since he had calmed down—since he had become his other self, his normal self which was apparently not what he was when he was texting her or alone on the internet—it might be more productive to be nice at least in this moment, at least until they could talk about what he had written to her and whether he had ever read *The Strange*

Case of Dr Jekyll and Mr Hyde. She remembered when she had wanted to leave a bar and he hadn't, downtown, he had acquiesced, and it would be the right thing to do to peaceably leave at this point. So she wasn't quite sure why she did the next thing she did.

In truth, she was excited about finally seeing the bad guys, genuine bad guys who would probably not even lie about being bad guys or pretend not to be. Or would they? Perhaps they would all claim that they didn't mean anything they said? She couldn't leave it alone. She had an opportunity now to find out how bad they really were, perhaps even to demonstrate to Daryn how bad they really were. She did not simply want to make Daryn squirm. But she wanted something to come to a head. She wanted to know, really, whether he was one of them or not.

So she waved.

The men were staring at her, at first, and then the tall one saw Daryn. His face changed from a kind of angry bafflement to an offended surprise.

"He's coming over."

Daryn looked up.

"Hey," said the tall guy. He put his knuckles on their table edge. "Dexter. Right?"

"Daryn."

"Daryn! That's right. Sorry bud. Daryn. You remember me?" The guy was smiling. He held out a fist and Daryn bumped it.

"How you doing," said Daryn.

"It's Jeb. You remember?"

"Of course I do. How you doing?" Daryn was giving a feeble smile.

"You been good, since our … thing?" Jeb's smile turned intense. He looked between Gloria and Daryn. "Hey," he said to her.

"This is—" said Daryn.

"—Jennifer," said Gloria. "Hi." She held out her hand. Jeb hesitated a second before taking it.

"Good to meet you. Jeb."

"*Very* nice to meet you."

"Nice dress." He was staring frankly at her chest. "What are you guys up to tonight?"

"We're just catching up," said Daryn.

"We're having a nice date," said Gloria.

"A date." Jeb nodded, smiling broadly. "Excellent. Good work man." He gave Daryn another fist bump.

"It's not really a date," said Daryn. "She's kidding."

"Hey, man, whatever. Don't sweat it. I was going to ask you guys if you wanted to watch the game with us. But I don't mean to interrupt."

"Some other time," said Daryn. "We're just about ready to go. Nice to see you."

"You live around here or what?" said Jeb.

"No," said Daryn. "We're just…happened to be around here."

"You happened to be around *here*? Who happens to be around *here*?" Jeb opened his mouth and laughed a cigarettey laugh. "I live just around the corner. Weird eh? I never run into anyone here. These are my buds, Gus and Jellico. Jellico's the big fellow. Over there. You want to say hi? Just for one sec. They have similar interests to you and me." Jeb looked intently at Daryn.

"No really," said Daryn. "We have to get going. We have a, she has this thing. A family thing. I'm just helping out, you know."

Jeb clapped him on the back and after some further entreaties to get in touch and stay cool and to have a great time whatever they were up to tonight, Jeb left them.

Daryn stood up. He was pulling his wallet out. "We'll leave money for the food. Let's go."

Gloria felt something in his urgency, his paleness, that told her this was something she should let go, or at least not fight about in front of these men.

On the street, she said, "I am really fucking hungry, you know that?"

He said nothing. He was walking quickly. This time she had to keep up.

She said, "Where are we going?"

"We'll find another place."

"You know what? No. You go find another place. I'm going back in there."

"Fine. Go ahead." He kept walking.

"You're really more afraid of those guys than you are of me?" She realized that this didn't sound right. "I mean you're more afraid of them than you care about me."

"I don't care about them. I just didn't feel like hanging around with them."

"How about here?" They stopped in front of the next place, another box in another parking lot. This one had fluorescent lights.

"It's like takeout chicken."

"Jesus Christ. I need to eat."

They went into the harsh light and looked at the video boards of sandwiches. There was country music in here, too.

They took their sandwiches to a plastic booth with a greasy tabletop. She said, "You told me you weren't on those forums anymore."

"I said I was sometimes. To help people."

"To help people. To *help* people?"

"I told you, exactly."

"So, you are still in contact with those guys. You still want their approval. Right?"

"No."

"You're still part of them. In which case I can't be a part of you. I mean I can't be anything to do with you. I'm not eating this here. This is gross." She wrapped up her chicken sandwich in the foil and stood up.

He did the same and followed her out. They walked in silence along the highway towards her place, and she did not stop him.

"This is kind of crazy," he said.

"Or maybe it's something else," she said. "Maybe you just knew that if you were to be seen with a girl, a woman, by those guys, that she'd better be a super-hot one, because that's the only kind of woman they care about, or maybe hate most, and I wasn't quite good enough."

"Okay that is really crazy."

"Is it?" She felt tears brimming now, and a hotness that was part rage and part shame, as if those things could be distinguished. "You know what I wish? I wish that once in my life, fucking once in my fucking life, a guy would be proud to be seen in public with me."

"That's not it. That's not it."

She wiped her eyes and walked. She knew, actually, that this was not it, but she could not stop the feeling. It was possibly as much about Florian as it was about Daryn.

He tried to put his arm around her and she pushed it off.

"I would be very proud to be seen with you, anywhere," he said.

Gloria wondered if she would ever be proud to be seen in public with him. He was good-looking, if a little young-looking, and tall, and she was aware of enjoying the way Kayleigh McGavin had perceived him. He wasn't rude to anyone or outwardly racist. There was nothing wrong with him. But he would be mocked by someone like Florian for his lack of sophistication or worldliness; he wasn't from downtown and didn't know the name of any bands or podcasts or microbreweries. He did not know anyone who ran a poetry-reading series. He wore a silver chain around his neck. Worse, one given to him by his mother. Which was both embarrassing and sweet, and which was of course exactly like all the boys around Gloria where she had grown up, and indeed exactly like her dad, her own father, whom she loved—and she even loved those boys from her high school because they knew no better and really they would save you from a fire or pull an overturned car off you if they had to, which was likely more important than being able to explain why lectins were bad for your gut biome—but the thing is she had been so overjoyed to leave them behind, to come here for university and to go to poetry readings herself, she had worked so hard for it, for what had felt like freedom, and so now she could not escape it, perhaps she had become Florian. Perhaps she was now incapable of anything but judgment. She had a sudden image of Isabel, laughing, and she realized that of everyone she knew Isabel was least likely to be embarrassed by Daryn; that Isabel would find him intriguing and real and ask him a lot of questions that seemed hostile but were really genuinely curious. So she would try to be proud of him too. She had to be proud of something.

They passed a glass bus shelter whose giant poster said, NOT SUICIDE. NOT TODAY. All these posters had pictures of average-looking people looking incredibly sad, and they had some help-line website in small letters, but of course you didn't see that, all you saw were these sad people.

They went into her apartment and finished the limp chicken sandwiches. Then all at once she felt an enormous fatigue pushing her down. She sat on the sofa with her head back. "This has been a long day," she said. "I'm very tired."

He sat next to her and put his hand on her thigh and she didn't push it off.

"I can hardly move," she said.

He nuzzled her neck and she let him. Then he began stroking her thighs and waist, and he unbuttoned the top of her dress, and she let him. Partly it felt nice and partly she was too tired to fight it. "I need to call Isabel," she said.

She got up and went into her bedroom, where she lay down and dialed Isabel, who didn't answer. Gloria sent her one long text about how loved she was and how Gloria needed her in her life. She reminded Isabel how she had helped Gloria move and how Isabel had spent the night with her when she had fever and let her sleep with Scott and when they did mushrooms at Harbourfront and probably lots of other kind things that she couldn't remember. Then she sent another saying Isabel should call her as soon as she could, even tonight, if she could. Gloria felt despair about sending these messages into silence; it was like opening one's curtains in the morning and seeing the window had turned to concrete.

Daryn came in and took off his shoes and lay down beside her. She let him kiss her neck but not her lips, and she let him run his hands up her thighs and cup her breasts. She lifted her arms over her head to let him pull her dress off, and she let him slip his hand up between her legs in their tights and rub her there. This was not unpleasant, and it was even arousing.

"Take off your clothes," she said.

She lay still, feeling a blanket of sleep pressing along her, and watched him pull off his T-shirt and carefully drape it over the back of the chair, and then his jeans, which he folded, and then his socks. He was aroused in his grey cotton boxers and she felt some pleasure in seeing them come off and his cock swollen and swaying.

"Wait," she said, before he could lie down. "Stay there."

"What?" he said.

"Just stand there." She stared right at his cock and it grew even stiffer, standing straight up, and he was blushing. "Very good," she said. "Touch it."

He rubbed at it rather half-heartedly, looking embarrassed. She unhooked her bra and pulled off her tights and underwear and lay there naked before him. "Go on," she said, "seriously." She spread her legs and licked her finger and touched herself, also not seriously. She wanted to see him become frustrated.

He stared intently at her crotch, then, almost frowning a little, as if concentrating on a problem, and took the shaft of his cock between his forefinger and thumb, just with the tips of his fingers, delicately, just beneath the head of his cock, and he pulled up and down slowly. The head grew large and tight and shiny and pink. Gloria watched his technique closely and was interested to see how careful it was, how precise: he did not grab his whole shaft in his fist as she had seen other lovers do—as she had made boys do this for her before—nor did he rub the whole head with his palm, as she had also seen; it was as if he was avoiding touching the head at all; perhaps it was so sensitive it would explode.

She noted, too, with interest, that one of his hands had crept to his chest and he was pinching his own nipple. She would remember that.

She let him do this until his breathing had grown more urgent. He was still staring at her crotch.

"All right," she said, "pleasure me, now." She rolled onto her front and folded her hands under her forehead. He kneeled on the bed and hesitated. "Rub my back," she said.

He began to do this rather roughly and she had to slow him down. "Gently," she said. "Just stroke me, don't paw me."

He was all right with her shoulders, as he had no doubt seen other people giving shoulder rubs but didn't know what to do as he moved further down. She spread her legs as he began rubbing her bum and arched her back a little.

"Why do you let me treat you so badly?" she said.

"Because I deserve it. Because I'm a loser."

She stiffened again as she heard this because it was the dark side, his conjoined twin who hated women and therefore her. "You're not a loser," she said.

"Oh yes I am. I am a pathetic piece of shit." His voice creaked and she felt a drop on her back.

She turned her head to glimpse his face all contorted. He was crying. She lay still and let him keep rubbing her. She was shocked, but she didn't think she knew how to argue with this in the moment. Perhaps it would pass. "Okay, stop that now." He sniffled and paused to wipe his nose. Then he continued stroking her and she let him. His fingers were between her thighs now and parting her, quite gently, and she was aroused. She spread her legs wide and said, into the pillow, "Use your tongue."

He knelt and pushed his face in between her cheeks and did so. She was very surprised and pleased by this, and even a little embarrassed that he was going so far. His nose was pushed against her anus as he licked. His whole face must have been getting wet.

She rolled over and pushed him off and then spread her legs and pulled him down onto her. She pushed his head down between her legs so that he would keep licking. She told him when to be gentle and when to speed up, and to move up, and to go in circles, and she felt, from a distance away, a wave of warm pleasure building, a wave of a different kind from what she had become used to, and she knew it would make her come, strongly, in a way she had not come with a boy for a couple of years, since she had been on the meds, and that she was no longer on the meds and that this was why, because it was coming without anyone pressuring her to come and she was going to feel it.

When it came she grasped his head and pushed it into her hard so he could not get away, to hold him there against her while it took her and pulled all her muscles together like rubber bands being stretched, and when finally she released him he was gasping as if he had been suffocating.

She didn't know if she had made noise or not. She was breathing hard and there were a few more little spasms. It took a while to subside.

Then he was lying on her and she felt the tip of his cock pressing against her and she let him in, aware that there was no condom and deciding that this was okay now, after so many times. He was quite large now and this made her come a little bit more, as if water would not stop rushing through the tap, and then she knew she was moaning and possibly biting his shoulder. Her pushed deep into her, quite slowly at first, and then when he began thrusting although it was intensely pleasurable she remembered to feel nervous and she said, "Don't come in me, remember. Don't come in me. I'm not on any birth control."

He was fucking her quite hard and fast then, and breathing hard and sweating, so she pushed him back and said, "No, no, stop," and he did stop, with a moan.

"Here," she said, and guided his cock on to her belly, and pulled him against her, and he understood and began rubbing against her, wet and slippery, and she felt him tensing all over and then he grunted loudly and sprayed hot all over her belly and even up over her breasts.

"Oh, boy," she said.

He lay on top of her, panting, very heavy and dead.

She waited; it was not unpleasant to feel him so heavy and hot and spent on top of her. She even felt drowsy, and thought she might sleep, until he was too heavy for breathing, and she rolled him off.

"I love you," he whimpered.

She did not say *oh fuck off* although she felt it. And then she was just thinking, *I came, I came.* Then she said, "This is kind of unhealthy," although she wasn't really sure whether she said it or just thought it, for she was falling asleep.

17.

SOME GREY LIGHT CAME THROUGH her little window. He was still there. He was sitting up and texting on his phone. The light from his screen was the same colour as the light from the window. Then he got up and started moving around her room looking for his clothes.

He saw that her eyes were open and he said, "Work."

She watched him pull the dark clothes over his pale limbs. She imagined what it would be like to have him move in with her. It had probably been foolish to imagine that they could talk about his workday and make breakfast for each other. It was playing house.

Then there was movement outside her door; the front door opening, something heavy being dropped. He froze.

She sat up. "My roommate," she said. She got up and pulled on a bathrobe. "Wait here," she said.

She slipped out, trying not to open the door too wide, and closed it behind her. Autumn was hauling her bags up the narrow stairs. She had left one suitcase on the floor of the living room. Gloria waited until she came puffing in and then greeted her as happily as she could and hugged her, which was somewhat comforting, as Autumn was so soft, and smelled of some cinnamony oil that she always wore. "I'll get this into your room," she said.

She knew that Daryn would wait obediently in the dark room until he was told the coast was clear, but it would never be clear, really, and she had no good reason for hiding him, except that she didn't want to remind Autumn that other people had sex. She said, "I have this guy over."

Autumn stopped. "Oh."

Gloria opened the bedroom door. "You dressed? Come on out."

He emerged and said hi to Autumn who said hi too quietly and did not try to shake his hand. She dragged the biggest of her bags into her room.

"Bye," Daryn said sadly and left.

Gloria went into Autumn's room. "It's not really a serious thing," she said. "He won't be over a lot. Maybe not at all. How are you?"

"Well I'm fucking furious, like everyone. Aren't you?"

"Furious?"

"At this fucking bill. This bill just totally guts university funding. Can you fucking believe it? Are you going to the thing?"

"What thing?"

"Oh my god, Gloria. Oh my god!"

"What?" She was thinking of how far Daryn would have to go to get his bus. With no jacket. He hadn't even had an orange juice when he left. The thought struck her that in many ways he was not needy, but hard. He was certainly tougher than Autumn.

"They went out of their way," said Autumn, "they went *out of their* way to target humanities departments—there's special tags on all the money for education that it can only go to certain departments, and they have cut out English, history, political science, gender studies—*of course*—sociology, all languages, like drama, art history, fine art, everything. It's just going to be all gone. And you should have heard that ignorant gumpo talking about it on TV, that smug fucking little frat boy, he's just smirking his—"

"When did this happen?"

"Yesterday. Where were you?" Autumn was opening bags and pulling out clothes and scarves. Gloria had to back into a wall. "It starts at noon. We're going to start on campus and then march to the legislature. You have to come." Autumn turned and stood very close to Gloria and took her hands in hers and said, "Please, will you come with me? Please? I will feel like I'm coming back to life, like I'm relevant again, and it would be so good for me, and I'm still a little fragile and I would just really really want you, really need you to come with me."

"I can't, sweetie, it's a workday for me. I have to produce two articles by the end of the day."

"Your boss has no right, no right to prevent you from protesting, that's your legal right, especially for an issue that's just so—"

"I don't really have a boss like that, Autumn, it's not a job like that. Most jobs are not like that, not anymore. You get paid for whatever you do. I can take any days off I like, but if I don't submit anything I don't get paid anything."

"And that's exactly the injustice you'll be protesting against," said Autumn.

"Ha. Nice idea. I would love to. But."

"Write your boss a note right now. Tell him how important it is."

"Okay. Sure." Gloria saw an opening and moved to the door. "It's great to have you back," she said from the doorway. "I'm so glad you're doing better."

SHE MADE COFFEE AND TOAST. She dressed. She sat at her computer and checked her phone. It was ablaze with protest: the word RESIST was in capital letters in every post, and calls to attend the protest came with exhortations to *Punch a fascist today*. Apparently there were rumours that some group called the Soldiers of the Nation were arranging a counter-protest. And maybe the anti-abortionists and the incels too. There was talk of borrowing bicycle helmets and gas masks and setting up first-aid tents. There was a great happy excitement at the idea of a big fight and injury.

Autumn came into her room. "I think you have a moral obligation to come," she said.

Gloria didn't turn from her computer. She didn't want to say anything angry about Autumn deciding what was and wasn't moral for her, especially on Autumn's first day back, and she was confused by her own hostility to this event, which was something she believed in, really—she should stand up to the Soldiers of the Nation or whatever, or someone should, they all should, she wasn't opposed to the demonstration, but she didn't truly believe the Soldiers of the Nation were going to be there in any large numbers, if at all, they would be a couple of heavy-breathing old guys with grey ponytails from small towns somewhere, and the excitement everybody felt about fighting them was really dishonest, because it was just excitement about fighting, about fighting anyone, and it had nothing to do with the budget of this stupid government, which no size of protest was ever going to change, because the government was really very popular, and it was popular because most people hated equally the Soldiers of the Nation *and* people like her and Autumn, people who complained that people like her and Autumn had basically taken useless courses at university and were trying to make everybody else feel bad about it. She could not explain this to Autumn without it sounding as if she agreed with this perception, which she did not, so it would be too difficult to try. She breathed deeply.

Autumn sat on her bed, and so Gloria said, "I have a really tight deadline."

Autumn sighed. "You don't think it's useful. Protest."

"No," said Gloria rather too sharply. "No, I do not." And then she regretted saying this as she could not get into an argument with Autumn right now.

"So we should all just accept whatever happens?"

As calmly as she could, Gloria said, "Protests would be great if they would get me some more money. But right now, I can't afford to protest because I have to work."

"Oh sweetie." Autumn got up and bent over her and hugged her, swamping her with her hair and her breasts and her arms.

WHEN AUTUMN WAS GONE, GLORIA texted Isabel to ask if she wanted to come over later.

She did not have any excellent ideas for Daily Self Care. She sent an email to the editor of a website called Tales from the Trenches, an online magazine made up of "stories about dating in the city" that was mostly a catalogue of male idiocy and cruelty. The editor was a woman Gloria had met who was younger than she was and running this whole stupid thing, it seemed, by herself. Gloria didn't know whether they paid anything for stories, but it was worth a try. She sent a pitch for an article about dating across class. "What do you do if you really like him but you're a bit embarrassed by him in front of your friends?" She wrote out a list of reasons not to be classist and concluded with a plea for empathy and compassion.

Her phone rang but it was from a number she did not recognize.

She checked HireMash, the job-search site where she had a membership. She had five credits for free job searches. The jobs that were listed for her were for a part-time copyeditor with the Canadian Association of Optometrists that paid $17.20 an hour and a content generator for Your Health News, a site that appeared to be based in China, which paid $10 per five hundred words of SEO-optimized text.

She texted Isabel, who had not replied to her first text, *How much do you think one could make hypothetically with an OnlyFans? Asking for a friend.*

An anxiety over Isabel was starting to take form in her, like a mass building in her abdomen, a feeling of actual illness.

The phone rang again with the same strange number. She squelched it again.

Then came a text. *Please call me, urgent. Harriet Feldman.*

This name was unknown and yet in some way familiar; it was like a character in a TV show she had seen or something. *Harriet* was especially familiar.

She stood for a moment with the feeling of unseen forces conspiring against her.

And then as she stood there repeating *Harriet Feldman*, it came to her in a great cold shock; Feldman was Isabel's mother's name. Isabel had taken her father's last name. Harriet was Isabel's mother.

18.

THE HOSPITAL WAS FAR IN the East End, and it took her an hour and a half to get there, because all the streetcars were diverting around the protest downtown. Gloria ended up on a sleepy streetcar through low-rise sprawl that ended up looking like a suburb. She had never been to this hospital before.

The lobby smelled of chicken noodle soup from the Tim Hortons, as hospital lobbies do. The line of people waiting for their coffees from the stand in the centre of the atrium snaked past the information desk and into the food court; people being pushed in wheelchairs had to ask politely to be let through. Gloria was to meet Jordan, Isabel's brother, here, and she did not know what he looked like and he did not know what she looked like, so she waited by the information desk. She felt shaky and knew she should eat something but could not. She had not cried; she was too frightened.

Jordan was a very pretty teenage boy with Isabel's dark hair and blue eyes. He smiled and nodded, and Gloria realized she must have seemed a bit hysterical and he was trying to calm her down. They would wait there for Isabel's mother and her estranged father, who was flying in from Dayton or Cincinnati or something. They could not see Isabel, who was in the ICU and not conscious.

Gloria and Jordan sat in a glass atrium on large armchairs. He offered several times to get her something from the food court. He said he didn't know much, really, all he knew was that Isabel's roommate had found her, last night. No one knew how long it had been since she had taken the pills. Jordan wasn't sure what she had taken. He knew she hadn't woken up yet.

Gloria got up and said she was going to find the ICU and see her and Jordan pulled her down again.

Isabel's mother arrived from the elevator, neat and small, with makeup and jewellery. She hugged Gloria and said to call her Harriet. Gloria asked if she could see her, and Harriet said no, but she, Harriet, had been with Isabel since she had arrived, and Isabel was intubated and non-responsive. She was alive, said Harriet, but there may have been brain damage, and she began to cry.

Jordan waved to a man walking towards them in a raincoat, wheeling a small suitcase. He looked to be in his forties, with abundant hair. He was not tall. He was introduced as Greg, Isabel's father. He hugged Jordan but not Harriet.

Harriet stopped crying and gave him the same update, quite soberly. "We're waiting for the scans," she said. "The brain scans." Then she began to cry again.

Gloria said she would go and get her some tea. She was aware as she walked away that she was not crying herself, but trembling a little, and a little dizzy, as if she herself had just had an accident. As she walked through the crowds, she had the sensation of not being present, of watching everything that unfolded before her as if it were on a screen and she, somewhere else. She had experienced this before, when drunk, or the one time she had tried ketamine. Her fingertips were tingling and her face felt tight, as if her muscles were seizing up. Her mouth was open, and she was breathing through her mouth.

Then she was sitting down on the floor with her back against a wall and two people were standing over her and asking if she was okay. She found she could not answer them, but she stood up and nodded until they went away. She was not aware of having fallen or how she had ended up on the floor.

As she walked, slower, aware that this was likely a panic attack and that she had caused herself to faint through hyperventilating, a thing she had done before, she tried the grounding exercises—she touched her clothing, touched walls, counted to twenty. If she was to be of use to Isabel and her family she would have to not be like this, she would have to be in the real world and not above it like this.

She was not crying, she thought, because it had not happened, it was not real; she wasn't even really there.

She knew she had to find Isabel's mother some tea but she also had to find Isabel; if she could not find Isabel in the hospital then she would know that none of it was real.

She stood in a line at a coffee stand and felt the buzzing throughout her body that warned her she was likely breathing too fast again and would soon find her face seizing up again like the time she had gone to emergency with paralysis and the doctor had given her an Ativan.

She had seen cats panting with their tongues out when they were very frightened, usually by being in a car.

Isabel was not dead, she kept telling herself, and Isabel would be okay.

She bought the tea, trying to keep her mouth closed. When she got back to the atrium only Jordan was there. Harriet and Greg had gone to meet with the doctors.

The afternoon passed like this, in waiting. She texted Surinder to say she had a family emergency and that she would be unable to file anything today. Surinder replied cheerily that it was no problem, which made Gloria wonder whether the copy was necessary to the site at all, ever. She supposed he had a bunch of freelancers he could call for extra copy. Or maybe he would just get someone to cut and paste stuff from the web. She wondered why he didn't just do that every day.

There was a new thing rising in her, another nausea, something dark blue and black: it was the horror of guilt. This was her fault, she knew, because she had been so distracted and had not been as attentive to Isabel as she should have. She went through all the times she should have checked in on her or pushed her to talk more or insisted she get help or just spent time with her.

In the late afternoon she was told she would be allowed to see Isabel if she really wanted to. She was given the ward number and rode the elevator up with a return of the first nausea, real physical nausea, the feeling again that it was not happening and she was elsewhere, so she told herself that Isabel was alive, and then she would see that she was alive and it would all be real, and that all Gloria had to do to help her was hold her hand.

If Isabel was alive and Gloria could see that she was alive then she would be okay, she would recover fully if Gloria could hold her hand and help her.

At the nurses' station she had to put on goggles and gloves and a mask and a hairnet and a gown. The units all had glass walls so you could see the four or six beds in each, with armies of machines around each bed and nylon curtains between the beds. There were people around the other beds, mostly silently sitting and watching old people with oxygen masks on their faces and their eyes closed. She was let into Isabel's room and allowed to stand by the bed. There was no chair. Isabel's face was covered by her oxygen mask. Her skin was grey and her eyes were closed. Her tiny chest inflated and fell again. The movement was so gentle you almost couldn't see it. Gloria would not let herself look at the vital signs on the display.

Isabel was flat in every sense. Her face looked as if it had been deflated. Gloria took her hand, which was quite cold. This was when she knew she was really there; she felt hot and then cold, and she began to cry. She stroked Isabel's arm and told her she loved her and she was going to be all right and all those things, and she wept freely until a storm of doctors came in, all following one older woman doctor, and it was clearly time for Gloria to go.

She left to take the streetcar and then the subway and then the bus home. All this was strange: the sky had opened; it was no longer a sky but a void; the world had changed to be simply a bearer of disaster, a hostile witness to disaster. The other strange thing was everyone else on the bus had not had their lives changed, were likely not feeling as if they were going to vomit, were on their way home to put a frozen pizza in the oven; she was outside them, perhaps could not even be seen by them.

There were many texts from her mother that she hadn't answered, and texts from Daryn, whom she hadn't told about anything. She spoke to her mother on the phone and cried, and her mother told her to come home for a few days, home to Fort Erie, which wasn't really home, and Gloria said she couldn't as she had to be close to Isabel, and she felt a great helplessness as she said this, for she knew she was of no help to Isabel at all, or to Isabel's family, or to anyone. Her mother said she needed to get some help, some grief counselling maybe, and Gloria got angry because Isabel wasn't dead. Then Gloria's mother asked her what medication she was taking and was she was sure it was adequate, and Gloria hung up.

She couldn't talk to Daryn, she didn't know why, perhaps because he would try to be nice about it in some inadequate way that would only make her angrier. She sent him a text that said, *My best friend Isabel attempted suicide yesterday and is in a coma. I will need some space alone to deal with this*. She knew she was sending this when he was possibly doing an evening shift in the store in the mall and that he would not see it until he got a break, which might be hours.

She thought about allowing him to try to comfort her, but it felt not right: for one thing he was responsible for Isabel's despair, in a way, because it had been Daryn distracting Gloria when Gloria should have been paying attention to Isabel and noticing what was wrong with her and helping her.

Of course that was ridiculous, it wasn't Daryn's fault, but it was men who had made Isabel so unhappy in the first place, not men like Daryn, admittedly—in fact, more like the kind of men Daryn probably hated and called Chads—but still, it was not the time for men. And she was afraid that she very much wanted to distract herself from her fear by having sex with Daryn, and this would encourage him. Because comforting was a thing that boyfriends did and it was not possible that he should become her boyfriend.

By the time she got home he had received her text and had called twice and left three texts asking her if she was okay and if there was anything he could do and could he come over. She texted that she was going home to her mother in Fort Erie and that she needed some privacy and that she hoped he would respect this boundary.

She texted Surinder and told him there had been a death in the family and she would need some time off.

Daryn texted, *I am really sorry that you are sad but what can I do??? Don't shut me out let me help you.*

She started texting, *I just can't right now* but deleted it. She did not have the energy to engage with Daryn or to anger him further by telling him, so she would just have to pretend she was too busy to answer.

19.

GLORIA WAS BACK AT THE hospital the next morning. In the elevator, on the way up to the ICU, there was a stout lady and her stout adult son. The lady looked tired and was talking about how she was going to feed him and Bert when they were all doing shifts like this. She said she had a lasagna for tonight and Tiffany was bringing a mac and cheese tomorrow. This was the first time that it occurred to Gloria that Isabel's hospital stay might be a long one and that she would herself now be entering the battlefield world of standing watch and feeding and being fed. "Lasagna for tonight," the old lady repeated as if to herself. "So we should be okay."

The son looked at his forearm, which was veiny and tattooed. He made a fist and stared at a tattoo that was some kind of a military crest, perhaps a ship's crest because it had an anchor in it. He stared at his tattoo and flexed it and did not answer his mother.

Gloria wished she was a better cook.

Gloria's mother was at Isabel's bedside, and it looked as if she had been there all night. She had not reapplied her lipstick and she looked older. There were cardboard coffee cups and muffin wrappers on a bedside table.

Isabel was grey and flat and she was breathing slowly and with a rasp.

Gloria stroked her hand and told her she was there. Isabel's eyes were closed and seemed to be gummy.

Gloria took Harriet Feldman's hand and told her she was sure Isabel was going to be okay, because the medicine was so good these days and the doctors were so good and she was in the best possible place, for care, the best place she could be.

Harriet looked at Gloria with eyes that seemed darker than before; eyes staring from the back of a cave. She asked Gloria to tell her everything, everything Isabel had said in the past week.

"She seemed sad, that's all. Just sad. But nothing like, nothing like this. She didn't tell me anything. I didn't know what was wrong. She didn't say anything about, you know, harming herself."

Harriet frowned and stared at Gloria and Gloria knew she had not believed her. "What else."

"I don't know. I really don't."

"I wonder if it was some man. You know that in the past, she had a—"

"Mr LaRusso. Yes, I know about that."

"She tends to get very mixed up." Here Harriet's voice cracked and got wavery. "About men." She wiped her eye and reached for a tissue. "She just doesn't know how to handle them. And they take advantage of her."

Gloria took her hand and squeezed it. There was no point in telling Harriet Feldman about the guy in the office, because there was nothing anybody could do about what had happened and blaming some dickhead wouldn't make Isabel well again.

"Why don't you take a rest," said Gloria. "I'll sit here for a while, and I'll call you if anything changes. Go home and have a real meal and a sleep."

And so Gloria and Harriet and Isabel's brother Jordan took turns that day; Gloria would stay until noon and then Jordan would come for the afternoon and Harriet could come back at night and Gloria would check in on her then. She got Jordan's phone number, and there was a lot of talk of transportation and meals. Harriet said she would bring in snacks in the evening and Gloria apologized more than once about not being better at cooking.

Daryn texted her several times.

Let me know what is going on.

Is your friend okay

What is really going on?

Where are you right now?

Who are you with?

JORDAN WAS LATE AND BY the time he arrived Gloria was hungry and feeling guilty about feeling hungry as Isabel was getting no food at all except for whatever they were dripping into her.

Jordan had brought a magazine—*The Economist*—to read while he stood watch and Gloria wondered how anyone could possibly read anything in that moment or ever again.

Going down to the lobby to get a bowl of soup, she had to wait while a large young man pushed a very old man in a wheelchair into the elevator. The young man was the same one who had been in the elevator with the lasagna lady that morning; she recognized him from the naval tattoo. The wheelchair had machinery in its base and the old man was connected to an IV stand and an oxygen tube and some other kind of monitor, so it took a while for the son to manipulate all this into the space. The old man was emaciated and had bruises in his stick arms where blood had been taken.

And there on the old man's forearm Gloria saw the same tattoo, faded, the crest with the anchor.

This caused tears to rush to her eyes for reasons she could not understand, and she was relieved to step into the lobby and cry unrestrainedly for a minute before she lined up for her soup.

Her phone rang and the screen told her the number belonged to Jianguo Transmountain Media, the company that owned The Hype Report. Perhaps she would be finally fired. She declined the call.

She had not filed any articles since she had heard about Isabel. She knew that at some point she would need to work, as the first of the month was coming up and rent, but this thought was distant, just another shifting shoal of anxiety she was floating above.

When she went back up to the ward, nothing had changed and Jordan told her she should go home, as they might need her tonight, and she needed rest. She said that it was true that she had to work at some point, as dumb as that sounded.

SHE SPENT MOST OF THE evening at the hospital and got home around midnight. She slept and dreamed of small children drowning.

In the morning there were more texts from Daryn.

I want to help you but why won't you talk to me

Are you really in Fort Erie

Am I really not that important to you

She decided she would answer him once she got some work done, if she could do any work at all. She would have to calm him down. She opened her computer and stared at it as a portal to another world, one from which she had been exiled.

Her phone told her that Jianguo Transmountain Media was calling her again. She answered.

"Gloria? It's Surinder."

She opened her mouth and said nothing. She had only ever spoken to Surinder once, when she had first been hired to write her column, and that chat had been brief. She had never met him in person. She had looked up photographs of him and seen a handsome brown man with glossy hair who looked to be about her age, possibly younger, indeed probably younger, as he hadn't wasted his time with any English degrees before he got this job. The photographs she had seen of him were at music and film and fashion festivals in front of walls of brand names. And he had had a headshot beside a column he had briefly written for *Marketing Week* on content generation and verticals.

Knowing then that she was about to be fired, she said, "Hi!" as cheerily and loudly as she could. She was in bed, with her laptop. She was looking at Isabel's Instagram, all her beautiful dresses and sad looks.

"How are you doing?" said Surinder. "How are you holding up? I'm really sorry for your loss. I'm not sure if it was a family member or, or anything I don't—I just want you to know that I think all bereavement is, is loss, and grief can be a hard thing."

"Thank you."

"I don't want to pressure you in any way," said Surinder, "if you're not ready to return to any kind of regular writing schedule?"

"I'm okay," she said. "I can do something. I need the money."

"Really? That's wonderful. That's great to hear."

It was only then that Gloria heard something in Surinder's voice that told her he was gay, and she liked him slightly better for it. "I just don't have a whole lot of ideas right now."

"Well, I'm calling you with an idea. If you're sure you're ready."

"Oh! Well, that's a surprise. I thought you were calling to fire me."

Surinder laughed. "Why would I do that?"

"Okay."

"As a matter of fact we need more content than ever right now. There are a few changes going on with the company, well, with the parent company, and they're going to affect us all, but I'm going to have to fill you in on that as we get a little more granular. I'll circle back. But I think you'll be excited."

"Okay."

"Anyway, that's not it, not right now. What I need, what I was thinking, was a piece that you would be just great for, on sex toys."

"Sex toys."

"Yeah—don't worry, not a review!" He laughed again. "I won't ask you to do that again."

"So, Surinder, like I said, I've had a thing, a family thing." Gloria felt her voice thicken and stopped so she would not cry.

"A what?"

"Someone, there's been a, someone is sick, very sick, close to me, and I'm not sure if..." Her voice wavered again.

"Yes, you told me, and I am very sorry to hear that. Are you not ready to work? That's fine. I can pass this on to someone. You can let me know when and if—"

"No. No. My rent is coming up. I do need the work. I really do. I'm sorry. I'll be fine. I can do it. Is this for a sponsor?"

"Yes, finally, a great one, and one that we're really excited to have on board. It's Circe."

"Circe."

"Right."

"I don't know what that is."

"You don't? You should. Huge, huge, online adult store."

"Okay."

"So we need some content. We need like a fun, funny piece that compares a whole bunch of sex toys."

"Surinder, I can't—"

"No, no, wait, don't worry, it's not reviews, you don't even have to see the products. It's dead easy. I'll get you the catalogue, you take ten sex toys from it, or okay, make it five maybe, so it's quick and easy. And we'll have a quiz out of it, like what kind of sex toy are you? We're going to handle that part of it, and Circe will help. But what we want you to do is like what's the most popular adult product in each Canadian city. Like, the Secret sells best in Quebec City, what does that say about the love life of French speakers, kind of thing."

Gloria sat up in her bed. She felt like getting dressed now, or completely undressed. "Do they have the stats on those things?"

"They're looking for them. But you know what, let's, we don't even have to wait for that. Make it more like a fun thing, like a made-up thing. Let's do which city is each sex toy, kind of thing. Like take the top five Canadian cities, assign a sex toy to it, and say, you know, like the Delver is Calgary, because of whatever Calgary is like. I don't know, make it up. You go and find some statistics on what Calgary is known for, and you say, I don't know, cowboys will love the Delver."

"Jesus."

"You can do this in your sleep. It's a listicle."

"Do I get any free product?"

"Ah, no. They didn't offer any. These things are like three hundred bucks each. They're not offering anyone any. But you get paid the normal rate."

"Okay. Send me the catalogue."

"It's online. I'll send you the list of ones you can do. Have fun with it. You know. You can be lively."

"Okay."

"How are you doing, though, really?" said Surinder.

"I am fine and happy to be writing a listicle about sex toys."

After she hung up, she sank back under the covers. She knew she had to reply to Daryn. She could ask him over, because he was probably getting angry about her going silent, and also because she should not be alone, and even if they were to have sex it would not be a bad idea, it would be a comfort, it would be feeling something physical through this numbness.

She would have to go back to the hospital that evening. But first she had to write about sex toys.

She had asked Isabel's mother whether Isabel had left a note, and Isabel's mother said that she had, but that it was for the family. Gloria wanted to beg to see it, but she did not. She was alone and it was her fault.

Her phone buzzed.

There was a text from Daryn. *I don't deserve to be treated this way. I am human. I have feelings. You cannot be so cold.*

She started typing a reply and then stopped and dropped the phone on the floor and hoped she had not broken it.

It was time to go to the hospital anyway, to relieve Jordan. She began to change, and her phone buzzed repeatedly.

You like causing pain. I know you do. Do you enjoy it?

I've had to miss work because I am in too much pain. I am walking in a park now. I am lost. I want to die.

I can cause myself more pain than you ever can. I am holding a lighter right now and I will burn myself with it. Do you want me to do this?

She picked up her phone and texted, *You need to get help. See a doctor. If you are going to harm yourself then call 911, not me.*

He replied, *I'm doing it now.*

Then came a picture of his hand holding a lighter. The background was grass.

I burned myself.

Gloria put on her raincoat and left the house. She was not going to respond to these. But her heart was pounding. She needed to walk.

She didn't check the phone again until she was at the bus stop.

You are a cunt just like all the other cunts.

At this she felt a slight relief, because she definitely did not need to answer him, now.

You disgusting slut. What a fucking whore. You are a fish-smelling cunt, you slime.

She switched her phone off.

She sat on the bus and did not cry. She would just not think about him, ever again; she would block him on every channel. He could be deleted from her life now, without guilt or hesitation.

She got to the subway and waited underground. She got on one train and took it downtown and then transferred to the long streetcar to the hospital. It was a warm but grey day, and she tried to watch people and count how many were carrying umbrellas. She tried to take pleasure when the umbrellas began to open.

When she entered the hospital lobby she had to phone up to the ICU and wait until she had permission to see Isabel. She felt hungry, suddenly, and afraid that there had been terrible news she had not been told, and she had nothing to do, so out of habit she took out her phone and switched it on.

There were six new texts.

I'm sorry, I didn't mean it. I hate myself.

I love you. Please answer.

I burned my arm and I have to go to the hospital.

I am going crazy. Please help me. I want to die.

I just need to talk. Please help me.

Please call.

And there, clicking through the lobby on heels, was Harriet, Isabel's mother. She had no makeup and her hair was uncombed.

"What is it?" said Gloria.

"There is damage," said Harriet in a high voice. "Gloria, there is damage."

"What kind of damage?"

"The scans," said Harriet, and she began to cough. "She was alone for so long, her brain didn't have enough oxygen. There was some kind of stroke." She was looking over Gloria's shoulder. Her eyes were wide and she looked as if she were far away. "There's Greg. We are all going up now. You can't see her today." She pushed past Gloria, and Gloria saw her joining Isabel's father. They both walked away very quickly, and Gloria was left alone in the soup-scented atrium with nowhere to go, and her phone heavy in her pocket.

She waited for an hour. She texted Harriet once to see if there was any news and did not receive a reply. She bought herself a muffin and waited another hour. She had to write her article.

On the long streetcar back, she texted Daryn. *Calm down. I'm here.*

20.

What are the ~~sexiest~~ horniest Canadian cities?

We've named the sex toy that most suits each big city in the country—you'll be amazed by number 8!

1. **Halifax** seems like the most likely place to enjoy the **Waveform** ($129.99), with its ocean-like pulse settings and fully water-resistant silicone skin. True mermaids can feel the sea-shanties filling their every pore with this powerful and programmable action. And isn't the port filled with discharged seamen?
2. **Quebec City** is just the spot for the **Petit Amour** ($89.99), a palm-sized prestidigitator with the discreet Gallic charm of a candlelit bistro. Snowy nights in the Old Town with red wine, checkered tablecloths and this wearable, remotely controllable yet powerful massager is the secret of every femme fatale. And it's small enough to fit into your baise-en-ville

(that's French for a little purse—but the literal translation is shocking. Look it up!)

3. **Ottawa** doesn't seem like the sexiest town on Earth, until you imagine all those brainy bureaucrats harbouring the **Diplomat** ($249), a unique communication device that passes one lover's movements to another's, remotely. (*need more on this one. Name Ottawa landmark.)
4. **Edmonton**'s macho charm finds its best expression in the **Cowboy** ($199.99), an enhancing device only for the boldest of prairie studs. It both penetrates and encircles, giving your western manhood a boost like the engine on an F150 truck (*need more on this one. Name Edmonton landmark.)
5. **Toronto** (*should be last really. Riff on banks and towers.)
6. **Victoria?**

THIS WAS ALL SHE COULD do without further information.

She texted Harriet again, and Jordan, asking if there was any news and when she could come again. She apologized for having to work and explained that she was self-employed and so had no sick days, then deleted that because obviously no one would care about that right now. She wrote instead that she could bring some food to the hospital if anyone would just tell her what time to come.

Then she stared at her silent phone with the sensation that Isabel was about to text her. Isabel would wake up and she would text Gloria.

Instead it was a text from Daryn that said *Here*.

She went down and let him in. It was six o'clock, an awkward time, because again she didn't have anything to feed him, but he didn't seem to care about that. She hadn't eaten all day, but this would be a good excuse not to eat at all. There was no law that said that people had to eat at certain times, especially when they were stressed.

His hand and wrist were bandaged.

"Did you do that yourself?" The bandage was loose, held together with what looked like Scotch tape. "I thought you went to the hospital," Gloria said.

"I decided not to. If they saw I'd done it myself they'd call in the psych people and then who knows how long they keep you."

"That's exactly what they should have done." She took off the bandage and inspected the burn. It was about two inches long and quite raw and blistered. "I think this is a third-degree burn."

"Yeah but it's small."

"You need to get disinfectant. And stuff."

"Don't you have any?"

"No. I don't even know what you're supposed to use."

There was a small first-aid kit somewhere that she'd been given and never opened. She had moved it from apartment to apartment since she had left home. She had to look for some minutes for it—in her closet, in kitchen drawers. On bathroom shelves. She found it on the kitchen shelves behind cans of lentils.

She got an ice cube and made him hold it to the wound, which made him wince. She had some memory about ice cubes and burns. She thought it might numb it a bit. Then she wiped it off with tissue and opened the first-aid kit. There was a small packet of gauze, which she opened, and some medical tape. She strapped the gauze to the wound. Daryn watched this dully, as if from afar.

When she had finished he just stared at it. He didn't say *thank you*.

She said, "So am I still a cunt?"

"What?"

She just stared at him then, and he looked away. "How is your friend," he said faintly.

"That is nice of you to ask. I don't know what's going on. She's not conscious and I don't really know why. I think she's really sick and I don't know... I don't know exactly what she did or what's going to happen."

"I'm sorry. I hope she's okay."

She said, "Did you have some kind of trauma as a child?"

He shrugged. "Who didn't?"

"I didn't, really. Everybody says they did but it's usually pretty normal stuff. Like their mother died or they had to go to hospital for a while. I mean real trauma. Like violence. Did anyone beat you up, when you were a kid?"

He shook his head. "Not that I remember. I don't remember much."

"That's interesting. Why not?"

"Not much to remember. I was always scared we'd have to move, because we had to move a lot. And I never had the right stuff, like clothes and backpacks and stuff. But my mom tried really hard. I had enough to eat, stuff like that."

"Were you scared to have friends? Because of where you lived and stuff?"

"Yeah, definitely. I could never have anybody over to my house because it was always crappy apartments in low-rises. We never even had a yard. We were close to a subdivision where there were real houses, so I went to school with those kids, so it was a little weird. Those were mostly Indian kids. It was like a Punjabi suburb or something."

"So you were like the only white kid."

"Not the only one, no." Gingerly, he touched the gauze on his arm. "It's hurting a lot now."

"That's because you're an idiot."

"I know that. I know that very well."

They sat in silence for a moment. He closed his eyes and then put his head down on the table, on his good arm. He let his bandaged arm sit in his lap as if he couldn't use it.

"I've got nothing to eat," she said. She checked her phone again.

Daryn said, "If she wasn't breathing for a while there's a chance that her brain had not enough oxygen and then ... I know a guy who ..." He stopped himself.

Gloria felt the same fatigue then, the fatigue that had been coming out of nowhere and flattening her, a deep depletion, an emptying, and she knew she had to lie down right away. She got up, went to her bedroom and stripped to her underwear. She got into bed. She left the door open.

In a minute she felt sleep lapping at her. She was sinking and then floating and then imagining large apartments, all empty airy rooms that led to other airy rooms. It was an apartment she was going to move into, but she didn't know how she was going to afford it.

Daryn was in the room with her and she heard him taking off his clothes. She couldn't move to stop him. And also she didn't mind.

He got into bed with her, his skin cool. He wrapped his thin arms around her from behind. He kissed her neck, and she let him because it felt nice. He pushed his pelvis against her, and she let him rub against her until he was hard. He was still wearing his underwear.

After a while she rolled on her back so that he could touch her properly. She didn't do anything for him, just lay still and let him touch her. Finally she turned and clung to him and without warning she was crying, quite loudly.

He didn't say anything but stopped stroking her between the legs. He held on to her tightly and let her cry.

She sobbed and shook for quite a few minutes. Then she felt it pass and she relaxed again, and the exhaustion had passed, too.

"She's probably going to be okay," he said. "Isabel."

"Don't. I just stopped. I'll start again."

"Okay."

"I don't know. I don't know how she is. She's not okay." She felt the tears seeping out again. "Don't, I'll start again."

"I'm sorry."

"See, when people want to end it, when they want to die, they don't talk about it. They don't tell anyone. They don't make threats. They just do it."

He thought about this. "Why do you think she did it?"

"Oh fuck off. Same reasons everyone wants to do it. But she had the addition of men fucking her around, fucking entitled men."

"A certain kind of man."

"You're right, You're right about that. Yes. A guy who can have all the women he wants. It is very very bad for men."

"See."

"Yeah, and also having shitty jobs all the time even though you have an education and did really well in school and you're always broke and there are always asshole men who are your boss, and then they want to fuck you too. Doing a really really boring job all the time is also part of it."

"You think she had to fuck him?"

"Oh shut up." She sniffled and held him tight again. There was a pain or a hollow, a sickness in her maybe, a drain somewhere with all of her flowing out of it.

He was still hard against her and she reached down and pulled down his shorts. He pushed them all the way down and wriggled out of them.

She pulled him on top of her and guided him between her legs. "Yes," she said. "Just do it. Push." She gasped a little as he did so, but she was ready. "Don't come in me."

He thrust until he was panting and moaning and so she pushed him off so that he wouldn't come.

"Hold still," she said, and she took his thigh between her legs and rubbed against it. "Hold still." She could feel his cock very hard against her side and he was quivering but holding still. She could feel her wetness smearing his thigh and she used it, kept at the slippery surface until she felt the tension building and she knew she could do it, come against him, and she kept at it, feeling it get close and then recede. He was yelping a little, his cock stiff against her ribs, and suddenly he convulsed and sprayed warm against her side, whimpering, and yet she did not let him go. The hot explosion against her and on her skin helped her and she gripped him hard and rubbed, slowly and steadily, until she came against his leg. She was mostly quiet, but it took a long time to subside. She released him and lay back and said, "I need to sleep now."

She slept for a while and dreamed of travelling in a desert with a great deal of equipment and some pets. When she woke up the light was dim and she felt the beginning of cramps in her belly. Daryn was still there, just lying naked beside her, staring silently at her. He looked grey and unhealthy.

"Listen," she said, "you can't stay over."

"Why not?"

She had no answer to this, knew that she would have to take a long time to think about her answer and that it would be important, it would have repercussions. She was feeling bad about having sex and enjoying it, because she knew now that she had constructed that, that it wasn't real, it had been a fantasy, it was a role play, a role play of a relationship, it was playing house, and she had always known that but he did not know that. So she lay still for a while.

"So you want me to go? After that? Just like that?" There was something high and petulant about his voice that made her stomach cramp even more.

"I'm not feeling well."

"What do you need?'

"I think I need to be alone."

"You're going to kick me out?"

She stopped herself from saying *yes*. "I'm just asking you for a favour. I'm not feeling well."

"It's freezing out."

"I'm sorry. I'm really sorry. I just can't let you—I can't have you... I can't be with anyone. Right now."

He sat up. "You think you can just treat me like a little piece of shit."

"Daryn."

"What am I, a little piece of shit? A little shit smear? That you can just use with your cunt?"

"What?" Gloria sat up. She pulled the duvet off him and onto her naked body. "Why are you talking like that?"

He ripped the duvet off her. He threw it on the floor. She covered her breasts with her hands.

"Stop it. Stop that. Calm down."

"You know what you did to me? You abused me."

"I what?"

"You tricked me. You misled me. You forced me into intimacy."

"Daryn. Daryn. How could I force you?"

"I wanted to protect myself, but you had to open me up. You broke down all my ... you forced me."

She glanced at the door. He saw her do this and moved in front of it. "I forced you. When did I force you?" She was trying to keep her voice level.

"That time. Last week. You said we were going to have, you know, you know what you said."

"I do not know. Please calm down and try to tell me."

"Real. Real." He spat this word. His face was twisted. "That was the one thing I wanted the most. And I was so afraid of it and that's what you forced me into. You seduced me." His voice broke and he was really crying now. "You know what that did to me? You fucking bitch. And now you want to just throw me away like a fucking tampon."

"Daryn. Daryn. There is no way I could force you into, into being *gentle*. Think about it. How could I—"

"You are fucking sick, you know that? You are a fucking witch that uses her cunt to make people weak."

She slipped off her side of the bed and ran to the door. She grabbed her bathrobe from the back of the door and went into the living room to try to put it on.

He followed her, naked, and pulled it from her hands. "Hide your cunt," he said. "Hide your pudgy cunt. Pudgy."

She was breathing wildly and knew she was about to cry. He was clenching his jaw, and his eyes were very wide. She darted behind the sofa, where there was little space, and held her hands out in front of her. "Please," she said, and her voice choked because she was crying. "Please stop. You're scaring me."

"What do you want me to do?" he shouted. "What do you fucking want from me? What do you want me to fucking do?" There was a white crust of semen on his belly.

She coughed as she often did when she was crying and breathing too hard. She remembered crying and trying to run away from a group of older girls at school.

"Just calm down," she said. "Just calm down."

He turned and went into the bedroom. She heard him putting on his clothes. She thought of calling the police, but her phone was in there. And in the time they took to arrive he would be further enraged. She picked up the bathrobe and put it on. She thought of running outside like that.

He came out dressed and said, "I'm sorry." His voice broke and he was crying too. "You can't treat me that way."

"I'm sorry," she said, as calmly as she could. "I won't. You need to go, now, and we'll talk about it later. Okay? You're not yourself right now."

"Oh I am myself," he said. "I am totally myself. I'm always myself." He grabbed his jacket from the back of the kitchen chair and left. He slammed the door. She heard his feet clumping very heavy all the way down the stairs. They stopped just before he reached the bottom door and she froze. There was a second's pause and then she heard the front door open and click shut.

She ran to the apartment door and locked it, then went to the one window that looked onto the street and looked out. She watched him walk quickly down the street, his shoulders hunched, his hands in his pockets. Without thinking, she reached for her phone, about to call Isabel, and then remembered she could not. She put the phone aside and stood very still, wishing for the first time ever that Autumn was there.

ABOUT AN HOUR AND A half later the apologetic texts began to come. They were abject and self-loathing and told her how he did not deserve to ever see her again and that she was a kind and genuine person and that she was the best thing that had ever happened to him. He did not deserve to live, and did not know how to love her properly, and he would go away and die, but she needed to forgive him. These went on for about an hour, then stopped—about twenty texts, altogether.

She screenshotted them all and emailed them to herself. Then she blocked him on all channels. She thought about how she needed to be close to Isabel but that she was not safe if she stayed in the city. She phoned her mother in Fort Erie to say she was coming to visit for a few days.

She was checking the bus schedule when her phone rang. It was Harriet Feldman. She said, "Gloria, we have some very sad news."

21.

SHE HAD TO GO BACK from Fort Erie to the city the night before the funeral to get the right clothes. Her mom did not want to go with her because she had the dogs to feed, and Gloria could not explain to her why she wanted her to stay in Gloria's apartment with her. There would have been no room for her mom anyway, as Autumn was there.

Gloria had thought of borrowing one of her mom's dresses, but they were all too large. Isabel would have wanted her to look nice at the funeral anyway.

And then there was to be some awful reception all afternoon, after the funeral, at Harriet's house in Scarborough.

Gloria had an appointment with her doctor in the morning, early, before the funeral, so that she could get some clonazepam or Ativan or even just zopiclone as she had not slept much in the last five days. She had stopped doing all her breathing and stretches as they were useless in the presence of death. The only thing that could enable her to face death, she thought, was a chemical, a real chemical, something from outside her, that would make her unconscious to the reality; something like death itself.

One day, Autumn had come out to Fort Erie to walk with her and that had actually been nice, although Autumn wanted to get her to cry and talk and hugged her too much. Gloria would have been happier to talk about the news, the riots, the people who had been arrested for planting bombs on Parliament Hill to stop the Illuminati or whatever they believed in, her old prof Avi Leibovitz, who had killed himself, who hadn't been such a bad guy anyway, anything.

THE BUS RIDE WAS VERY long. On the bus there was a person with one leg who walked with canes, one homeless person of indeterminate sex who was surrounded by bags stuffed with rags that were all the same grey-brown colour, one construction worker covered in dust who appeared to be asleep standing up, and a smell of fried chicken and alcohol. The rest of the people were all square and squat and also looked very tired. She had to take it all the way downtown and then back out to where she lived with two trains and a bus. She was hungry when she began walking up her street, which she supposed was a good sign, as she hadn't been eating much.

She made sure Autumn was home before she arrived and told her to check the street to see if anyone was waiting outside, and Autumn thought she was being a bit crazy but promised she would.

Gloria walked a long way around her building so that she could come down the street from a different direction, and she walked on the other side of the street, where the cars were parked, to have time to see if anyone was waiting. She texted

Autumn and Autumn answered that no one had come by and she hadn't seen anyone on the street.

Gloria dashed across the street and to the door.

And even when she was inside the vestibule and felt the front door click behind her, she felt a slight disappointment that he was not there, that he would not even wait that long for her, and wondered if perhaps he had moved on, as he should have, after having been blocked for five days. There was no way, of course, that he could have heard about Isabel, because he did not know her or anyone she knew.

She would have tea and maybe some of Autumn's baked tilapia, which would be nice.

It would also be nice, it occurred to her from nowhere, to have sex, as she did not think of sex much at her mother's and here she was back in the city again, a place where one could have sex, and sex would be feeling something. It would be better than crying. Sex was a pleasure like a hot bath or a shot of vodka and it was all she could do now anyway, what else was she going to do now, read a book?

And it wasn't just pleasure, either, sex, it was flattery, it was what Autumn would have called validation: the being desired was more important than the desire, and frankly Daryn had been good for her that way, especially after Florian, and she should be grateful to him, she really should—she could hear him saying this now, whining that she couldn't just discard him, since he had served a purpose for her; had she just used him, could she be free of him without guilt, for was he not a human too? And was she not opposed to disposing of people like chattel once they had served their purpose? Wasn't that what she hated in so many men, in men like Isabel's douche idiot, who had killed her, really, killed her as simple as murder?

And the truth was that Daryn was the way he was now, so completely crazy, because of her, because she had come into his life and fucked it up; she could have left him alone, and he would just be in front of his computer right now and he wouldn't be trying to hurt himself or threatening to hurt her; he would be sad but he would be normally sad like a lot of people, and he was who he was after all, there was nothing he could do about it.

And it occurred to her then, from a distance, that she was thinking of this thing, this pulsing weight, weighing and poking the black, swelling, shifting mass of it, with its guilt and its blame, as if it were a tumour, a part of her. This was probably how someone would think of a chronic illness, something one had to accommodate one's whole life, that one could never be free of. People did live with chronic illness. And if she was free of him, and if he really did hurt himself as a result of her, which he probably wouldn't, but still, you were always supposed to take that stuff seriously; if he did then would it be a murder *she* would carry, a hole in her that would be worse, maybe, than the chronic illness?

But she had to admit that the thought of him being dead was not terrible, actually, it was like a vision of a door to a garden, to some new life you could walk into, like leaving the hospital after your illness, and this thought, this vision, was terrible, terrible.

She could call Daryn, and he would be there that evening.

If she could have some clonazepam now she would not be thinking like this.

Autumn welcomed her with tears and brought her into her breasts. The apartment smelled of fish.

AFTER THE FUNERAL HOME THEY went to Harriet Feldman's house which was flat and suburban and surrounded by lawn. There was no sidewalk on the street but lots of driveways. The house was filled with flowers and people. There were flowers piled outside the front door and up against the wall of the entrance hall, mostly in crinkly plastic, but some in decorative pots and jars. They had no smell, but perhaps they were overpowered by the hot oven and its trays of pastry-puff things. Harriet had two caterers to take them out of the oven and serve them on other trays, pale women Gloria's age. For a moment Gloria was envious of them: she would have liked to be busy handing out food. The young women were very grave, as of course they were supposed to be, and Gloria wondered whether she should try to talk to them and make them feel at ease. It would be weird to be working in such a sad place. She also wondered how much they made doing this. Harriet was very busy supervising the two girls and carrying around trays herself. She was in a fitted black dress and heels and black hose and carried a whiff of perfume around her with the trays. Harriet was very lively and had also stopped crying. There was a big urn of coffee and a table of cups that must have been rented.

There was a table in the hall set with many framed pictures of Isabel. Gloria could not look at these as she had stopped crying, momentarily, and was happy with that, very relieved to be out of the funeral home where she had wept unstoppably for an hour and a half.

It was strange, the crying. Her body was broken open and floods of liquid were coming from it but she didn't feel anything. It was a physical ailment rather than an emotional one. She had heard the speeches at the funeral home and seen everyone else crying, and waves poured from her with the same discomfort one feels with vomiting or uncontrollable shitting, but she wasn't sure whether this was actually grief or some kind of injury, something like an allergy; she was not feeling the loss of Isabel because she could not be dead; she had been alive and healthy just days before and she had not suffered any illness. Gloria had been told Isabel was dead but she could not imagine it and therefore she was not. She supposed this was what people meant when they said *shock*.

Once, as a child, Gloria had been hit by a car while riding her bicycle. She had flown off and hit her head on the asphalt; she had seen the asphalt rising towards her in the last second before she hit, upside down, the moment of realization that something very bad and irreversible was happening, and then she had been looking at bits of gravel very close to her eye and did not know where she was. In the subsequent hours, from sitting up and being told to lie down again to her parents arriving to the hospital and its machines, she had had the sense of not being there, of watching everything on a screen, the ketamine feeling. The feeling of being distant had been interrupted by brief flashes of terror, which increased in frequency as her concussion dissipated and she began to be aware of pain. The greatest of these moments had come when she had tried to eat a bowl of apple sauce that had been given her in the hysterical light of the observation ward and found that her mouth was mushy, that she was missing a tooth and spitting blood. Only then had the realization come to her, as from a great distance, that the repercussions of the blow were yet to be felt, but when they came they would be far worse than what she was already experiencing. (And they were, for she had cracked her cheekbone.) This was how she felt now.

She was aware of this, that the grief would be worse when it finally came, and so she was happy for now to float in this non-reality—a non-reality in which she was still expected to—had to—write articles about stress-busting diets or how to update your resumé or hand out canapés, which she honestly wished she could do.

Gloria's mother was there in a green dress and was being very quiet and good and was holding Gloria's hand a lot. Gloria cried every time she took her hand, mostly because she knew that her mother hated travel and had not complained once about it, and also that she did not like wearing dresses and would not be comfortable in Harriet Feldman's fancy house, and Gloria was very grateful to her and wanted to say this repeatedly but couldn't because it would make her cry more, so she kept withdrawing her hand.

She went around to every family member and hugged them and told them she was sorry, again, as she had already done this at the funeral. And many people came up to her and said the same thing. A few of Isabel's brother's friends were there, young men maybe still in or just out of high school, in their good pants and their cotton shirts with button-down collars. One of them had not tucked his shirt in and wore a baseball cap in the house and still he looked sweet. They looked like a boy band. They were too shy to talk to Gloria and stood together murmuring and giggling. When they looked over at Gloria, in her own black dress, she felt like a ripe fruit. She felt she could cause any one of them to fall over just by looking at him, like some kind of magic ray or beam. This was a good feeling and a bad feeling, as she was not really very interested in any of them, except to look at, and besides, maybe she was very wrong about it all and they would just laugh at her.

She had not looked at her phone since the funeral, in case Daryn had found some new way to contact her and she would not be able to resist answering him, but she took it out furtively now and looked at it with her back to the crowd. There were three texts from Florian, who said he was terribly sorry for this terrible news and hoping he could be of assistance to her.

She thumbed quickly back *thanks*.

He responded right away that he wanted to help and that she could reach out to him any time. He said he knew she was strong and a beautiful person.

This didn't even make any sense and yet it brought tears to her eyes again.

She considered unblocking Daryn so she could hear some words of consolation from him too.

She was not quite sure why she did what she did next, which was to take a quick selfie, standing next to some white flowers, with what she hoped was a sad or at least neutral face.

She held the phone high and angled it down. The black dress was quite fitted in the bust.

She sent it to Florian. She knew this was a self-centred thing to do in the moment and probably not wise but it was a thing one did, she supposed, when one was lonely and surely she could count herself as lonely now.

She waited three minutes before Florian responded with five flames.

This was the stupidest response she could have imagined and she castigated herself for having sent the picture.

Florian wrote: *When can I see you?*

She did not reply.

She quickly skipped around her social feeds. She had a new follower on her Instagram, called Ignore Me. Ignore Me had not made any posts. She set all her posts to private. There was a Facebook friend request from a person with a new account and no photo called D. Knight. She set all her posts to private. Her LinkedIn told her she had received a new message. It was from an account also called D. Knight and it said simply *You will talk to me.*

She went to Boredcitygirl, Isabel's anonymous Instagram account, and it was still up. The last photo Isabel had posted was still up. It was a new one. It was Isabel's body on a bed—her own bed, Isabel's bed, which Gloria recognized—in grey afternoon light, in cotton panties and a cotton bra, and ankle socks. Her head was cut off by the frame. Her skin was perfectly smooth and pale, and her hipbones jutted out; it was an image of perfect desirability.

Gloria put her phone away.

Her mother had to leave at five because she had to take the train back, and Gloria said she would stay, she had to stay to be with the family, but she wasn't really sure why. She wasn't sure why to do anything.

There were still people there at six o'clock and she was tired of standing. She had had many cheese puffs and coconut-crusted shrimp and felt a little queasy. She saw Harriet settling up with the two server girls in the kitchen, and they left. Gloria envied them going out into the cool evening, together.

At one point she tried to remind herself that Isabel was gone, but she still could not believe it.

Harriet began bustling in the kitchen with her sister, a woman who looked like an older Harriet, and told Gloria she was welcome to stay, she'd be putting some food together, Gloria said no, she had to go.

She was relieved to be out on the sidewalk in front of the house, as the evenings were getting long and she felt she could walk, but it was all suburban lawns and nowhere to go. She didn't even know which bus to take to get out of there. She could look it up on her phone, but that seemed like a daunting task at the moment. She wished she had gone with her mother.

She waited at a bus stop on a road so wide and bleak it could have been a parking lot. A poster was taped to a telephone pole. It said DON'T TEXT ME. Nothing else was written on it.

She got on the first bus, which would probably end at a subway line somewhere.

On the bus she checked her phone. There was text from Autumn, saying she would not be home that night, because her mother had bought her a trip to New York as a mental-health break, but she really hoped Gloria was okay and she was thinking of her and sending sister love.

Then she checked emails. There was a long one from Surinder.

It began by expressing his condolences that she had suffered a bereavement. It then went on to announce that the site she wrote for, The Hype Report, had been sold to Guavax Media Holdings, and that this would entail a pivot in mandate that would affect all of them. The site would henceforth be focusing solely on product reviews, and these reviews would be entirely user-generated. This meant that The Hype Report would no longer be requiring original content. He thanked her for her immense contributions to the site's success so far and hoped that she could continue to be a member of the Guppy Media team (a subsidiary of Guavax) in a freelance capacity. As a result of this sale, Surinder would no longer be employed by The Hype Report and was herewith ceasing to be her contact. All of her enquiries should be sent to the communications department of Guppy Media.

She could tell that aside from the first line about bereavement Surinder had not written any of this himself. She felt sad, momentarily, for Surinder, who had not been such a bad guy really and who had seemed to believe that it was a real thing they were doing. He would be looking for a job as a content generator now, or as a brand narrative experience manager, or whatever it was that jobs were called. She told herself she would write to him but she knew that she never would. Because Surinder would never have written to her.

Clouds had surreptitiously covered the sky and the suburb went grey through the window. The bus was passing through a Sri Lankan strip of street and she stared at the restaurants, as if she could regenerate some hunger by seeing the pictures of rice dishes in the windows, and she saw a few women in colourful saris, but soon they were through it and back on blank streets of schools and car dealerships. She shivered and missed the sun.

She was a little puzzled by Guppy Media; as far as she knew Guppy was a video texting app that made a cartoon avatar for you. Perhaps the site had always been owned by Guppy, and she had simply not been aware. Perhaps all the websites and newspapers were owned by Guppy.

She stared out the window and stopped thinking about it.

It took her almost two hours to get home after that. She had ended up on a streetcar to the subway and then to her usual buses. On the streetcar was a mom with four children, one crying in a stroller, one strapped to her, and two on foot, slapping each other. On one bus everyone looked pretty much exactly as she thought she looked; no one looked anything like people in advertisements or movies, and every single one of them was tired from an awful job, which may yet have been better than having no job at all, which was now Gloria's state.

By the time she got to her street the sun had set and it had grown cold. She had not brought a coat and wrapped her arms around herself, and her silly handbag dangled from her wrist and banged on her hip.

She stopped at her front door and searched in the bag for her keys.

"Gloria," said his voice, and she jumped and swivelled.

He was right there, very close, as if he had been standing there all along.

He had his usual black bomber jacket on, but also some heavy boots she had never seen him wear, and a T-shirt with an American flag and something written on it. His face was pasty and damp and he had a sharp unwashed smell. And for a second she felt pleasure, she felt pleased that he had come. It was the first emotion aside from pain she had felt in five days.

"Stand back," she said quickly, and then, to soften that, she said, "a bit. Just stand back a bit."

"I need to talk to you."

She took a deep breath. "My best friend died five days ago. I'm coming back from the funeral. I need to be alone now."

His mouth opened and then closed again. He blinked. "I'm sorry. What happened?"

"You know what happened." She had her key in her hand, now, and put it in the lock.

He reached out and put a hand on her arm. "Wait."

"Take your hand off me."

He dropped his hand, and she opened the lock. "I'm sorry," he said. "I'm sorry about your friend."

She opened the door and he held it open with his hand.

"Let's just talk. Please."

"I can't right now, Daryn." She felt exhaustion now, that sense of numbness creeping over her that would not leave until she was asleep. She had to get to her bed. "I am very sad. I am very tired. I've been at a funeral all day. Why don't you call me tomorrow?"

"I've tried calling you. I'm blocked. You won't answer. Wait."

She pulled on the door. "You have to go."

His foot was blocking it. "You can't," he said, his voice high, "you can't just abandon me, I can't live, I'm really really fucked up, listen to me."

"Tomorrow. Tomorrow, I promise, I will talk to you. Just let me go in, now."

"Okay, that's it. Tonight, right now, I'm going to end my life. I'll do it right now."

He was shouting, and she heard a thump nearby as someone moved in the stairway next door. She shivered, too. She had to get under her covers.

"Okay then. Go ahead. Good luck."

"You mean it? You really mean that?" He pushed in then, so he was fully inside the door, and she backed up against the stairs.

She had no choice but to walk up a few steps, backwards. The staircase was narrow. The overhead light was yellow and flickering. He stood at the bottom of the stairs with his back to the door. Then he stepped up onto the first step.

"Daryn," she said, "you're scaring me. Don't come up. Go back."

"Sure, as soon as you are honest with me and you tell me what's been going on. You must have a reason, you don't just dump someone."

"I'm not dumping you, okay? We'll talk tomorrow. I can't right now."

"Are you lying? Are you lying to me?" He stepped onto the second step.

She pulled her purse to her front and reached in for her phone. "Okay," she said, "if you don't go I'm calling the police." She pulled the phone out. Her hand was shaking. She kept backing up, one stair at a time. He followed her. Each time she backed up, he climbed another step. She was aware of his height then, that he was taller than she was, so that although he was below her his face was always close to hers. The staircase was so narrow he blocked it entirely. The steps were linoleum tile with a metal ridge at each lip to stop slipping; still, she knew, they were slippery. She stopped with her back to her door. He was one step down, his face just below hers.

"You would call the police on me?" He began shouting hoarsely. "Is that how you treat someone you love? Someone who loves you?"

She typed in her password, and as she looked down to do this, he reached out to grab the phone. She pulled it back in front of her face. He swatted at it again and knocked it from her hand into her face, where it hit her hard on the nose, and she jerked her head back, hitting it against the door. He caught the phone as it fell and stepped back, down two steps, where he stared into it with a fearful expression, and in the white light from the phone began to tap away at it with his thumbs.

"What are you doing? Give me my phone."

"What are you afraid of? Huh? What am I going to find on here? Huh? I'm going to find everything."

She was grabbing at the phone now and he ducked and flinched, batting her hands away with his free hand. His head was about level with her waist, and she could kick him.

"What are you so scared of? What can't I see? Who it is? Who is it, anyway? It won't take me one second to find out. I can't wait. I'm going to see who you're whoring yourself out to. Florian? Who is Florian? Is that a guy? Oh here he is. Little simp guy with beard. You fucking slut. I knew it."

"You're scaring me. Stop."

"I won't fucking stop. I won't fucking stop until I know what a whore you are."

He put his foot onto the next step, the step below the one she was standing on, as if he was going to lift himself next to her, or against her. "Nice pic," he said, his voice shaky. "Nice pic, you fucking slut. Four flames from Florian. How long—"

She brought her knee up into his chest and pushed, and he fell backwards. He grabbed at the railing and missed and went right down the stairs. His head hit the other wall with a very loud bang and then he tumbled completely over, down the last few steps, and his head hit the floor with another thump that sounded like a rock on ice.

He flinched once and then lay there still. His body was twisted: one leg was under him unnaturally, and his head was jammed against the wall at too sharp an angle.

She went quickly down the stairs and picked up the phone where it lay a couple of steps above him. She tried to pull him away from the wall, but he was too heavy, and she felt sickened to do it, as if perhaps she would hurt him more by moving him.

She dialled 911 and waited. She had to hold.

She didn't want to reach down and touch to see if he was breathing. She did not want him to be dead. She did not want to have killed him, and wished she had let him kill her, or encouraged him to kill her as she was all alone then, there. She felt cold and she was shaking, perhaps from the cold.

"What is your emergency," said the voice, a woman. "Fire, police or ambulance."

"Ambulance," she said, "and police too. I—someone has fallen down the stairs, and he's hit his head and he's not conscious."

She gave the address, and the dispatcher asked if he was breathing, the man who had fallen.

"I don't know. I can't tell."

"You have to check, honey. You have to try. Just tell me if he's breathing."

"I can't. I can't look. I think not. Maybe."

"Can you find a pulse?"

"He's all twisted up. His neck. I don't want to move him."

"Okay. Don't move him. But I have to know if his airway is obstructed."

"I think he's dead."

"So he's not breathing?"

"I don't know. Can't you send someone?"

"I have sent someone. They're on their way. But you have to see if you can keep him breathing till they get there."

"I can't do that."

"Why do you need the police, sweetheart? What's going on?"

"It's totally my fault. I should never have let him in. I should never even have tried anything with him."

"Why do you need the police, sweetheart?"

"Because he was, he was threatening me."

"So you had a fight?"

"Yes."

"How old are you, sweetheart?"

"How old am I? Why?"

"I just need to know what's going on, honey."

"Oh my god. Oh. I'm not a kid. I'm an adult."

"Oh. Okay. Ma'am, have you been hurt?"

"No. I don't think so. I don't know. But I'm really cold." As she said this she began to shake. Her teeth started chattering. And then she started crying, quite hard, and gulping as she tried to stop.

"Ma'am. You haven't been injured?"

Gloria sobbed so hard she couldn't speak.

"Ma'am. I can't hear you."

"I can't stop shaking."

"Okay. Are you sitting down? The ambulance will be there soon. Are you losing any blood?"

"There's nowhere to sit down. He's all smushed up here against the wall." She sobbed until she was wailing. She heard voices through the wall and then saw heads through the reinforced glass pane. Someone trying the front door. There was a slight space between Daryn's shoulder and the door, so she could probably open it if she could get to it.

"Ma'am? Talk to me."

"I should have just let him kill me. Now I don't know if I've killed him or not. I think I have.

"I'm sorry?"

"No he didn't really want to kill me. I know that. He wasn't going to kill me, he didn't even want to hurt me, he just, he just, I think he did love me, he really did, he just made me, I had to defend myself, didn't I? It's not my fault but I wish I hadn't started the whole fucking thing because why did I fucking think he could ever be anyone else?"

"Okay. You just calm down now. Are you losing any blood?"

Gloria wailed. "Isabel's never coming back. I know she isn't. I knew it, I mean, I knew it as soon as she went into the coma, I knew she wasn't coming back. I knew she was gone. And she didn't love me enough to stay. And I loved her so so much, so so much, you know? Do you know?"

"Ma'am. Stay where you are. They're coming. We are coming to help you. They will help you."

The people from next door, or maybe just from the street, were pounding on the front door. Faces were at the glass. Then Gloria heard the sirens. When she heard the sirens, she knew she could move away from Daryn. She stopped crying, stepped over him and opened the door.

THANKS

Martin Ainsley
Claire Cavanagh
Victoria Hetherington
Sam Hiyate
Jessica Latimer
Sophie McCreesh
Nancy Ellen Miller
Vanessa Stauffer
Aley Waterman
Dan Wells

The writing of this book was refused funding by the Canada Council, the Ontario Arts Council and the Toronto Arts Council.

The painter James Lahey gave me a private grant to help me finish the book. I am deeply grateful.

RUSSELL SMITH is the author of nine books, eight of them fiction. His books have been nominated for the Giller Prize, the Governor General's Award, the Trillium Prize, the Rogers Writers' Trust Fiction Prize, the Impac Dubin Award, and the Smithbooks/Books In Canada First Novel Award. He was a weekly arts columnist for the national *Globe and Mail* for twenty years, and hosted the popular CBC Radio series "And Sometimes Y" for two seasons. He lives in Toronto.